# VISION OF DESTINY

Zor knew it as well as Dolza. Drifting in a near-delirium, feeling surprisingly little pain, he heard exchanges about the dimensional fortress. Thankful that the starship had escaped, he smiled to himself, though it hurt his scorched face.

Once more, he saw the Vision that had decided him to dispatch the ship; as the master of the limitless power of Protoculture, with his matchless intellect, he had access to hidden worlds of perception and invisible paths of knowledge.

He saw again an infinitely beautiful blue-white world floating in space, one blessed with the treasure that was life. He sensed that it was or would be the crux of transcendent events, the crossroads and deciding-place of a conflict that ráged across galaxies.

"Zor, if you die, the mission is over, and I must return in defeat and humiliation," Dolza said.

"I have thwarted the Robotech Masters' plan to control the universe." Zor had to cough and regain his breath, with a rattle in it that spoke of dying. "But a greater, finer mission is only beginning, Dolza..."

Zor coughed again and was still, eyes closed forever.

The ROBOTECH™ Series
*Published by Ballantine Books:*

GENESIS #1

BATTLE CRY #2

HOMECOMING #3

BATTLEHYMN #4

# ROBOTECH™ #1:

# GENESIS

## Jack McKinney

A Del Rey Book

BALLANTINE BOOKS • NEW YORK

# PROLOGUE

*I'VE BROUGHT DEATH AND SUFFERING IN SUCH MAGNI-tude*, Zor thought. *It's only right that I spent the balance of my life bringing life.*

He looked out from the observation bay of his temporary groundside headquarters upon a planetary surface that had been lifeless a mere four days before. He saw before him a plain teeming with thriving vegetation. Already the Flowers of Life were sprouting, reaching their eager, knob-tipped shoots into the sunshine.

Zor, supreme intellect of his race and Lord of the Proto-culture, nodded approvingly. At times the memories of his own past deeds, much less those of his species, seemed enough to drive him mad. But when he looked down on a scene like this, he could forget the past and be proud of his handiwork.

And above him, blocking out the light of the nearby pri-mary, his gargantuan starship and super dimensional for-tress was escaping, as he had directed. The satisfaction he felt from that and from seeing the germinated Flowers made it much easier to accept the fact that he was about to die.

He was tall and slender, with a lean, ageless face and a thick shock of bright starlight hair. The clothes he wore were graceful, regal, cut tight to his form, covered by a short cloak that he now threw back over one shoulder.

Zor could hear the alarm signals ring behind him, and the booming voice of a Zentraedi announced, "Warning! Warning! Invid troop carriers are preparing to land! All warriors to their Battlepods!"

Zor gazed away from the beauty of the exterior scene, back to the harsh reality of the base, as towering Zentraedi dashed about, preparing for battle. Even though the appearance of the Invid had taken them by surprise, even though they were badly outnumbered and at a disadvantage since the enemy held the high ground, there was a certain eagerness to the Zentraedi; war was their life and their reason for being.

In that, they had met their match and more in the Invid. Zor found bitter irony in how his own poor judgment and the cruelty of the Robotech Masters—*his* masters—had turned a race of peaceful creatures, once content with their single planet and their introspective existence, into the most ferocious species in the known universe.

While subordinates strapped armor and weapons on his great body, Dolza, supreme commander of the Zentraedi, glared down at Zor. His colossal head, with its shaven, heavy-browed skull, gave him the aspect of a stone icon. "We should have departed before the Flowers germinated! I warned you!"

Dolza raised a metal-plated fist big enough to squash Zor. Unafraid, Zor looked up at him, though his faithful aide, Vard, was holding a hand weapon uneasily. Around them the base shook as armored Zentraedi and their massive fighting pods raced to battle stations.

"What of the super dimensional fortress?" Dolza demanded. "What have you done with it?"

"I have sent it away," Zor answered calmly. "To a place far removed from this evil, senseless war. It is already nearing the edge of space, too fast and far too powerful for the Invid to stop."

That much, Dolza knew, was true. The dimensional fortress, Zor's crowning technological achievement, was the mightiest machine in existence. Nearly a mile long, it incorporated virtually everything Zor had discovered about the fantastic forces and powers springing from the Flowers of Life.

"Sent it where?" Dolza demanded. Zor was silent. "If I weren't sworn by my warrior oath to protect you"—Dolza's immense fist hovered close—*"I would kill you!"*

A few pods from the ready-reaction force were already on the scene: looming metal battle vehicles big enough to hold one or two Zentraedi, their form suggested that of a headless ostrich, with long, broad breastplates mounting batteries of primary and secondary cannon.

"I don't expect you to understand," Zor said in carefully measured tones, as explosions and shock waves shook the base. They could hear the Zentraedi communication net crackling with reports of the Invid landing.

"You were created to fight the Invid; *that* is what you must do," Zor told the giant as the headquarters' outer wall heaved and began to crumble. "Go! Fulfill your Zentraedi imperative!"

As Zor spun and ducked for cover, Vard shielded him with his own body. Dolza turned to give battle as the wall shuddered and cracked wide. Through the showering rubble leapt Invid shock troopers, the enemy's heaviest class of *mecha*, advanced war machines. Forged from a superstrong alloy, bulky as walking battleships, the mecha resembled a maniac's vision of biped insect soldiers.

They were every bit as massive as the Zentraedi pods, and even more heavily armored. Concentrated fire from the few pods already on the scene—blue lances of blindingly bright energy—penetrated the armor of the first shock trooper to appear. Even as the Invid returned fire with streams of annihilation discs, the seams and joints of its armor expanded under the overwhelming pressure from the eruptions within. It exploded into bits of wreckage and white-hot shrapnel that bounced noisily off the pods' armor.

But a trio of shock troopers had crowded in behind the first, and a dozen more massed behind them. Annihilation discs and red plasma volleys quartered the air, destroying the headquarters command center and equipment, setting fires, and blasting pods to glowing scraps or driving them back.

Armored Zentraedi warriors, lacking the time to reach their pods, rushed in to fight a desperate holding action, spraying the Invids with hand-held weapons, dodging and ducking, advancing fearlessly and suffering heavy casualties.

A swift warrior ran in under an Invid shock trooper, holding his weapon against a vulnerable joint in its armor and then triggering the entire charge all at once, point-blank. The explosion blew the Invid's leg off, toppling it, but the Zentraedi was obliterated by the detonation.

Elsewhere, an Invid mecha seized a damaged pod that could no longer fire, ripped the pod apart with its superhard metal claws, then dismembered the wounded Zentraedi within.

Scouts, smaller Invid machines, rushed in behind the shock troopers to scour the base.

It took only moments for one to find Zor; the Invid had been searching for him for a *long* time and were eager for revenge.

As the scout lumbered toward them, Vard tried to save his lord by absorbing the first blast himself, firing his little hand weapon uselessly at the Invid monster. He partially succeeded, but only at the cost of his own life—immolated in an instant by a disc. The force of the blast drove Zor back and scorched him.

The rest of the discs in the salvo were ignited by the explosion, but, having been flung aside, Zor was spared most of their fury. Still, he'd suffered terrible injuries—skin burned from his body until bone was exposed, lungs seared by fire, bones broken from the concussion and the fall, tremendous internal hemorrhaging. He knew he would die.

Before the Invid scout could finish the job, Dolza was there, firing at it with his disruptor rifle, ordering the remaining pods to concentrate their fire on it. "Zor is down! Save Zor!" he thundered. Switching to his helmet communicator, he tried to raise his most trusted subordinate.

"Breetai! Breetai! Where are you?"

The scout was blown to fiery bits in the withering fusillade, but its call had gone out; the other scouts and the shock troopers were homing in on their arch-enemy.

Dolza, with the remaining warriors and pods, formed a desperate defensive ring, unflinchingly ready to die according to their code.

Suddenly there was a massive volley from the right. Then an even more intense one from the left. To Dolza's astonishment, they were directed at the Invid.

Breetai had arrived at the head of reinforcements. Some of them were wearing only body armor like himself, but most were in tactical or heavily armed officers' Battlepods. The Invid line began to collapse before a storm of massed fire. More pods were arriving all the time. Dolza couldn't understand how—an invasion force was descending by the thousands from a moon-size Invid hive ship, its troopers as uncountable as insects. Surely the base must be covered by a living, swarming layer of the enemy.

But the enemy *was* being driven back, and Breetai was leading a countercharge on foot, just as a small wedge of shock troopers threatened to make good on a suicide rush at Dolza and Zor. A disc struck a pod near Breetai even as he was firing left and right with his rifle; blast and shrapnel hit his head and the right side of his face.

Breetai dropped, skull aflame, but the Zentraedi countercharge went on—somehow—to drive the Invid back to the breach in the wall.

Finally Dolza wearily lowered his glowing rifle muzzle. Pursuit of the retreating Invid could be left to the field commanders. He began to take reports from the newcomers, thus learning the details of the unexpected Zentraedi victory.

Most of the Invid had been diverted in an attempt to stop or board the dimensional fortress and had been wiped out. Even now, word of the attack was going back to the Robotech Masters; a punitive raid would have to be mounted. Breetai was being attended to by the healers and would live, though he would be scarred for life.

But all of that was of little moment to Dolza. He looked

down on the smoking, broken body of Zor. Healers crowded around the fallen genius with their apparatus and medicines, but Dolza had seen enough combat casualties to know that Zor was beyond help.

Zor knew it as well as Dolza. Drifting in a near delirium, feeling surprisingly little pain, he heard exchanges about the dimensional fortress. He smiled to himself, though it hurt his scorched face, thankful that the starship had escaped.

Once more, he had the Vision that had made him decide to dispatch the ship; as the master of the limitless power of Protoculture, with his matchless intellect, he had access to hidden worlds of perception and invisible paths of knowledge.

He saw again an infinitely beautiful, blue-white world floating in space, one blessed with the treasure that was life. He sensed that it was or would be the crux of transcendent events, the crossroads and deciding place of a conflict that raged across galaxies.

A column of pure mind-energy rose from the planet, a pillar of dazzling force a hundred miles in diameter, crackling and swaying, swirling like a whirlwind, throwing out shimmering sheets of brilliance, climbing higher and higher into space all in a matter of moments.

As he had before, Zor felt humbled before the mind-cyclone's force. Then its pinnacle unexpectedly gave shape to a great bird, a phoenix of mental essence. The firebird of transfiguration spread wings wider than the planet, soaring away to another plane of existence, with a cry so magnificent and sad that Zor forgot his impending death. He wept for the dreadful splendor of what was to come, two tears flowing down his burnt cheeks.

But he was buoyed by a renewed conviction that the dimensional fortress must go to that blue-white planet.

The sounds of the last skirmishes came from the distance as Zentraedi rooted out and executed the last of the Invid troops. Dolza stood looking down at Zor's blackened body as its life slipped away despite all that the healers could do. Dolza suspected that Zor did not wish—would not *permit* himself—to be saved.

Whatever Zor's plan, there was no changing it now. The ship *itself*, along with a handful of Zentraedi loyal to Zor alone, had jumped beyond the Robotech Masters' reach—at least for the time being.

It was of little comfort to Dolza that final transmissions from the dimensional fortress, in the moments before transition through a spacefold, indicated that the traitors aboard had been badly wounded during the battle to get past the Invid surprise attack.

"Zor, if you die, the mission is over and I must return in defeat and humiliation," Dolza said.

"I have thwarted the Robotech Masters' plan to control the universe." Zor had to pause to cough and regain his breath, with a rattle in it that spoke of dying. "But a greater, finer mission is only beginning, Dolza . . ."

Zor coughed again and was still, eyes closed forever.

Dolza stood before a screen that was large even for the Zentraedi. Before him was the image of a Robotech Master. Dolza spoke obsequiously.

". . . and so we have no idea where the dimensional fortress is, at least for the moment."

The Master's ax-keen face, with its hawkish nose, flaring brows, and swirling, storm-whipped hair, showed utter fury. Dolza wasn't surprised; Zor, who'd given the Masters the key to their power, *and* the mighty dimensional fortress gone, at a stroke! Dolza wondered if the Invid realized just how much damage they'd inflicted in a raid that would otherwise have been an insignificant skirmish.

The Robotech Master's voice was eerily lifeless, like a single-sideband transmission. "The dimensional fortress must be recovered at all costs! Organize a search immediately; we shall commit the closest Zentraedi fleet to the mission at once, and all others will join in the effort if necessary."

Dolza bowed to the image. "And Zor, my lord? Shall I have his remains interred in his beloved garden?"

"No! Freeze them and bring them back to us personally. Guard them well! We may yet extract information from his cellular materials."

With that, the Master's image disappeared from the screen.

"Hail, Dolza! Breetai reporting as ordered."

Dolza looked him over. A day or two of Zentraedi healing had the senior commander looking fit for duty; though he was again the fierce gladiator he'd always been, he was far different.

The damage done by the annihilation discs of the Invid could not be completely reversed. The right half of Breetai's black-haired scalp and nearly half his face were covered by a gleaming alloy prosthesis, a kind of half cowl, his right eye replaced by a glittering crystal lens.

Breetai had always been given to dark moods, but his mutilation at the hands of the enemy had made him distant, cold and wrathful. Dolza approved.

Dolza had summoned Breetai to a spot on the perimeter of the reinforced base where Flowers of Life were sprouting underfoot. The supreme commander quickly outlined the situation. The details of the long struggle between Zor and the Masters, and Zor's secret plan for the future of Protoculture, shocked Breetai, as did certain other information that was Dolza's alone to tell.

"You're my best field commander," Dolza finished. "You will lead the expedition to retake the dimensional fortress."

The sunlight glinted off Breetai's metal skullpiece. "But —it *jumped*!"

Sympathy was not part of the Zentraedi emotional spectrum. Dolza therefore showed none. "You must succeed. You must recover the fortress and its Protoculture factory before the Invid do, or we'll have lost everything we've worked for."

Breetai's features resolved in taut lines of determination. "The dimensional fortress will be ours, on my oath!"

# CHAPTER
# ONE

*I had misgivings like everybody else, but I thought [the appearance of SDF-1] just might be a good thing for the human race after all when I saw how it scared hell outta the politicians.*

Remark attributed to Lt. (jg) Roy Fokker in *Prelude to Doomsday: A History of the Global Civil War*, by Malachi Cain

**W**HEN THE DIMENSIONAL FORTRESS LANDED IN 1999 A.D., the word "miracle" had been so long overused that it took some time for the human race to realize that a real one had indeed come to pass.

In the late twentieth century, "miracle" had become the commonplace description for home appliances and food additives. Then came the Global Civil War, a rapid spiraling of diverse conflicts that, by 1994, was well on its way to becoming a full-scale worldwide struggle; in the very early days of the war, "miracle" was used by either side to represent any highly encouraging battle news.

The World Unification Alliance came into existence because it seemed the best hope for human survival. But its well-meaning reformers found that a hundred predators rose up to savage them: from supranational conglomerates, religious extremists, and followers of a hundred different ideologies to racists and bigots of every stripe.

The war bogged down, balkanized dragged on, igniting every corner of the planet. People forgot the word "miracle." The war escalated and escalated—gradually, it's true,

but everyone knew what the final escalation would be—
until hope began to die.

And in a way nobody seemed to be able to stop, the
human race moved along the path to its own utter obliter-
ation, using weapons of its own fashioning. The life of the
planet was infinitely precious, but no one could formulate
a plan to save it from the sacrificial thermonuclear fire.

Then, almost ten years into the Global Civil War, the
thinking of *Homo sapiens* changed forever.

The dimensional fortress's arrival was a coincidence
beyond coincidence and, in the beginning, a sobering catastrophe.

Its entry was that of a powered object, and it had appeared from nowhere, from some unfathomable rift in the
timespace continuum. Its long descent spread destruction
and death as its shock waves and the after-blast of its
monumental drive leveled cities, deafened and blinded
multitudes, made a furnace of the atmosphere, and somehow awakened tectonic forces. Cities burned and fell, and
many, many died.

Its approach rattled the world. The mosques were
crowded to capacity and beyond, as were the temples and
the churches. Many people committed suicide, and, cur-
iously enough, the three most notable high-casualty-rate
categories were, in this order: fundamentalist clergy, certain elected politicians, and major figures in the entertain-
ment world. Speculation about their motives—that the
thing they had in common was that they felt diminished
by the arrival of the alien spacecraft—remained just that:
speculation.

At last the object slowed, obviously damaged but still
capable of maneuvering. Its astonishing speed lessened to a
mere glide—except that it had little in the way of lifting
surfaces and was unthinkably heavy. It came to rest on a
gently sloping plain on a small island in the South Pacific,
once the site of French atomic tests, called Macross.

The plain was long and broad, especially for such a tiny
island, but it was not a great deal longer than the ship itself.
A few hundred yards behind its thrusters, waves crashed

against the beach. A short distance ahead of its ruined bow were sheer cliffs.

Its outer sheath and first layers of armor, and a great portion of the superstructure, had been damaged in the course of its escape, or in the controlled crash of its landing. It groaned and creaked, cooling, as the combers foamed and bashed the sand on an otherwise idyllic day on Macross Island.

The human race began assessing the damage in a dazed, uncoordinated way. But it didn't take long for opposing forces to convince themselves that the crash was no enemy trick.

For the first few hours, it was called "the Visitor." Leaders of the various factions of the civil war, their presumed importance reduced by the alien vessel's appearance, took hasty steps toward a truce of convenience. The various commanders *had* to move quickly and *had* to sacrifice much of their prestige to accommodate one another; all eyes were turned to the sky and to Macross Island. The Global Civil War looked like a minor, ludicrous squabble compared to the awesome power that had just made itself felt on Earth.

Within hours, preparations were being made for an expedition to explore the wreckage. Necessary alliances were struck, but safety factors were built into the expeditionary force. Enemies at the top had accomplished an uneasy peace.

Now, those who'd *fought* the war would have to do the same.

The flight deck of the Gibraltar-class aircraft carrier *Kenosha* retreated beneath the ascending helicopter, a comforting artificial island of nonskid landing surface. Lieutenant (jg) Roy Fokker watched it unhappily, resigning himself to the mission at hand.

He turned to the man piloting the helo, Colonel T.R. Edwards, who was flying the chopper with consummate skill. Roy Fokker was more used to those occasions when he and Edwards were doing turns-and-burns, trying to shoot each other out of the skies.

Roy Fokker was an Internationalist, right down to his soles. His uniform bore the colors of his carrier aviation unit, a fighter squadron: the Jolly Roger skull-and-cross-bones insignia. The colors were from the old United States Navy, the renowned and justly feared VF-84 squadron off the USS *Nimitz* that had hunted the skies in F-14 Tomcats, then Z-6 Executioners, right up to Roy's own production-line-new Z-9A Peregrine.

Roy wished he was back there in his own jet, in his own cockpit.

For so important a takeoff, it would have been normal to see the *Kenosha*'s skipper on the observation deck under phased-array radar antenna and other tower shrubbery—the deck the aviators called Vulture's Row. Admiral Hayes and the other heavy-hitters were all there, but Captain Henry Gloval wasn't. Today, Captain Henry Gloval was belted in the rear of the helo with a platoon of marines and some techs and more scientific equipment and weapons than Roy had seen packed into a bird before. That the Old Man should actually leave his command and go ashore showed how topsy-turvy this spaceship or whatever it was had turned matters on Earth.

It was as oddball a mission as Roy had ever seen; it made him uncharacteristically nervous, *especially* since the opposition junta had picked Edwards as its representative on the team.

The last time Edwards and Roy had crossed contrails, Edwards had been in the hire of something called the Northeast Asian Co-Prosperity Sphere. There was no telling who he was *really* working for now, except that he was *always*, without exception, out to benefit Colonel T.R. Edwards.

Roy told himself to stop thinking about it and do his job. He fidgeted in his seat a little, uncomfortable in web gear weighted with about a hundred rounds of weapons, ammo, and survival and exploration equipment.

He pushed his unruly mop of blond hair back out of his eyes. He wasn't sure why or when long hairstyles had become the norm among pilots, but now it was practically de rigueur. Some *Samurai* tradition?

He glanced over at Edwards. The mercenary was perhaps thirty, ten years older than Roy, with the same lean
height. Edwards had tan good-looks and sun-bleached hair
and a killer smile. He seemed to be enjoying himself.

Roy's youth didn't make him Edwards's inferior in
combat experience or expertise. The practical philosophy
of the old-time Swiss and Israelis and others like them
was now the rule: Anyone who could fly well did, and
they flew as leaders if they merited it, regardless of age or
rank.

All the tea-party proprieties about a flyer needing a college education and years of training had been thrown out as
the attrition of the war made them untenable. Roy had
heard that kids as young as fourteen were in the new
classes at Aerial Combat School.

Edwards had caught the glance. "Want to take over,
Fokker? Be my guest."

"No thanks, Colonel. I'm just here to make sure you
don't mess up and spike us into the drink."

Edwards laughed. "Fokker, know what your problem is?
You take this war stuff too personally."

"Tell me something: D'you *like* flying for a bunch of fas-
cists?"

Edwards snorted derisively. "You think there's that
much difference between sides, after ten years of war? Besides, the Neasians pay me more in a week than you make
in a year."

Roy wanted to answer that, but his orders were to avoid
friction with Edwards. As if to remind him of that, a sudden
aroma wafted under his nose. It was pipe tobacco, but to
Roy it always smelled like a soap factory on fire.

Gloval was at it again. But how do you tell your com-
manding officer that he's breaking regs, smoking aboard
an aircraft? If you are a wise young lieutenant (jg), you
do not.

Roy turned back to study Macross and forgot Gloval,
Edwards, and everything else. There lay the blackened
remains of a ship like nothing Earth had ever seen before.

"*Great God!*" Roy said slowly, and even Edwards had
nothing to add.

* * *

The wreck was cool, and radiation readings were about normal. Previous fly-bys hadn't drawn fire or seen any activity. The helo set down a few dozen yards from the scorched, broken ruin. In another few moments the team was offloading itself and its equipment.

Gloval, a tall, rangy man with a soot-black, Stalinesque mustache, captain's hat tilted forward on his brow, was establishing security and getting ready for preliminary external examination of the wreckage. He was square-shouldered and vigorous, looking younger than his fifty-odd years until one saw the lines around his eyes.

But while the preparations were going on, Lance Corporal Murphy, always itching to be on the move, couldn't resist doing a little snooping. "Hey, lookit! I think I found a hatch!"

Gloval's voice still retained its heavy Russian accent. "You jackass! Get away from there!"

Murphy was standing near a tall circular feature in the battered hull, waving them over. With his back to it, he didn't see the middle of the hatch open, the halves sliding apart. He couldn't hear his teammates' shouted warnings, as several long, segmented metal tentacles snaked out.

In another moment, the unlucky marine was caught and lifted off his feet. The service automatic in his hand went off, then fell from his grasp, as he was yanked within. None of the others dared to shoot for fear of hitting him.

The hatch snapped shut. Gloval spread his arms to hold back Roy and some of the others; they would have charged for the hatch. "Stand where you are and hold your fire! Nobody goes any closer until we know what we're dealing with!"

An hour later things *had* changed, although the explorers didn't know much more than they had at the beginning.

At Admiral Hayes's insistence, Doctor Emil Lang had been choppered ashore to supervise. Lang was Earth's premier mind, by decree of Hayes and Senator Russo and the

others in the alliance leadership, the final authority on interplanetary etiquette.

Lang ordered everyone into anticontamination suits,
then directed a human-size drone robot to make preliminary
exploration of the ship. When the robot, essentially a bulbous detector/telemetry package on two legs, stopped dead
in front of the hatch as the hatch reopened, Lang looked
thoughtful.

The robot refused to respond to further commands, the
hatch stayed open, and there was no sign of activity within.
Lang's eyes narrowed behind his suit's visor as he concentrated.

Lang was a man just under medium height, slight of
build, but when it came to puzzling out the unknown, he
had the courage of a lion. Disregarding his orders, he
directed Gloval to select a party to explore the wreck.
Gloval picked himself, Roy, Edwards, and eight of the
grunts.

"Get those spotlights on," Lang instructed. "And you
may chamber a round in your weapons, but leave the safe-
ties on. If anyone fires without my direct order, I'll see that
he's court-martialed and hung."

Unnoticed, T.R. Edwards made a wry face inside his suit
helmet and flicked his submachine gun selector over to full
auto.

The lights they'd brought—spotlights mounted on the
shoulders of their web gear—were powerful but not powerful enough to reach the farthest limits of the compartment in
which they found themselves. Lang and Gloval only studied
what was before them, but from the others were soft exclamations, curses, obscenities.

It resembled a complex cityscape. The alien equipment
and machinery was made of glassy alloys and translucent
materials, with conduitlike structures crisscrossing in midair and oddly shaped contrivances in every direction. The
spacecraft was built to a monumental scale.

Readings still indicated no danger from radiation, atmospheric, or biological contamination; they removed the
suits.

"We will divide into two groups," Gloval decided, still in

charge of the tactical decisions. "Roy, you'll take four marines. Dr. Lang, Edwards—you'll be in my group."

They were to work their way forward, following opposite sides of the wreck's inner hull, in an attempt to link up in the bow. Failing that, they would observe as much as possible and fall back to their original point of entry in one hour.

They started off. No one heard the inert probe robot suddenly reactivate and step through the open hatch in their wake, moving more nimbly than it had a few minutes before.

Fifteen minutes later, in a passageway as high and wide as a stadium, Roy paused to shine his shoulder-mounted lights around him. "This place must be playing tricks on my eyes. Does it look to you like the walls're moving?" he asked the gunnery sergeant behind him.

The gunny said slowly, "Yeah, kinda. Like there's a fog or somethin' flowin' through all the nooks and crannies."

Roy was about to get them moving again when he heard someone calling softly, "Caruthers. Hey, *man*, where y' at?"

Caruthers was the man walking drag at the rear of the file; they all turned back to see what was going on. Caruthers had fallen far behind for some reason; but he was rejoining them, his spots getting nearer. But something about the man's movement wasn't normal. Moreover, his head hung limply and he appeared to be moving considerably above them, as if on a catwalk.

They flashed their beams his way and stood rooted in astonishment and stark terror. Caruthers's body hung on a line, like a tiny puppet, held in the hand of a humanoid metal monster seventy feel tall.

The armored behemoth swung its free hand in their direction. They didn't have time for permission to react; they wouldn't have listened if Lang had denied it, anyway.

Roy and the gunny and the other marines opened fire, the chatter of their submachine guns loud in their ears.

Their tracers lit up the darkness, as the bullets bounced off the monster's armor as if they were paper clips.

Its right hand loosed a stream of reddish-orange fury. A marine disappeared like a zapped bug, turned to ash in an instant.

■ ▪ ■ ▪ ■ ▪ ■ ▪ ■ ▪ ■ ▪ ■ ▪ ■ ▪ ■ ▪ ■ ▪ ■ ▪ ■ ▪ ■ ▪ ■

# CHAPTER
# TWO

*I suppose, in the back of my mind, I was aware that fate had
sent my way a chance to be mentioned in the same breath with
Einstein, Newton, and the rest. But to tell the truth, I thought
little of that. Before the lure of so much new knowledge, any
scientist would've made poor old Faust look like a saint.*

Dr. Emil Lang, *Technical Recordings and Notes*

R OY AND THE OTHERS EMPTIED THEIR WEAPONS TO NO
avail. The looming weapon hand swung to a new target as
they ducked, switching their turned-and-taped double magazines around to lock and load a fresh one.

A second stream of superheated brilliance blazed, and
another marine was incinerated.

Roy realized the radio was useless; it was in Hersch's
rucksack, and he'd just been fried. Roy turned, spotted the
RPG rocket launcher dropped by the first victim, and made
a dive for it.

The gunnery sergeant gave him a look of misgiving but
kept his peace. Firing the weapon might be suicidal for a
number of reasons, including secondary explosions from
their attacker, but Roy saw no other options; their escape
was cut off, and there was no cover worthy of the name.

The RPG was already loaded. Roy peered through the
sights, centering the reticle, and fired at the thing's midsec-
tion, where two segments met. The resulting explosion split
the metal monster in half; it toppled, venting raging energy.
The secondary blast knocked Roy off his feet.

He lost consciousness for a second but came to, momentarily deafened, with the gunny shaking him. Roy managed to read his lips: *"It's still alive!"*

Blearily Roy followed the pointing finger. It was true: Segments of the shattered behemoth were rocking and jouncing; those that had some articulation were trying to drag themselves toward the intruders. Other pieces were firing occasional beams, most of which splashed off the faraway ceiling.

The gunny got Roy to his feet and began dragging him around the remains in what seemed like the direction from which they'd come. Even though he couldn't hear, Roy could feel heavy vibrations in the deck. He turned and found a second monster approaching. He couldn't figure out how the first one had come upon them so silently, and he didn't wait around to find out.

The thing halted by the smoldering debris of the first as Roy staggered off behind the gunny.

". . . remember coming through here," Roy dimly heard the gunny say when they paused after what seemed like a year of tottering along the deck. Evidently, the gunny had covered his ears to avoid the rocket's impact; he was listening as well as looking for more enemies.

"Neither do I," Roy said wearily. "But all our other routes were blocked."

"They could've polished us all off, Lieutenant," the gunny said.

Roy shook his head, just as confused as the marine. "Maybe they're herding us along somewhere; I dunno."

They took up their way again. Roy's hearing was coming back, accompanied by a painful ringing. "Maybe they don't want to kill all of us because—"

The gunny screamed a curse. Roy looked down to see that the deck plates were rippling around their legs like a running stream, engulfing them.

Gloval gripped his automatic resolutely. "Are you getting all this on the video, Dr. Lang?"

Lang put his palm to his forehead. "Yes, but those shapes keep shifting . . . gets me dizzy just looking . . ."

"Kinda like . . . vertigo . . ." T.R. Edwards added.

Gloval was feeling a little queasy himself. He called a halt for a breather, sending Edwards to peer into the next compartment. Gloval watched Lang worriedly; with the arrival of the alien ship, Lang became the most indispensable man on the planet. Lang must be kept safe at all costs, and the fact that Gloval couldn't raise Roy's party or the outside world on the radio had the captain skittish.

Edwards was back in moments, face as white as his teeth. "You'd better brace yourselves." Edwards swallowed with difficulty. "I found Murphy, but—it's a little hard to take." He swallowed again to keep from vomiting.

One by one they went to join him at the entrance to the next compartment, from which an intense light shone. Lang caught the edge of the hatch to steady himself when he saw what was there.

In a large translucent tank wired with various life support systems floated the various pieces of Lance Corporal Murphy in a tiny sea of sluggish nutrient fluid.

They drifted lazily, here an arm, there the head—sightless eyes wide open—a severed hand bumping gently against the stripped torso. The fluid was filled with fine strands glowing in incandescent greens. Tiny amoebalike globules flocked to the body parts and away from them again, feeding and providing oxygen and removing wastes.

Gloval turned to the marine behind him. "Establish security! Whoever did this may still be around." The men shook off their paralysis and rushed to obey.

All, that is, but one, who was about to pluck out a leg by a white, wrinkled foot that had bobbed to the surface. "We can't leave 'im like this!" Through the grinding war, the marines had maintained their honor and their high traditions proudly; *esprit de corps* was like the air they breathed. To leave one of their own on the battlefield was to leave a part of themselves.

But Lang pulled the grunt back with surprising strength. "Don't touch him! Who knows what the solution is? You want to end up pickled in there too? No? *Good!* Then just draw a specimen with this device and be careful!"

Gloval, carefully gauging the alien topography to keep

his mind—and eyes—off Murphy's parts, determined that his suspicions were true: The internal layout of the place was changing around them. There was no way back.

He quickly formed up his little command and got them moving, grimly satisfied that Edwards wasn't so cocky anymore.

Moments later, as the party moved through a darkened area, he felt a marine tug at his shoulder. "Cap'n! There's a—"

And all hell broke loose as armored behemoths set upon Gloval's group from the rear, blasting and trying to stamp the puny humans into the deck.

One marine gave the beginning of a shriek and then blew into fragments, the moisture in his tissues instantaneously converted to steam, the scraps of flesh vaporized in the alien's beam.

The humans cut loose with all weapons, including a man-portable recoilless rifle and a light machine gun whose drum magazine was loaded with Teflon semi-armorpiercers. A second marine was cremated almost instantly.

They had better luck than Roy's team in that the machine gunner and the RR man both happened to aim for the lead monster's firing hand and were lucky enough to find a vulnerable point, blowing it off.

The fortress's guardian staggered and shook as the fire set off secondary explosions. "Gloval! *In here!*" screamed Edwards, standing at the human-size hatch to a side compartment. The survivors dashed to it, crowding in, two of the marines hauling Lang between them while the doctor continued recording the scene as the injured machine-thing shot flame and smoke and flying shrapnel through the air.

"We can hold 'em off from here—for now," Edwards said, throwing aside a spent pair of magazines and inserting a fresh one in his Ingram MAC-35.

"Concentrate fire on anything that approaches that door," Gloval told the marines, and turned to survey the rest of the compartment. It was quite tiny by the standards of the wreck: Perhaps eight paces on a side, with no other exit.

Lang was shaken but in control, *willing* his hands to be

steady as he took what videos he could of the scene in the outer compartment. Gloval was about to command him to get back out of the line of fire when the floor began to move.

"Hey! Who pushed the up button?" Edwards shouted, pale again.

"*Security wheel!*" Gloval bellowed. "Doctor Lang in the center!"

Lang was thrust into the middle of the rising elevator platform as the others put their backs against him, weapons pointed out before them. The ceiling was about to crush them, but suddenly it rippled like water, letting them pass through. They came up into a brighter place and heard a familiar voice.

"Well, well. 'Bout time you guys got here."

"Roy!" The lieutenant stood leaning against a stanchion in the most immense chamber they'd seen yet, lit as bright as day.

When stories were exchanged, Gloval said, "All right, then, we've been herded here. But why?"

Lang pointed to a bridgelike structure enclosed by a transparent bowl, high to the stern end of the compartment. It was big but seemingly built to human scale.

"I'm betting that is the ship's nerve center, skipper, and that is the captain's station."

"It's our best shot, so we shall try it," Gloval decided, "but you stay with the main body, my good doctor, and let Roy go first."

"What an honor." Edwards grinned at Roy.

Zor's quarters were as he had left them, so long ago and far away. The sleep module, the work station, and the rest were built to human scale and function. Lang stared around himself as if in a dream.

Despite the many objects and installations that were impossible to identify, there was a certain comprehensibility to the place: here, a desk unit, there, a screen of some kind.

Roy, Gloval, and the others were so fascinated that they didn't notice what Lang was doing until they heard the pop and crisp of static.

"Lang, you fool! Get away from there!"

But before Gloval could tear him away from the console, Lang had somehow discovered how to activate it. Waves of distortion chased each other across the screen, then a face appeared among the wavering lines.

Gloval's grip on Lang's jacket became limp. "Good God . . . it's *human!*"

"Not quite, perhaps, but close, I would say," Lang conceded calmly.

Zor's face stared out of the screen. The wide, almond eyes seemed to look at each man in the compartment, and the mouth spoke in a melodious, chiming language unlike anything the humans had ever heard before.

"It's a 'greetings' recording," Lang said matter-of-factly.

"Like those plates and records on the old Voyagers," Roy murmured.

The alien's voice took on a different tone, and another image flashed on the screen. The humans found themselves looking at an Invid shock trooper in action, firing and rending.

"Some kind of war machine. Nasty," Lang interpreted.

As the others watched the image, Roy touched Gloval's shoulder and said, "Captain, I think we'd better get out of here."

"But *how?* This blasted ship keeps rearranging itself."

"*Look!*" cried Edwards, pointing. The deck rippled as a newcomer rose up through it. All weapons came to bear on it except Lang's; the doctor was dividing his attention between what was going on and the continuing message on the screen.

A familiar form stood before them. "It's the drone robot, the one that broke down," the gunny said.

Edwards's eyes narrowed. "Yeah, but how could it have followed us?"

"It appears to be functioning again," Gloval said. "Maybe we can use it to contact the base."

Lang crossed to the robot, which waited patiently. He opened a rear access cowling and went to inspect the internal parts there, then snatched his hands back as if he'd been bitten.

They all crowded around warily, ready to blast the machine to bits. "This isn't the original circuitry," Lang said, sounding interested but not frightened. "The components are reshaping themselves."

As they stared, wires writhed and microchips changed like a miniaturized urban renewal project seen from above by time-lapse photography. Things slid, folded, altered shape and position. It reminded Roy of an unlikely cross between a blossoming flower and those kids' games where the player slides alphanumeric tiles around into new sequences.

"Perhaps it's been sent here to lead us out," Gloval suggested.

"But why'd the other gizmos attack?" Edwards objected.

Lang shrugged. "Who knows what damage the systems have suffered? Perhaps the attacks are a result of a malfunction. Certainly, the message we just saw was intended as a warning, which implies good intentions."

"But what's it all mean, Doc?" Roy burst out.

Lang looked to him. "It means Earth may be in for more visitors, I think. *Lots* more."

"All right, all of you: Get ready," Gloval said. "If we can get the drone to lead us, we'll take a chance on it. We've no alternative."

While the others readied themselves, dividing up the remaining ammunition, reloading the last two rocket launchers, and listening to Gloval direct their order of march, Lang went back to the screen console.

He had been right; this *was* the ship's nerve center, and the console and its peripherals were the nucleus of it all. Lang began form-function analysis, fearing that he would never get another chance to study it.

Certainly, the ship used no source of power that he could conceive of. Some uncanny alien force coursed through the fallen ship and through the console. Perhaps if he could get some data on it or get access to it . . .

At Lang's cry they all turned with guns raised, as strobing light threw their shadows tall against the bulkheads. The command center flashed and flowed with power like an unearthly network of electronic blood vessels.

The console was surrounded by a blinding aurora of harsh radiance that pulsed through the spectrum. Lang, body convulsed in agony, holding fast to the console, shone with those same colors as the enigmatic forces flooding into him.

*"Don't touch him!"* Gloval barked at Roy, who'd been about to attempt a body check to knock Lang clear. Edwards moved to one side, well out of range of the discharges, to get a line of fire on the console that wouldn't risk hitting Lang. Edwards made sure his selector was on full auto and prepared to empty the magazine into the console.

But before he could, the alien lightning died away. Lang slumped slowly to the deck.

"Captain, the robby's leaving!" The gunny pointed to where the deck was starting to ripple around the drone's feet.

There was no time for caution. Roy slung Lang over his shoulder, hoping the man wasn't radioactive or something else contagious. In another moment they were all ranged around the robot, sinking through the floor.

Air and matter and space seemed to shift around them. Lang was stirring on Roy's shoulder, and Roy was getting a better grip on him, distracted, when one of the marines hollered, "Tell me I'm not seein' this!"

The ship had changed again, or they were in a different place. And they were gazing at the remains of a giant.

It was something straight out of legend. The skeleton was still wearing a uniform that was obviously immune to decay. It also wore a belt and harness affair fitted with various devices and pouches. But for the fact that it would've stood some fifty feet tall, it could have been human.

The jaw was frozen open in an eternal rictus of agony and death; an area the size and shape of a poker table was burned through the back of its uniform, fringed by blackened fabric. Much of the skeletal structure in the wound's line of fire was gone.

"Musta been some scrap," a marine said quietly, knowingly.

Lang was struggling, so Roy let him down. "Are you all right, Doc—"

Roy gaped at him. Lang's eyes had changed, become all dark, deep pupil with no iris and no white at all. He had the look of a man in rapture, gazing around himself with measureless approval.

"Yes, yes," Lang said, nodding in comprehension. "I *see*!"

There was no time to find out just what it was he saw, because the robot was in motion again. Roy took Lang in tow, and they moved out, only to round a corner and come face to face with two more of the armored guardians.

The gunny, walking point right behind the robby with one of the RPG launchers, let fly instantly, and the machine gunner and the other RPG man cut loose too as the red lines of tracers arced and rebounded off the bright armor.

## INTERLUDE

> *Listen, take the Bill of Rights, the Boy Scout oath, and the*
> *Three Laws of Robotics and stick 'em where there's no direct*
> *dialing, jerk! "Good" is anything that helps me stay at the top;*
> *"bad" is whatever doesn't, got it?*
>
> Senator Russo to his reelection committee treasurer

"**A**ND, IN BRIEF," ADMIRAL HAYES FINISHED, "Captain Gloval's party made it back out of the ship with no further casualties, although they encountered extremely heavy resistance."

Senator Russo puffed on his cigar, considering the report. "And Doctor Lang?"

"Seems to be all right," Hayes said. "They wanted to keep him under observation for a while, but he's absolutely determined to resume research on the alien vessel. And you know Lang."

Indeed. Earth's foremost genius, the man to whom they would all have to look now for crucial answers, made his own rules.

"I should add one more part of the aftermission report that I still find it difficult to credit," Hayes grudged. "Captain Gloval estimates, and his and the others' watches corroborate this, that they were inside the ship for some six hours."

Russo blew a smoke ring. "So?"

Hayes scratched his cheek reflectively. "According to

27

the guards posted outside the ship and *their* watches, Gloval and the others were only gone for approximately fifteen minutes." He sat down again at the conference table.

Russo, at the head of the table, thought that over. He knew Hayes was too methodical an officer to include a claim like that in his report without having checked it thoroughly.

Senator Russo was a florid-faced, obese little man with a gratingly false-hearty manner and a pencil mustache. He had fat jowls and soft white hands bearing pinkie rings. He also had a brilliant tailor, a marvelous barber, and enough political clout to make him perhaps *the* most important figure in the emerging world government.

Now, he looked around the top-secret conference room aboard the *Kenosha*. "Whoever sent this vessel may come to retrieve it. Or someone else might."

He broke into an unctuous smile. "If something like this hadn't come along, we'd've had to invent it! It's perfect!"

The other power mongers gathered there nodded, sharing the sly smile, their eyes alight with ambition.

The timing of the crash was indeed astounding. Not a month before, these same men had been part of a group that had met to lay the groundwork for one of the most treacherous plots in history. It's true they were confronting the ultimate crisis—the likelihood that the human race would destroy itself. But their solution was not the most benign, just the one that would be most profitable for them.

They'd been intent on creating an artificial crisis, something that would stop the war and unite humanity under their leadership. A number of promising scenarios had been developed, including epidemics, worldwide crop failure, and a much less spectacular version of the very thing that had taken place in Earth's atmosphere and on Macross Island.

Russo's smile was close to a leer. "Gentlemen, I don't believe I'm being presumptuous when I say this is destiny at work! The blindest fool can see that mankind *must* band together."

*Under our rule*, was the unstated subtext. Russo saw that the true power brokers there understood, while Hayes and a few other idealistic dupes were almost teary-eyed with dedication and courage. Suckers...

It had never really mattered to the power brokers what side they served, of course; the ideologies and historical causes of the Global Civil War meant little or nothing to them. Russo and others like him had given those mere lip service.

The important thing was to use the opportunity, to gain prestige and power. Russo had joined the Internationalists —the world peace and disarmament movement—because they offered personal opportunity. If they hadn't, he'd have thrown in with the factionalists without a qualm, so long as they promised him a route to power.

Hayes was saying, "We must act with all possible speed, throw every available resource into understanding the science behind that ship, into rebuilding it, and using this amazing 'Robotechnology,' as Doctor Lang insists on calling it."

*Absolutely beautiful!* Russo thought. An enormous tax-supported defense project, more expensive and more massive than anything in human history! The opportunities for profit would be incalculable. In the meantime, the military could be kept distracted and obedient, and all political power would be consolidated. More, this incredible Robotechnology business would ensure that the new world government would be absolutely unchallengeable.

Russo frowned for a moment, considering Hayes again: good soldier, obedient and conscientious, but a plodding sort of fellow (which was Russo's personal shorthand for someone prone to be honest).

Yes, Hayes might present a problem somewhere down the road—say, once Earth was rebuilt and unified and ready to be brought to heel, when it was time to make sure that those in power stayed there for good.

But there would be ways to deal with that. For example, didn't Hayes have a teenage daughter? Ah, yes. Russo recalled her now: a rather plain, withdrawn little thing, as the senator remembered. *Lisa.*

In any case, there'd be plenty of time to neutralize

Hayes and those like him once they'd served their purpose. Have to keep an eye on that Lang, too.

But this Colonel Edwards, now; he seemed to be a bright young fellow—knew which side his bread was buttered on. He was already passing secret information to Russo and keeping tabs on Gloval and the others. Edwards would definitely have his uses.

"Let's have Doctor Lang, eh?" Senator Russo proposed.

Lang came in, lean and pale, emitting an almost tangible energy and purpose. The strange, whiteless eyes were unsettling to look at.

"Well, Doctor," Russo said heartily. "We've had a miracle dropped from heaven, eh? But we want you to give us the straight gospel: Can that ship be rebuilt?"

Lang looked at him as if he were seeing Russo for the first time—as if Russo had interrupted Lang during some higher contemplation, as, of course, he had.

"Rebuild it? But of course we will; what else did you think we would do?" It sounded as though he had doubts about Russo's sanity, which was mutual.

Before Russo could say anything, Lang continued. "But you used the word 'miracle.' I suppose that may be true, but I want to tell all of you something that Captain Gloval said to me when we finally fought our way out of the ship."

He waited a dramatic moment, as his whiteless eyes seemed to take in the whole conference room and look beyond.

"Gloval said, 'This will save the human race from destroying itself, Doctor, and that makes it a kind of miracle. But history and legend tell us that miracles bear a heavy price.'"

# CHAPTER
# THREE

*There's a movie my grandfather loved as a boy, and my father sat me on his knee and showed me when I was a little kid, The Shape of Things to Come.*

*The part that made the biggest impression, naturally, was when the scientist-aviator climbs out of his futuristic plane and looks the local fascist right in the eye and tells him there'll be no more war. Babe, how many times I've wished it was that easy!*

Lt. Comdr. Roy Fokker, in a letter to Lt. Claudia Grant

"**F**IREWORKS," LIEUTENANT COMMANDER ROY Fokker murmured to himself, neck arched back so that he could watch the bright flowers of light. The gigantic mass of Super Dimensional Fortress One blocked out much of the sky, but he could still see skyrockets burst into brilliant light above every corner of Macross City. There were banners and flags, band music, and the constant laughter and cheering of thousands upon thousands of people.

"Fireworks instead of bombs; celebrations instead of battles." Roy nodded. "I hope it's always like this: parades and picnics. We've seen enough war!"

Macross Island had changed a lot in ten years—all for the better, in Roy's opinion. After the World Government made rebuilding the alien wreck its first priority, a bright modern city had been erected around the crash site, along with landing strips used to airlift supplies and equipment, construction materials, technicians and workers and their families, and military personnel.

A busy deep-water harbor had been dredged, too. Two colossal aircraft carriers were anchored there, though they were dwarfed by the vessel in whose shadow Roy stood. Flights of helos and jetcraft made their passes overhead, rendering salute to the Earth's new defender, Super Dimensional Fortress One.

Roy glanced up at the SDF-1 again. Even after a decade, he was still awed every time he gazed at it. Its hull and superstructures gleamed, sleek and bright now, painted in blue and white. The vast transparent bubble of the bridge bulged like a spacesuit facebowl, giving the eerie impression that the fortress was keeping watch over the city.

Roy still found himself wondering what the ship had originally looked like before its terrible crash. How close had Lang and his team come to restoring it to its original state?

One thing was certain: Lang and the others had performed the most amazing technical feat in Earth's history. Not all the battle fortress's secrets were theirs, not yet; but that seemed only a matter of time. In the meantime they'd gotten the SDF-1 fully operational, and given the Earth the means to build its Robotech Defense Force—the RDF.

And today, for the first time, the general populace was going to see things that had been classified top-secret.

A flight of Veritech fighters, wings swept back for high speeds, performed a fly-by. They were from Skull Team, Roy's command. "Wait'll we show 'em what we can do," he said, smiling.

Across town, a motorcade made its way with flashing lights and wailing sirens toward the SDF-1's platform, already late for the ship's scheduled launch on its maiden flight. Motorcycle outriders led the way, followed by a *long* stretch limousine. Bunting and pennons hung everywhere.

Not everyone in town was overjoyed with the day's festivities. Macross City's mayor, a small, stocky man who usually showed good humor, scowled in disapproval as the motorcade rolled in his direction. Vern Havers, who ran one of the town's more prosperous appliance stores, stood by his side, watching.

"Now what's wrong, Mr. Mayor? What's all that sighing about?"

Mayor Tommy Luan shrugged. "Aw, after all these

years, it's hard to believe we may be looking at the old girl for the last time." Both men gazed at the colossal ship, which dominated the city and the island, its running lights blinking and flashing.

Of course, SDF-1 was only leaving for a test flight, to be followed by a short shakedown cruise if everything checked out well; but the mayor could be right—there was no telling when the fortress might return.

Certainly, Macross would never be the same place again.

"We'll all miss her," Vern conceded. "But aren't you proud to see her launched at last?"

"Of course. But if the test is successful, we'll all be unemployed!" the mayor burst out. Vern wasn't looking forward to closing down his business either, but he remembered the war very well. He had to admit he liked the idea of the battle fortress being out there in space, guarding the planet, a lot better than the mayor seemed to.

Vern sighed. A lot of people had forgotten just why Macross City existed. But Vern kept his opinion to himself.

The motorcycles and limousine roared by. "The big shots making their grand entrance!" The mayor sniffed. It was well known that the mayor hadn't been invited to any of the important ceremonies; the world leaders were keeping the prize honors for themselves.

"Captain Gloval doesn't seem too happy about it," Vern observed, hoping it would make Tommy Luan feel a little better.


Not happy, indeed. As the limo shot along, Russo, sharing the back seat with Gloval, waved tirelessly, flashing his smile to everyone with the bland relentlessness of a career politician.

Without turning from the crowds, he chided, "Don't look so sour, Gloval! It's our big day! Surely you realize all those loyal citizens out there consider you their hero! You could at least wave to them."

Gloval grunted, chin sunk on his chest, arms folded. He was wearing his dress uniform, and some pushy liaison officer had seen to it that every decoration Gloval was entitled to wear was in place. Gloval had certainly won more than his share of medals and "fruit salad" over the years, but he didn't much like being in the spotlight. He was grumpy.

Still, there was something to what Russo had said. The senator might consider it *his* big day, but it was those people out there who'd worked like mad these last ten years, sacrificed and hoped, all in the name of peace and security for future generations.

"All right, I'll wave," said Gloval, hoping the speech-makers' foolishness and the political hacks' patting themselves on the back wouldn't last long. Gloval only wanted to be out in space with his new command.

At SDF-1, all was controlled commotion. The Veritech demonstration was due to begin at any moment, and final preparations to get the fortress under way were still not on schedule. Comcircuits and the ship's intercoms rang with checklist items: engine room and astrogation systems, communications and life support, combat and support squadrons, and more. Literally millions of items had to be double-checked by the SDF-1's thousands of crew members during those final days of preparation.

Up on the bridge, Commander Lisa Hayes arrived to make sure everything would be squared away for launching. Admiral Hayes's daughter had always made it a point of honor to show more merit, more skill at her job, and more dedication to the service than anyone around her so that there could be no question of favoritism when the time came for promotion.

She'd carved out an amazing career for herself. At twenty-four, she'd been made First Officer of SDF-1. A lot of that was due, no doubt, to her familiarity with the ship's systems: With the exception of Doctor Lang, no one had such a complete and comprehensive knowledge of the vessel's every bolt and button.

But there were her endless commendations and top evaluations as well, and two decorations for courage under fire. Some people thought her too severe, too single-minded in her obsession with duty, but no one accused her of not earning her rank.

She paused to survey the bridge, a slim, tall, pale young

woman with blond-brown hair that bobbed, confined in graceful locks, against her shoulders. Her subordinates were already at their duty stations.

Claudia Grant seemed to have things well in hand, speaking into an intercom terminal from her position at the Bridge Officer's station. "Roger, engine room; that's affirmative."

Vanessa, Sammie, and Kim, three young female enlisted-rating techs, completed the bridge complement; Gloval liked running things with as little confusion and as few people as possible.

Vanessa was feeding computer projections of fuel consumption to the engine room while Kim finished up the astrogation checklist and Sammie saw to the manual systems. They were all young, like Lisa—like most of SDF-1's crew. Robotechnology and the weapons and machines it had spawned were a whole new game; taking people while they were young and instilling its strange disciplines in them had proved more workable, in most cases, than trying to get veterans to unlearn what they'd already taken to heart.

Lisa sighed, brushing her hair back with her hand, making her way to her station. "The ceremony starts in fifteen minutes. I hope the captain gets here in time. The scuttlebutt is that he didn't get much sleep last night."

Claudia gave a smile, her brown face creasing, eyes dancing. "Yeah; the flag-rank officers threw a farewell party for him. They probably sat up all night telling each other war stories. *You* know how they are."

Lisa hid a mischievous smile. "And where were *you*, Claudia? Hmm?"

Claudia was taken off guard. "What're you talking about?"

"You didn't get back to your quarters until four in the morning, that's what! You must've been partying too."

Claudia stuck her nose in the air and struck a glamorous pose. She was taller than Lisa and several years older, with exotic good looks crowned by a cap of close, coffee-colored curls.

"You jealous? I had a late dinner with Commander Fokker."

Lisa had been joking, assuming Claudia had spent her last groundside leave visiting with her family, but suddenly the First Officer was angry.

"Claudia! You stayed out all night, knowing you and Roy both have flight duty today?" Duty was everything to Lisa; she had trouble understanding how anyone could be so casual about such an important mission.

But there was also something else, something about Claudia's love affair with the handsome, heroic Roy Fokker—not jealousy, but rather a feeling of Lisa's own loneliness. It brought an uncharacteristic confusion to her, a sudden emptiness that made her doubt the principles by which she lived her life. She shied away from it, reasserting control over herself by acting every inch the First Officrer.

But Lisa wasn't the only one who was angry. Claudia set her hands on her hips. "So? What's the big fuss about, Lisa? We won't let it affect our performance on duty. After all, we're not children—and you're not our mother!"

Lisa felt her cheeks growing red. "Your responsibilities to the ship come first, Claudia!"

Neither one was backing away from the confrontation, and Claudia looked like she was running out of patience. And given her size and temper and the fact that she was an accomplished hand-to-hand fighter, Claudia was nobody to antagonize unnecessarily.

"My private life is my own business! Nobody else's!" Claudia stopped herself just short of some cutting remark: *Why don't you try loosening up for a change, Lisa?*, for example.

But she got hold of herself instead. "Now then, let's get to work, all right?" She pointed toward Lisa's duty station. "Get outta here."

Lisa hesitated, unused to backing away from a fight, and still angry but feeling she'd overstepped her authority. Just then Vanessa said slyly, "Lisa doesn't understand about men, Claudia. She's in love with this spaceship."

Claudia couldn't resist a grin, and Kim threw in, "Yeah, you got that right!"

That stung Lisa terribly, though she'd have died before admitting it. She knew she had a reputation as a cold fish among most of the ship's complement; maybe that was why, against the rules of good discipline, she'd found herself becoming close with the other women with whom she spent so much time on the bridge. Besides, Captain Gloval's informal and even indulgent way of running the bridge —rather fatherly, really—made it it easy to make friends.

But now Lisa felt herself flush angrily. "That wasn't funny, Vanessa; we have an important job to do here—"

Claudia, still steaming, interrupted her: "You act like I don't care about our mission at all!"

Sammie, at twenty the youngest of the bridge crew, couldn't bear to hear her friends fight anymore. "Oh, don't argue!" she cried.

She was so plaintive that the danger level lowered a little. "I'm not the one who keeps butting into everybody's business," Claudia pointed out.

Not quite ready to retreat, Lisa let out a growl she'd somehow picked up during her time with Gloval. Even as she began, "I'm warning you—" she was aware of a new sound in the bridge, cutting through her anger.

Claudia wore a haughty look, nose in the air again. "I hate to interrupt, but hadn't you better check your monitor, *Commander*?"

Then Lisa realized that an insistent signal was sounding from her duty station. She crossed to it, trying to put the argument out of her mind as Kim called out, "It's an unidentified incoming aircraft, Lisa!"

Checking her monitors, Lisa saw it was on an approved approach path and signaling for landing instructions. Since none of the many military aircraft flying patrol around Macross Island had challenged or interfered with the new arrival, it could be nothing but a peaceful visitor.

Lisa opened a communication link, resolving to try to smooth things out with her friends. She'd so much wanted the day to be right, to be marked by excellence and top performance! Why couldn't anyone share her drive for perfection? Perhaps she was simply fated to be the outcast, the oddball—

"Attention, aircraft approaching on course one-zero-seven," she said coolly. "Please identify yourself."

A youngish male voice came in response. "This is Rick Hunter. I have an invitation for today's ceremonies, invitation number two-zero-three."

Lisa checked it against another computer display, although she found herself irked by the job. The SDF-1 was set to launch, and she was expected to act as an air traffic tech!

But she responded, "That's confirmed as an invitation from Lieutenant Commander Fokker." *Fokker!* Lisa kept emotion out of her voice and avoided meeting Claudia's eye, finishing, "Follow course five-seven for landing."

"Roger," the voice said cheerfully, and signed off.

*With all the important things I have to worry about,* Lisa mumbled to herself, *they also have to saddle me with babysitting the Rick Hunters of this world?*

# CHAPTER
# FOUR

*All right, you win, "Big Brother." I'll come to your party. I'll even put up with all those military types you hang around with. But try not to make it too boring, okay?*

Rick Hunter's RSVP to Roy Fokker's invitation to the SDF-1's launch ceremonies

**H**IGH ABOVE MACROSS ISLAND, AN UNUSUAL AIRcraft began to descend into the complex flight patterns of Launching Day, following course five-seven for landing, just as Lisa Hayes had instructed.

Rick Hunter whistled as he got a better look at the SDF-1. The descriptions and the newscasts just didn't begin to do justice to the astonishing *size* of the thing! The two supercarriers anchored among the flotilla of ships in the harbor were of the new Thor class—each longer than a 150-story office building resting on its side—yet they were modest in comparison to the battle fortress.

And the sky was full of the sleekest, most advanced-looking fighters Rick had ever seen—Robotech fighters, the newscasts had called them. Whatever that meant. For a moment Rick couldn't blame Roy Fokker for dedicating himself to this Robotech stuff.

After a decade of secrecy, the United Earth Government promised the wonderful new breakthroughs made on Macross would be revealed. To Rick, it simply meant that Roy wouldn't have to be so hush-hush about what he was doing, and perhaps their friendship could get back on its old footing.

Rick maneuvered his ship smoothly through the traffic, relying not on his computers but on his own talent and training—a point of pride. He was the offspring of a proud, daring breed: last of the barnstormers, the stunt fliers and the seat-of-the-pants winged daredevils.

He was eighteen years old and hadn't been outflown since—well, long before his voice had changed from a kid's to a young man's.

His plane was a nimble little racer of his own design. A roomy one-seater, white with red trim, powered primarily by an oversize propfan engine but hiding a few surprises under its sleek fuselage. Rick had named it the *Mockingbird*, a fittingly arrogant name for the undisputed star of the last of the flying circuses.

He tossed a dark forelock of hair back and adjusted his tinted goggles, then went into a pushover and power dive for the SDF-1. This Robotech stuff *looked* impressive... but maybe it was time somebody showed these military flyboys that it was the *pilot* that mattered most, not some pile of mere metal.

Far out beyond the orbit of Earth's moon, a portentous tremble shook the spacetime continuum as if it were a spiderweb. It was only a preliminary disturbance, yet it was exacting and of great extent. A force beyond reckoning was making tentative contact on a day that marked a turning point in the history of the unsuspecting earth.

On Macross Island, in the shadow of the SDF-1, Roy didn't have time to notice the tiny racing plane making a pass over the ship's bow, thousands of feet above him. The public address system carried an announcement to the tens of thousands gathered there.

"And now we present an amazing display of aerial acrobatics, demonstrating the amazing advances we have made through Robotechnology. Lieutenant Commander Roy Fokker, leader of the Veritech fighters' Skull Team, will describe and explain the action for us."

Roy made his entrance to enthusiastic applause; he was known to and well liked by most people on Macross Island. Tall and handsome in his uniform, the blond hair still full and thick, he stopped before the microphone stand. He gave a snappy salute, then fell into parade rest and began his address.

"Today, ladies and gentlemen, you'll see how we've applied human know-how to understanding and harnessing a complex alien technology."

Overhead, a half dozen swift, deadly Veritech fighters peeled off to begin their performance.

"Keep your eyes on planes two and four," Roy went on as two and four lined up for the first maneuver, engines blaring. "Flying at speeds of five hundred miles per hour, only fifty feet above the ground, they will pass within just a few yards of one another. Robotechnology makes such precision possible."

Roy looked out over the crowd with satisfaction. All eyes were gazing up in amazement at the onrushing fighters.

But the show would build from there. Precision flying was nothing compared to the *other* forms of control Robotechnology gave human beings over their new instruments. At long last average citizens would get to see Guardian and Battloid modes in action, Robotechnology applications that until now had been used only in restricted training areas or drills far out at sea, when the Veritechs were launching from the decks of the *Daedalus* and the *Prometheus*.

Those people in the throng, the ordinary citizens of Macross, were the ones who deserved the first live look at what the SDF-1 project had brought forth. They'd earned that right—much more than all the politicians, who had merely voted how much time and work and money would be spent—time and work and money that were invariably *not* the politicians'.

Today, all the rumors and speculations about Robotechnology would be put to rest, and the people of Earth would find out that the reality surpassed them all.

Roy was thinking about that happily as he spoke, waiting for the inevitable gasps from the crowd as the first high-speed pass was executed. It took him a few seconds to realize that the people below the speakers' platform weren't gasping.

They were laughing.

Roy whirled, craning his head to look up. Two and four had been forced to peel off from their pass by the sudden appearance of an interloper, a gaudy little stunt plane, absurdly out of place among the modern miracle machines.

*A circus plane!* "Oh no-o-o!" Roy didn't have to guess who it was; he'd arranged for the invitation himself, and he was regretting it already. He grabbed the microphone out of its stand and flipped the switch that would patch him through to the aircom net.

"Rick! Is that you, Hunter?"

The little *Mockingbird* gave a jaunty waggle of its wings in salute as Rick banked slowly overhead. His reply came patched through the PA system.

"Roy! It's good to hear your voice, old buddy! They tell me you're a lieutenant commander now. The army must really be desperate!"

Furious, Roy yelled into the mike. "Are you crazy? Get that junk heap out of here!" He forgot that he was still patched through the PA, so that the whole crowd followed the exchange. Of course, as loud and angry as Roy was, the people up front would've had no trouble hearing him anyway.

The people below thought it was great, and the laughter started again, even louder. Roy was shaking one fist at the little stunt plane, holding the mike stand aloft with the other, like Jove brandishing a lightning bolt. "Hunter, when I get my hands on you, I'm gonna—"

Roy didn't get to elaborate on that; just then the bottom half of the telescoping mike stand dropped, nearly landing on his foot.

Roy caught it just in time—at thirty, he was one of the oldest of the Veritech fighter pilots, yet his reflexes hadn't slowed a bit—but couldn't quite get it to fit back together. Fumbling, forgetting what he'd been about to say, he was ready to explode with frustration.

He abruptly became aware of the laughter all around him. The crowd was roaring, some of them nearly in tears.

One young woman in front caught his eye, though. She looked to be in her mid teens, slender and long-legged, with a charming face and hair black as night. She was standing behind a kid, possibly her brother, who was laughing so hard, he seemed to be having trouble breathing.

At some other time, Roy might have tried to catch her eye and exchange a smile, but he just wasn't in the mood. His face reddened as the laughter washed over him, and he unknowingly echoed Lisa Hayes's sentiments of a few moments before: *Why today, of all days?*

Roy covered the mike with his gloved palm and stage-whispered to one of the techs. "Hey, Ed! Switch this circuit over to radio only, will you?" It was going to be awfully hard to chew out his men about com-procedure discipline after today.

It took only a second or two for Ed to make the change.

"What're you trying to do, Rick, make a perfect fool of me?"

Roy could hear the laughter in his old friend's voice. "Aw, nobody's *perfect*, Commander!"

Roy was just about grinning in spite of himself. People who didn't watch their step every moment were liable to become Rick Hunter's straight men. Roy decided to give him back a bit of his own. "You haven't changed a bit, have you, kid? Well, this isn't an amateur flying circus; my men are *real* pilots!"

"Amateur, huh?" Rick drawled. He looked off in the distance and saw the Veritech fighters in a diamond formation for a power climb, preparing to do a "bomb-burst" maneuver. "I'm gonna have to make you eat those words, Commander. Comin' in."

"Stop clowning around, Rick—look out!"

*Mockingbird* swooped down in a hair-raising dive, barely missing the speaker's platform, so low that Roy had to duck to avoid getting his head taken off. A lot of people in the crowd hit the dirt too, and most of them cried out in shock. Roy caught another glimpse of the pretty young thing in the front row; she seemed thrilled and happy, not in the least frightened.

Roy spun as the *Mockingbird* zoomed off, building on the acceleration it had picked up in its dive. Suddenly, as the little aircraft was safely away from the crowd, covers blew free from six booster-jet pods mounted around the turbofan cowling at the rear of the ship, and powerful gusts of flame lifted it into a vertical climb. The crowd went *"Oh!"*

Leaving streamers of rocket exhaust, the *Mockingbird* went ballistic, quickly overtaking the slower-moving formation of Veritechs.

"Get out of there!" Roy yelled up at him, not even bothering with the mike, knowing it was pointless. "Headstrong" was a word they'd *invented* with Rick Hunter in mind.

Rick cut in full power, came up into formaton perfectly, becoming part of the display, as the Veritech fighters completed their climb and arced away in different directions, like a huge version of the afternoon's skyrockets.

The crowd was applauding wildly, cheering. Roy shook his fist again, furious—but a part of him was proud of his friend.

Out in space, vast forces were coalescing—nothing Earth's detectors could perceive yet, though that would happen soon. Soon, but too late for Earth.

Contact had been made; an inconceivable gap was about to be bridged, a marvel of science put to hellish use.

As *Mockingbird* floated in for a perfect landing, Roy leaped from the speaker's platform, so eager to get at Rick that he forgot to let go of the mike, yanking the stand over and nearly tripping on the microphone cord. The cord snaked along behind him as he ran.

Rick raised the clear bubble of the cockpit canopy as he taxied to a stop, his forelock of dark hair fluttering in the breeze. He pushed his tinted flying goggles high on his forehead. "Whew! Hi, Roy."

Roy was in no mood for *hi*'s. "Who d' you think you are? What were you trying to do, get yourself killed?"

Rick was nonchalant, pulling off his headset and goggles and tossing them back into the cockpit as he hiked himself up. "Hey, calm down!"

Not a chance. Roy still had the mike in one hand, a few yards of cable attached to it. He flung it down angrily on the hardtop runway surface. "And while we're at it, where'd you learn to do that, anyway?"

Rick had his hands up to hold the much bigger Roy at bay. He gave a quick smile. "It was just a simple booster climb. You taught it to me when I was just a kid!"

"*Ahhh!*" Roy reached out, grabbed Rick by the upper arm, and began dragging him off across the hardtop.

"Hey!" Rick objected, but he could see that he'd taken a lot of the voltage out of Roy's wrath with that reminder of old times.

"I have to admit, those guys up there were pretty good," Rick went on, jerking his arm free, straightening his dapper white silk scarf. "Not as good as *me*, of course."

Roy made a sour expression. "You don't have to brag to me, Rick. I know all about your winning the amateur flying competition last year."

"Not amateur; *civilian*!" Rick bristled. Then he went on with great self-pleasure. "And actually, I've won it eight years in a row. What've *you* been doing?"

"*I* was busy fighting a war! Combat flying and dogfighting kept me kind of occupied. Hundred 'n' eight enemy kills, so they tell me."

"You're proud of being a killer?"

They'd touched on an old, sore subject. Rick's late father had rejected military service in the Global Civil War, though he would have been the very best. Jack "Pop" Hunter had seen combat before and wanted no more part of that. He had instilled a strong sense of this conviction in his son.

Roy stopped, fists cocked, though Rick continued walking. "*What?*" With anyone else, a serious fistfight would have resulted from this exchange. But this was Rick, who'd been like family. More than family.

Roy swallowed his fury, hurrying after. "There was a war on, and I was a soldier! I just did my duty!"

They made a strange pair, crossing the hardtop side by side: Roy in his black and mauve Veritech uniform and Rick, a head shorter, in the white and blazing orange of his circus uniform.

They stopped by a vending machine unlike any Rick had seen before, which offered something called Petite Cola. Rick fed it some coins while the machine made strange internal noises. He took a can of ice-cold soda for himself, giving Roy the other.

"You promised my dad that as soon as the war was over you'd come back to the air circus. Why'd you go back on that, Roy?"

Roy was suddenly distant. "I really felt guilty about letting your father down, only . . . this Robotech thing is so important, I just couldn't give it up."

He pulled the tab on his soda, torn by the need to explain to Rick and the knowledge that some parts of the original mission to Macross Island, and of Robotechnology, were still classified and might be for decades more. He felt a debt, too, to the late Pop Hunter.

Roy shrugged. "It gets into your blood or something; I don't know."

Rick scowled, leaning back against the Petite Cola machine. "What *is* Robotech, anyway? Just more modern war machinery!" Somewhere, he could hear a kid raising a ruckus. "And the aliens—*huh*?"

He couldn't figure out how he'd lost his balance, sliding along the vending machine. Then he realized it was moving out from behind him.

The Petite Cola machine was rolling eagerly toward the child, a boy of seven or so who was throwing a terrible tantrum.

"Cola! I wanna *cola*! You promised me you'd buy me a cola, Minmei, and I want one right now!" He was dressed in a junior version of a Veritech pilot's uniform, Rick saw disgustedly. *Teach 'em while they're young!*

Roy looked around to see the commotion. He was suddenly very attentive when he saw the person trying to reason with the kid—"Minmei"—was the young lady who'd been standing at the edge of the speaker's platform.

She was charming in a short red dress, pulling on the boy's arm, trying to keep him from the vending machine that was closing in for the sale. "Cousin Jason, behave yourself! I already bought you one cola; you can't have any more!"

Jason wasn't buying it, stamping his feet and screaming. "Why? *I wanna cola-aaahh!*"

To Rick's amazement, the scene turned into a combination wrestling match and game of keepaway: Minmei was trying to prevent Jason from reaching the machine and was crying, "Cancel the order, please, machine!" while Jason struggled to get past her. In the meantime, the machine, circling and darting, made every effort to reach him short of rolling over Minmei. With its persistence and agility, the vending machine somehow gave the impression that it was alive.

"Never saw anything like *that*." Rick blinked.

Roy gave him an enigmatic smile. "Robotechnology has a way of affecting the things around it, sometimes even non-Robotech machines."

Rick groaned. "Robotech again?"

"Jason, you'll make yourself sick!"

"I don't care!" Jason wailed.

"Maybe you could tie a can of soda to a fishing pole and *lure* him home, miss?" Roy suggested.

Minmei turned to him, still deftly keeping the kid from scoring the Petite Cola. She broke into a winsome smile. She was of Chinese blood, Roy figured, though she had strange, blue eyes—not that he was interested! Claudia would probably take a swing at him (and connect) if she found out he was roving. Still, something about Minmei's smile made her irresistible.

"Oh! You're the officer from the stage! You were very, very funny!" Minmei giggled, then turned to the little boy sternly.

"That's it! We're going home! Come on, Jason; don't make me spank you!" She lugged the boy away as the Petite

Cola machine made halfhearted attempts to clinch a sale against all hope.

"Well, Roy," Rick commented, elaborately droll, "I see you're still a big ladies' man."

In deep space, dimensions folded and transition began; death was about to come calling.

# CHAPTER
# FIVE

> *From the first, there were anomalies about the situation on*
> *the target world, things that gave me pause. The second-*
> *guessers would have it that I was remiss in not advising caution*
> *more strongly. But one did not antagonize great Breetai with too*
> *much talk of circumspection, you see—not, at least, without*
> *great risk.*

> Exedore, as quoted in Lapstein's *Interviews*

**T**HE STARS SHIMMERED AND WAVERED AS IF SHIVERING
with dread. And well they should.

The forces that bound the universe were briefly snarled
by a tremendous application of energy. The dimensional
warp and woof pulled apart for a moment.

In a precisely chosen zone of space beyond Luna's orbit,
it was as if a piece of the primordial fireball that gave birth
to the cosmos had been brought back into existence.

Motes bright and hot as novas, infinitesimal bits of the
Cosmic String, were spewed out of the rift in spacetime like
burning sparks of gunpowder from some unimaginable cannon shot; the burning detritus of nonspace moving at
speeds approaching that of light itself, consumed almost as
soon as they came in touch with three-dimensional reality.

Larger anomalies, like furious comets, flared here and
there in the wash of light. Then there was another explosion
beyond any description: the pure emission of unadulterated
hell. It pushed outward from a rip in the fabric of the universe, taking on shape and shedding a raging wave of in-

candescence as if it were water. The shape became longer, more forceful, menacing.

The Zentraedi had come at last.

First was the great flagship, sheets and wind racks of ravenous light streaming away behind it to reveal its shape: nine miles long, an irregular blunt-nosed cylinder.

A vessel many times the size of SDF-1, the flagship was a seemingly endless span of mighty weapons and invulnerable shields, of combat-ship bays and mountainous armor and incalculable firepower. The pride of the Zentraedi fleet, searching the solar system in an instant and knowing where its prey waited.

The flagship had been built with only military conquest, warfare, and destruction in mind. Manning it was a race of beings bred for that single purpose.

The ship was like a leviathan from the deepest oceans of human nightmares, with superstructure features that might be gills here or titanic eyes there, huge spines that were sensor spars, nubbles of the secondary and lesser weapons batteries, projections like questing fangs. Lighted observation ports, some of them a hundred yards across, suggested bulging, multiple eyes.

Behind it came a fleet surpassing any the Zentraedi had ever assembled before, cascading from the spacefold warp that had been their shortcut past the endless light-years. They were a school of gargantuan armored fish numerous enough to fill all the oceans, plated and scaled in sinister greens and browns and blacks, with pale underbellies in sickly grays and blues.

There were more of them than the visible stars. They were the mightiest Zentraedi armada ever seen, and yet they were cautious. They followed a flagship that knew no equal in any fleet they'd ever encountered, and yet they were wary.

If translated into human terms, their caution would mean something like: *Even wolves can be prey to the tiger*.

Having pursued the single wounded tiger across space and time, the fleet of so many hundred thousand ships formed up around the flagship.

In the transparent bowl of the Supreme Commander's

flagship, Breetai, tall and stiff in his dress uniform, gazed down on his operations center. Even for a Zentraedi, he was a mighty tower of bone and muscle, as strong as any trooper under his command and as good a fighter. Like many of his engineered race, his skin was a mauve shade suggestive of clay.

A projecbeam drew a two-dimensional image of the target planet in midair, a puny and an unremarkable blue-white sphere, nothing much to look at. Rather disappointing, really.

Breetai reached up one hand to touch the cold crystal-and-metal half cowl that covered much of his head, thinking back to the day so long ago when Zor had died, and the dimensional fortress had been lost. The failure still burned at him.

He'd accepted that with a warrior's fatalism, and with a warrior's lust for triumph he contemplated the final victory that would be his this day.

Breetai studied the Earth coldly. "The finder beam has locked on this planet. Are you sure this is the source of those emanations?" His voice was huge and deep, with a resonance that shook the bulkheads.

Off to one side, Exedore, Breetai's adviser, kowtowed slightly, showing deference from habit even though he wasn't in Breetai's line of vision. "Yes, sir, I'm positive."

Breetai pursed his lips in thought. "They *could* have executed a refold." The thought of losing his quarry again was almost unbearable, but Breetai allowed no emotion to show.

"It's doubtful, sir," Exedore said quickly. "There was no evidence of a second jump into hyperspace."

Savagely, Breetai thought again of those traitors to his race and their narrow escape. "Hmm. They couldn't have gone far in their condition. And they would have to land in order to repair the ship." He looked to Exedore. "That's a logical conclusion, I think."

Exedore inclined his head respectfully. "I agree. It *would* seem very likely, sir."

Breetai was used to acting on his own instincts and deductions; but it was reassuring that Exedore, the most brilliant intellect of the Zentraedi race, was in accord.

Breetai considered Exedore for a moment: small, almost a dwarf by the standards of their species, and frail into the bargain. Gaunt, with protruding, seemingly lidless eyes and a wild thatch of odd, rust-red hair, Exedore was still the embodiment of Zentraedi law and tradition—and more valuable to the towering commander than any battlefleet. Yet with all that, he was loyal, almost selfless in his devotion to Breetai.

Breetai gave Exedore a curt nod. "Very well; dispatch a scout team for a preliminary reconnaissance."

In the Zentraedi warrior religion, efficiency was a virtue ranking only behind loyalty and courage in battle. The words were scarcely out of Breetai's mouth when two of the fleet's heavy cruisers detached themselves and advanced on the unwary planet.

At the festivities in the shadow of the SDF-1, Rick was getting his first close look at a Veritech fighter that had been put on display. Because he was accompanied by Roy, Rick was allowed into the roped-off area around the craft and permitted a hands-on examination of the ship.

"Whew, this fighter's a real beauty, all right." He looked at it enviously; he had no desire to fly combat, but that didn't stop him from longing to sit at the controls of the fantastic machine, high in the blue.

He ran his hand along the fuselage. "It looks great. How does it handle?"

Roy thought that one over. "Hmm. Well, why don't you climb aboard and see for yourself?"

"You really mean that?"

"Uh huh. I'll ride piggyback behind you." It was, perhaps, bending the rules a bit, though familiarization flights were scheduled for VIPs later in the day. Still, a little sample of what the Veritech could do might change Rick's attitude about military service, and the service could sure use a flier like Rick Hunter.

Rick was already scrambling up the boarding ladder, peering into the cockpit. "The controls look pretty complicated," Roy called up, "but I'll check you out on them."

Rick looked down and smirked,. "I'm not worried. If *you* can learn to fly one of these things, I sure can."

Roy snorted, "Don't be so modest!"

When Rick was in the pilot's seat and Roy was in the rear seat, Roy handed Rick a red-visored Robotech flight helmet.

Rick turned it over in his hands, examining the interior. "Whoa, what kind of helmet is this? What's all this stuff inside?"

"Receptors. They pick up electromagnetic activity in your brain. You might say the helmet's a mind reader, in some ways."

The receptors were just like part of the helmet's padding: soft, yielding—no safety hazard. But Rick wasn't so sure he liked the idea of having his head wired. "What're they for?"

"For flying a Veritech, buddy boy. You'll still handle a lot of manual controls, but there are things this baby does that it can only do through advanced control systems."

Rick hiked himself around in his seat and leaned out to look back at Roy. "Look, I saw your guys flying, remember? What's so special about these crates that you have to wear a thinking cap just to steer one?"

Roy told him, "The real secrets aren't supposed to go public until the politicians are through with all their blabbing, but I'll tell you this: The machine you're sitting in isn't like anything humans have ever built—it's as different from *Mockingbird* as *Mockingbird* is from a pair of shoes.

"Because you don't just pilot a Robotech ship, Rick; you *live* it."

On the main reviewing stand high above the crowd, Senator Russo stood at the speaker's rostrum, his voice echoing out over the throngs, amplified so that it reached to the farthest shores of the sea of people. Flags snapped in the wind, and the moment felt like a complete triumph.

"This is the day we've all been looking forward to for ten years! The Robotech project has been a tremendous asset to the economy of Macross City and to the welfare of our people!"

Captain Gloval, standing to one side with a few other dignitaries, tried to keep from yawning or simply throwing up his hands in disgust. So far, all Russo and his cronies had done was take credit for themselves and do some not-too-subtle electioneering.

Gloval cast a critical eye at the weather and gave it his grudging approval. He was impatient to launch; various other Earth military forces were already deployed in space, patrolling and awaiting the start of the SDF-1's first space trials. But the politicos didn't care who they kept waiting or what careful timetables they spoiled when they had the spotlight.

A liaison officer came up the steps at the rear of the reviewing stand and approached Gloval as Russo went on. "More important, though, is the fact that the technology developed here will benefit all mankind, now and in the future. And I need not mention what it means to the defense of our great planet, Earth!"

The liaison cupped his hand to Gloval's ear and said, "Excuse me, sir: urgent message from the space monitoring station. A strange flash of light and an explosion, tremendous radiation readings, accompanied by irregularities in solar gravitational fields."

In spite of the warmth of the day, Gloval suddenly felt cold all over. "The same sort of event occurred ten years ago. You know what happened then, don't you?"

The aide was trying to conceal his fear, nodding. "That's when the alien ship arrived."

Gloval assumed the icy calm of a seasoned captain. "Better check it out. Come with me."

Gloval was descending the platform steps as Russo announced what a great honor it was to introduce the commander of SDF-1, Henry Gloval.

For once, Russo didn't know what to say. "Come back here! You have to make a speech!" he shouted.

Gloval never even looked around. The time for speeches was over.

\* \* \*

On the SDF-1 bridge, the women who were the battle fortress's heart worked furiously to make some sense of the sudden chaos around them.

"What's going on here, anyway?" Claudia demanded, trying everything she could think of to interpret her instruments and reassert some control over the ship's systems.

"Claudia, give me a readout!" Lisa called calmly. All around her, the bridge was a din of alarms, flashing indicators, malfunctioning controls, and overloaded computers.

Claudia looked up from her hopeless efforts. "Every system on the ship is starting up without being turned on!"

Unprecedented, impossible-to-interpret mechanisms had self-activated in the ship's power plant—the great, sealed engines that not even Lang had dared open. And the many different kinds of alien apparatus connected to it were doing bewildering things to the SDF-1's structure as well as its systems, making the humans helpless bystanders.

"The defense system is activating the main gun!" Claudia reported, horrified.

Far off at the great starship's bow, gargantuan servomotors hummed and groaned. The huge twin booms that made up the forward portion of the ship moved to either side on colossal camlike devices. The booms locked into place, looking like a fantastic tuning fork. The ship's reconstruction had the bow high up now, pointed out above the end of Macross Island's cliff line at the open sea.

Lisa's mind raced. The main gun had never been fired; no one was even sure how powerful it was. That test was to be reserved for empty space. But if it salvoed now, the ensuing death and destruction might well be greater than that created by the ship's original crash.

At the same time, everyone aboard could feel the supership shifting slightly on the massive keel blocks—the monolithic rests on which it lay. Warning klaxons and horns were deafening.

*The SDF-1's aiming its gun*, Lisa realized. *But at what target?*

"Shut down all systems!" she ordered Claudia.

Claudia, trying the master cutoff switch several times to no effect, looked at Lisa helplessly. "It doesn't work!"

A sudden glare from the bow lit the bridge with red-orange brilliance, throwing their flickering shadows on the bulkhead behind them.

Around and between the forward booms, tongues of orange starflame were shooting and whirling and arcing back and forth. The fantastic energy cascade began sluicing up the booms toward their tips, sparks snapping, seemingly eager to be set free.

And still Lisa could think of nothing she could do.

Just then the hatch opened and Gloval hurried in so quickly that he bumped his head on the frame. He didn't spare time or his usual swearing at the people who'd refitted the largest machine ever known for not providing a little more headroom.

"Captain, the main guns are preparing to fire!"

Gloval assessed the situation in seconds, but Lisa could see from his expression that he was as much at a loss as she.

"I can't control them!" Claudia told Gloval. "What'll we do?"

Lisa absorbed a terrible lesson in that moment. Despite what they might teach in the Academy and the War College and Advanced Leadership School, sometimes there was nothing you could do.

The energy storm around the booms had built to an Earth-shaking pitch, a noise like a million shrieking demons. Then huge eruptions of destructive energy streaked off the booms.

The bolts streamed off into the distance, thickening into a howling torrent of annihilation, a river of starflame as high and wide as SDF-1 itself, shooting out across the city.

Lisa expected to see everything in the volley's path consumed, including the gathered populace.

But that didn't happen. The superbolt went straight out over the cliffs and over the ocean, turning water to vapor and roiling the swells, raising clouds of steam that wouldn't settle for hours. The shot was direct, the curve of the Earth falling away beneath it as it lanced out into space.

And just as Lisa Hayes was registering the fact that the city still remained, intact and unharmed—that her father was down there somewhere, still alive—new information began pouring in on scopes and monitors.

The Zentraedi heavy cruisers, closing in on the unsuspecting Earth, barely had time to realize that they were about to die. By some unimaginable level of control, the blinding shaft of energy split in two.

The twinned beams holed each heavy cruiser through and through, along their long axes. Armor and weapons and hull, superstructure, and the rest were vaporized as the beams hit, skewering them. They expanded like overheated gas bags, skins peeling off, debris exploding outward, only to disappear, blown to nothingness, an instant later in globes of bright mass-energy conversions.

From his command station, Breetai watched impassively, arms folded across his great chest, as the projecbeam displayed the death of the two heavy cruisers.

"Now we know for sure: The ship is on that planet!" This time he didn't bother soliciting Exedore's advice. "All ships advance, but exercise extreme caution!"

The Zentraedi armada took up proper formation, ships-of-the-line moving to the fore, and closed on the target world.

Clouds of superheated air blew out across the ocean; gulls cried in the aftermath of the SDF-1's single volley.

Gloval was at the bridge's protective bowl—its "windshield"—his face all but pressed against it, scanning through the steam and fog. He breathed a prayer of thanks that the city was unharmed.

"Some sort of magnetic bottling," Sammie reported, focused on her work. "All the force was channeled directly out into space, except for some very marginal eddy currents."

"We have control over all systems again, sir," Claudia announced calmly. "What happened, sir?"

Gloval suddenly felt old—older than the ship, the island, the sea. He wasn't about to speculate aloud, not even to his trusted bridge gang, but he was just about certain he knew. And if he was right, it put the weight of a planet on his shoulders.

# CHAPTER
# SIX

*While Captain Gloval gets admittedly deserved credit for his handling of the disaster that day, male historians frequently gloss over Gloval's straightforward statement that if it weren't for the women on SDF-1's bridge, their nerve and gallantry and professionalism, the Robotech War would have been over before it had fairly begun.*

Betty Greer, *Post-Feminism and the Global War*

**T**HE GROUND HAD STOPPED SHAKING, AND THE SKY was clearing. The Veritech fighter stopped its trembling dance, and Rick Hunter caught his breath. The air seemed a little hotter in his lungs, but not terribly so.

He called back to Roy in a subdued voice, "Wow. What were all those fireworks about?"

*Fireworks!* Roy thought. *'Fraid not!* Aloud, he said, "I dunno. I better go check. Wait here; I'll see what's goin' on."

He put aside his flight helmet—the "thinking cap," as Rick had called it—and hiked himself up out of the fighter cockpit. If what Roy feared the most had come to pass, Rick would be as safe where he was as anywhere else. And he'd also understand why some people could spend their lives preparing for war.

"The space monitor report's coming in," Sammie sang out. "It shows what our gun was firing at."

"I have it here, Sammie," Lisa cut in, studying her monitors. "Two large objects, probably spacecraft, origin unknown, on Earth-approach vector, approx two hundred miles out."

Gloval was nodding to himself without realizing it. The ship could be raised or lowered, the booms traversed for— what, a few insignificant minutes of arc? And the SDF-1 hadn't been moved, except to lift it onto the keel blocks, since it crashed. The range was incredibly long, making for a greater field of fire; but still, such a shot, such a series of events, could only come about with some forewarning, or intuition, or—*We forgot that whoever built this vessel had to some extent mastered time; could, perhaps, see through it. Could see this very moment?*

"Both objects were struck dead center by the beam and were destroyed—disintegrated," Claudia said. "Orbital combat task forces are deploying for defense, with Armor One and Armor Ten—sir? Captain Gloval?"

Sammie, Vanessa, Kim—they exchanged looks with one another as Lisa and Claudia traded facial signals. Gloval was laughing, a deep belly laugh, his shoulders shaking. Claudia and Lisa saw that they were both thinking the same thing: If Gloval, their source of strength and calm, had lost his grip, all was lost.

"Captain, what is it?" Lisa ventured. "What are you laughing about?"

Gloval stopped laughing, crashing his fist against the observation-bowl ledge. "It was so *obvious*! We should have known! A booby trap, of course!"

Claudia and Lisa said it at the same time, "Booby trap, sir?"

"Yes, it's one of the oldest tricks in military history! A retreating enemy leaves behind hidden explosives and such."

He clamped his cold pipe between his teeth. "The automatic firing of the main guns means that enemies have approached close enough to be a threat to us." He drew his tobacco bag out of the breast pocket of his uniform jacket.

"Captain Gloval!" Sammie was up out of her chair. Everyone turned to her, wondering what the new alarm was.

"No smoking on the bridge, sir!" Sammie said. "Strictly against regulations!"

Claudia groaned and clapped a hand to her forehead. Lisa reflected, *Nothing throws Sammie*.

"I was just holding it; I wasn't going to light it," Gloval said defensively. The unreality of the situation retreated with Sammie's interruption. There were both good things and bad things about having one's bridge crew be like family.

But doubts were past now. Gloval barked, "Hot-scramble all fighters and sound general quarters! I'm declaring a red alert!"

Down below, the crowds milled uncertainly as helos and other aircraft veered away to report to battle stations. Suddenly, launch crews were scrambling to get Veritechs into the air. Out on the carriers, all catapults were busy, while the SDF-1's own warcraft rushed up from the ship's interior and groundside runways to establish a protective shield overhead.

Out in the void, armored spacecruisers, human-designed vehicles incorporating some of the principles learned from Robotechnology, moved their interceptors and attack craft out of the bays and into fighting position.

It wasn't long before the swarm of human defenders had sensor contact, then visual sighting, on the aliens; the Zentraedi wouldn't have had it any other way.

A Scorpion interceptor pilot reported back to Armor One over the tac net, "Enemy approaching on bearing niner-zero. We are engaging. Commence firing!"

Scorpions and Tigersharks and a dozen other types of Earthly combat spacecraft, ranging up to the mammoth Armors themselves, rushed to close with the aliens' first attack wave.

Missiles—Stilettos and Piledrivers and Mongooses— were launched at extreme range so that all but the glows of their drives were lost to sight until the blackness blossomed with the spherical explosions characteristic of zero-g, the bursts overlapping one another, thicker than a field of dandelions.

The Zentraedi ships-of-the-line forged through the intense fire with few losses, closing the gap in seconds. The formations broke up to lock in a fierce, pitched battle.

The Armors launched all their missiles. Lasers, kinetic energy weapons—rail-gun autocannon and such—were the other main Terran weapons. The Zentraedi's were far superior; their warcraft simply outclassed the defenders', whose design involved fewer Robotech innovations.

Earth's forces fought with savage determination, but the unevenness in technologies was instantly apparent.

Aboard the alien command ship, Breetai studied the engagement solemnly in the projecbeam images and monitors, listening to his staff's relayed readouts with only a small part of his attention.

"Very heavy resistance, sir," Exedore observed.

"Yes," Breetai allowed. "But why are they using such primitive weapons? Our lead ships have broken through. It's unbelievable, this sacrifice they're making! Some sort of trick, no doubt."

Exedore considered that. "Yes, it is puzzling."

Breetai whirled on him. "It makes no sense, then? Even to you?"

"There has to be a reason, but it's beyond me. Surely, the Robotech Masters—"

He was interrupted by an urgent message from the tech at the threat-prioritization computers. "Commander Breetai! Two enemy cruiser-class vessels are approaching; they could be the ones who launched the missile bombardment."

Breetai smiled, but his single eye was chilly. "Destroy them!"

Specially designated main and secondary batteries opened fire: phased particle-beam arrays and molecular disruptors, long-range and fearsomely powerful.

Armor Two was hit on the first volley as hundreds of spears of high-resolution blue fury ranged in on it. It tried to evade the barrage; house-size pieces of armor and superstructure were blown from it. Many of the smaller defending craft were completely disintegrated.

Breetai, waiting for effective counterfire, lost patience. Perhaps the foes' hesitation to use reflex weaponry fit into some strange plan, but to forgo use of *any* advanced technology, to sacrifice troops to this kind of slaughter, was perverse.

Incredulous, Breetai wondered if somehow this victory was going to be far easier than it had seemed when that first mighty bolt rose from Terra. "Those idiots behave as though they don't even know how to use their own weapons! Full barrage, all cannon!"

The Zentraedi command ship cut loose again with all forward gun turrets. Armor Two was instantly holed through in a hundred places, the enemy beams penetrating it like ice picks through a cigar box.

Hull integrity went at once, and internal gravity; hatches and seals blew, and space began sucking the atmosphere from the cruiser, tossing crew and contents around like toys. Still more hits made a sieve of the pride of the orbital defense command and destroyed its power plant. A moment later it disappeared in a horrendous outpouring of energy, while lesser ships all around it met a similar fate.

Lisa, more pallid than ever, kept her voice even as she reported to Gloval: "Armor Two is destroyed and Armor Ten is heavily damaged, sir. Other losses extremely heavy. The Orbital Defense Forces are no longer even marginally effective. Alien fleet is closing on Earth."

Gloval sat in his command chair, fingers steepled, chin resting on pressing thumbs. "I had hoped this moment wouldn't come in my lifetime. SDF-1 kept us from exterminating ourselves and let us achieve worldwide peace, but now it has brought a new danger down upon us. We face extinction at the hands of aliens whose power we can only guess at."

Henry Gloval's mind ranged back across a decade to that first investigation of the wrecked SDF-1. *Miracles have a price. And this one, I think, will be very, very high.*

Claudia and Lisa and the other members of the bridge crew swapped quick, worried looks.

"I had hoped that war was a thing of the past. We all had." Gloval looked up from his distraction like a knight at the end of his prayer vigil, ready to take up a shining sword, a gleaming shield.

"But here we go again, like it or not." He rose to his feet, shoulders back, and a vivid current of electricity that hadn't been there a moment before hummed in the air. Gloval was suddenly strong as an old oak.

"All right. Give the order to move out!"

"Yes, sir." Lisa relayed the command crisply. "All forces, deploy in accordance with Contingency Plan SUR-TUR."

More Veritechs launched all across the island as Lisa's words reverberated to every corner of it, like the gods' final war song. "We are under attack by alien invaders in sector four-one-two. This is not a drill, I say again: This is not a drill."

Roy Fokker, clambering into his fighter, pulling on his flight helmet, gasped, then hissed. He'd been so busy saddling up Skull Team when word came that there was trouble that he'd forgotten all about Rick!

Then he calmed. The fighter in which Rick was sitting had been seconded from active duty for the public relations events; it wasn't as if some angry pilot would be wrestling him out of the cockpit. So Rick was as safe there as anywhere else for the time being.

Lisa's voice rang across the airfield. Roy didn't mind it, but he couldn't help wishing it were Claudia's.

Then Roy got back to the job at hand, settling the all-important helmet on his head. He switched on the tactical net, trying to sound casual, just about bored. The fighter-pilot tradition; dying was something you sometimes couldn't help, but losing your cool was unforgivable.

"Well, boys, you heard her. This is the real thing." Roy practically yawned.

The sky was filled with climbing flights of fast-moving aircraft, vectoring off to their assigned coverages. Dozens, hundreds had arisen from the carriers and the island. The flattops were making ready to stand out to sea so that the foe couldn't concentrate his attacks; that would take some time. But at least with the combat squadrons aloft, Earth wasn't as vulnerable to a single, concentrated strike.

Lisa's voice came over Roy's flight helmet phones. "Wolf Team has cleared. Skull Team, prepare for takeoff."

"Skull Team ready." Roy knew the men in the other parked Veritechs would be watching him as well as listening over the tac net. He gave a quick thumbs-up. "Awright, boys; this is it."

More fighters were streaking up from the flight decks of the carriers, launched out from the waist catapults or propelled out into the air over the Hurricane-style bows.

"Let's go," drawled Roy Fokker. Robotech engines shrilled.

"What a disorderly arrangement!" Breetai exclaimed, studying Macross City on long-rage scanners. The populace, the military forces—they were so unbelievably concentrated! "These people must be completely ignorant of spacewar tactics!"

The sensor image panned until an image-interpretation computer locked it in. Breetai leaned closer to the fishbowl surface that protected his command post.

"What's this? The battle fortress! But—what's happened to it?"

Exedore took that as leave to speak. "It appears to have been completely redesigned and rebuilt, perhaps by the inhabitants of that planet."

Breetai set his fists on his hips. "Mere primitives couldn't possibly have captured a Robotech ship."

Exedore fixed Breetai with his great, protruding eyes, their eerily pinpoint pupils hypnotic, mystical. "Perhaps it crashed on their planet and they managed to salvage it."

"But what about the crew? Zor's traitors wouldn't just let these creatures have the vessel!"

"Maybe they perished in the fighting with the Invid, or in the crash," Exedore suggested delicately. It was an answer of high probability; Breetai saw that at once, chose not to contest it, and congratulated himself on having a friend and adviser like Exedore.

"Even so . . ." The commander sidestepped the discomfitting idea that the primitives were antagonists to be feared. "The ship would have been terribly damaged. And these primitives wouldn't have the technology to repair it."

*This Zentraedi arrogance of ours gets worse with every generation*, Exedore thought, even as he readied his answer. *Someday we may all pay for it.*

"I know, sir, but is there any other explanation? It *is* a Robotech vessel, and we know they have—"

"Reflex weaponry!"

"Precisely. And this makes them very dangerous. So we must exercise extreme caution."

Breetai turned back to the projecbeam displays, uttering a feral growl. The instruments and transparent bowl rang with it.

A command center coordinator's voice came up over the intercom. "Target pinpointed, Commander. We're launching fighters!"

Breetai and Exedore contemplated the image of the dimensional fortress.

# CHAPTER
# SEVEN

*If there exists on record a stranger familiarization flight than Rick Hunter's VT shakedown, I have been unable to find it.*

Zachary Foxx, Jr., VT: *the Men and the Mecha*

**Z**ENTRAEDI COMBAT SHIPS OF EVERY KIND CUT DOWN through Earth's atmosphere in tight, well-maintained formations, plunging at Macross Island and its surrounding waters. The alien pilots were confident, swelled with their swift and smashing victory against the target world's outer defenses.

The bright streaks of their plummeting drives seemed as numerous as raindrops. They were primed for easy kills and a swift capture of the battle fortress that had to be captured whole and undamaged, as Breetai had ordered. The invaders had had it pretty much their own way so far.

All at once that changed . . . and the rout suddenly became a battle again.

Protective covers had been raised from the SDF-1's missile racks; almost all incoming ordnance was intercepted and exploded in midair. Fighters of types the Zentraedi hadn't encountered before boiled up to lock in combat with them. And the elite warrior race found out, to their extreme unhappiness, that the primitives had indeed puzzled out quite a bit of Robotechnology.

In Earth's slaughterhouse skies, the dying began again.

* * *

Snoozing comfortably, Rick Hunter began to rouse a bit. If the weather had turned so bad—there was constant thunder—maybe he ought to make sure all the windows were shut. Only, he didn't seem to remember where he was. Besides, there was this bothersome voice in his ear; it had the ring of authority, and that was something that never failed to antagonize him.

"This is SDF-1 control calling VT one-zero-two. You down there, on the exhibition grounds! We're on combat alert! Why haven't you taken off?" Lisa Hayes had a million other things to do; prodding slowpoke fighter jocks was the last problem she needed, and it made her mad to have to take time she couldn't spare to do it.

Rick sighed and stretched, then tilted the strange flight helmet back on his head, leaning forward and blinking groggily at one of the cockpit's tiny display screens. A young woman's face peered angrily out of it: pale and intense, impatient. Rick Hunter was used to being regarded as something pretty special, particularly by the opposite sex; he therefore decided at once that whoever she was, she had a pinched and grumpy look.

"You don't mean *me*, do you, lady?" But just then he became aware of distant explosions—not thunder but the reports of incoming fire. And there were blazes in the city, and smoke and damage. Crewpeople were rushing everywhere, fueling and arming and guiding planes, getting them airborne. Meanwhile, up in the *air* . . .

What *were* all those intertangled contrails and afterburner glows and explosions and tracers?

"Huh? What?" Rick Hunter asked himself weakly. People were scrambling around the plane in which he sat, readying it.

"Don't waste any more time!" the pale face in the screen scolded. "Take off immediately and join your wingman! The fighter squadron's outnumbered as it is!"

Rick gritted his teeth. "What d'you mean take off? The runway's demolished!"

And so it was, one of the primary Zentraedi targets, one

of the few to be hit effectively. The young woman on the screen appeared to be counting to control her temper.

"Runway two is operable. You're fully armed, and your engines will overheat very quickly at high standby, so prepare for immediate takeoff!"

Now that she mentioned it, he could hear the high-pitched whine of an engine, could feel it through his seat, but it was not like any he'd ever heard before—and Rick Hunter had heard 'em all.

Rick leaned out of the cockpit for a look. Sure enough, the Veritech was armed to the teeth, external hardpoints and pylons loaded with ordnance, the jet also carrying odd pods that he couldn't quite figure out.

Then a ground crewman was next to him, standing on the boarding ladder. "All set, sir! Good hunting!" The man did something or other, and the cockpit canopy descended.

Rick was to admit later that that would have been a very good time to come clean and admit that he had no idea what was going on, that he was a noncombatant and needed to be shown to a shelter. But that would have entailed admitting that he didn't know how to fly the aircraft in which he was sitting, that he *couldn't*. That he was, in short, nothing but a bystander, a hick, just like the people who gawked up at him at the flying circus.

And when you regard yourself as the greatest pilot in the world, an admission like that is extremely difficult. Besides, there was that irritating female on the screen.

"Well, okay. If you insist."

Rick drew a deep breath, took the controls, and gave himself a quick run-through, remembering all the stuff Roy had told him. He waggled rudders and played around for a second, then increased throttle, taxied out, and stood the fighter nearly on its tail, like a meteor in reverse.

A late Zentraedi missile blew a hole the size of a city block where he'd been parked a few seconds before. He was hoping the ground crews had all gotten clear as the Veritech responded to his demands for speed.

*Wow!* The proverbial bat.

He adjusted wing sweep and camber and angle of attack, going ballistic, wingtips leaving wispy lines of contrail like spider's thread. And though he would never have admitted it, he was more than a little intimidated. He was riding a rocket.

He punched a hole in a cloud, then found himself in the middle of a vast, swirling gladiatoral combat, the biggest dogfight since the close of what they called WWII.

"Whoa-ooooooo!"

Robotech craft were everywhere, and planes of some design that made no sense to Rick; not aerodynamic but devilishly fast and mounting unprecedented firepower. Explosions flowered all around him, rocking the ship, just as a lazy, familiar voice came over the tac net.

"Skull Leader to Veritech squadron. Intercept new invader flights at zone four-two-eight. Traffic's pretty heavy out here, boys, so break formation, but *don't leave your wingman!*"

"*Roy!*" He sounded short of breath. Rick looked up, open-mouthed, as a Veritech flying the Jolly Roger insignia bagged an alien recon craft shaped something like a flying bottle.

Debris was raining everywhere; pilots from both sides screamed in agony as they were blown to oblivion up where sky met space.

And, because dogfighting was so incredibly demanding physically, the tack net was loud with gasps and grunting. Dogfighters trained themselves to lock the muscles of their lower bodies—turn their legs to iron; suck their gut to their spine. Anything to keep the blood up high in the head. Up in the brain, where it was needed even more than in the heart.

The pressure on the pilots' diaphragms was fearsome; they could draw only short, hard-won breaths, if they were in high-g maneuvers.

The tac net sounded like eight or ten wrestling teams had been paired off for the championship.

And the trophy was Earth.

"Hey, Fokker! Wouldja mind telling me what's going on around here?"

Roy had just finished dusting a bogie off Skull Eight's

tail. He switched a communications screen over to ship-to-ship and was, he admitted, not all that surprised to see Rick Hunter's face.

"How's it feel to be a fighter pilot?"

"What're you talkin' about, Big Brother? I'm not a fighter pilot; in fact, I—uhhhh!"

That last, as a wash of light came through Rick's canopy, and Roy's screen dissolved into a storm of distortion. There had been explosions just before the cutoff; in fighter jocks' lingo: *he tuned out*. Tuning out was terminal.

But Roy cut in maximum thrust, checking his situation displays, heading for his friend's location. "Hold on, Rick; I'm coming."

The Veritech's thrust pushed him back, deep into his seat. Roy felt tremendous relief when he sighted VT one-two-zero flying level and unharmed.

Roy caught up and fell in on Rick's wingtip. "You weren't hit; it was just a close one. You all right?" The alien that had come so close to nailing Rick was coming around for another try.

*"Whew!* Yeah, I'm okay," Rick decided.

Roy moved into the lead just a bit. The enemy fighter was closing fast. "Combat flying's scary for everyone first time out," he said. "You'll get used to it, though; it's not that much different from the good old days at the flying circus."

So saying, Roy thumbed the trigger on his control stick and sent two air-to-air Stilettos zooming to score direct hits on the invader and blow it to flaming bits.

"Yeah, but I never got shot at in the circus, Roy." Funny, but now the flying circus seemed like another life, a million years ago.

"You'll get used to it. Just tag along with me and we'll start your on-the-job training—*if* you can keep up with me."

The old smirk was back on Rick's face. "If? I'll do my best not to leave you in my backwash!"

"Let's go get 'em, Little Brother." Roy increased airspeed, beginning a climb, wings folding back for high-speed dogfighting. Out of nowhere, an enemy fighter came in at

Rick from six o'clock high, chopping at him with energy bolts.

He let out a cry as he began to lose control, the fighter shaken and bounced by the near misses.

"Climb and bank!" Roy called out, trying desperately to bring his ship around. "Rick!" He himself was dodging Zentraedi cannon fire a moment later. With Rick's ship out of control and nosediving in a spin, the Zentraedi had broken off his attack and turned on the Skull Team leader. The two fighters joined in a vicious duel.

Rick tried everything he'd ever learned but couldn't regain control of the Veritech. "I think I've had it, Roy. I'm getting no response from the controls at all!" Macross Island pinwheeled up at him.

Just then a voice he recognized came up over the net. "This is SDF-1 control calling VT one-two-zero. Pull out! You're diving straight at us!"

"Lady, don't you think I'd like to? But all the controls have lost power."

"Have you tried switching to configuration B?" Lisa Hayes demanded.

"Huh? B? What're you talking about?"

"You don't know?" *This one must've really lost it—complete panic!* "Listen, pulled down the control marked B on the left side of your instrument panel."

The ground was very near. Rick, dizzy and almost unconscious from the g forces, somehow guided his hand to the knob in question, having a little trouble sorting it out from an identical one next to it marked G, moving it down in its slot.

The Veritech abruptly slowed in its tailspin, stabilizing, beginning to level off. At the same time, Rick could feel the entire ship start to shudder and shift, its aerodynamics changing in some way that he couldn't comprehend. He could feel vibrations, as if the fighter was—*changing*.

"What's it doing?" The fighter was still descending, the streets of Macross City looming up before the canopy. Rick had been a pilot long enough to know that since its flight characteristics had changed so dramatically, there was no other answer except that the shape of the Veritech had somehow altered.

What he didn't realize, and couldn't see from the cockpit, was that the ship had begun undergoing a process Doctor Lang had dubbed mechamorphosis. It was no longer configured like a conventional fighter but had, instead, gone to Guardian—G—mode, on its way to B.

In this transitional state it resembled a great metal bird of prey, an eagle, with sturdy metal legs stretched to set down and wings deployed, humanlike arms and hands outstretched.

But before Rick could figure out what had happened or the fighter could complete the shift to B, the Veritech crashed into the upper floors of an office building at an intersection in Macross City.

Fortunately, the alert had the population indoors or underground in the sprawling shelter system, and so no one was killed. The Guardian carved a path of devastation through the upper stories of an entire block, its fantastically strong armor and construction resisting damage.

Bricks, concrete, and girders flew in all directions; clouds of plaster went up like a dust storm. Signs crashed down, and broken plumbing gushed; severed power lines spat and snapped. The Guardian's engines cut out as the machine became aware of its situation and reacted to emergency programming.

Rick Hunter could still feel the plane shifting, changing, all around him. In fact, in some way he couldn't figure out, he could sense it—could actually *feel* it.

Rick sat where he was, realizing that he didn't know how to eject, even if the system was a "zero-zero" type that would let him survive a standstill ground-level ejection, which was far from the case.

It felt as if the crazy Robotech fighter was coming to a stop; he readied himself for a quick escape, not wishing to be in the neighborhood if a few tons of highly volatile jet fuel suddenly took a notion to catch fire. But the Robotech ship had one last surprise for him; the relatively smooth slide became a lurch as the plane snagged on some final obstruction. The fighter heaved, and Rick's helmeted head slammed into the instrument panel.

If he hadn't been wearing the flight helmet, it would have been the end. As it was, he saw stars and nearly lost consciousness.

But the Veritech was unhurt. With a creaking of girders and the racket of tons of rubble being moved, the machine began to extricate itself. The mechamorphosis to B mode was complete, and the fighter was now a Battloid.

It looked for all the world like a man in armor, a super-technological knight sixty feet tall. The electric gatling gun that had been pod-mounted under the Veritech's belly was now aligned along its right arm, the giant right hand gripping it like an outlandish rifle.

The cockpit section was unrecognizable, now incorporated in the turretlike "helmet," the Battloid's head. Its visor swung this way and that, taking in the situation, seeing the explosions of the dogfight continuing high above.

The Battloid knew the enemy was there; it was ready to do what it had been designed to do. It awaited orders.

Rick shook his head groggily. "What d'ya know? I'm alive!" Then he saw that something was wrong with his perspective—that he was high above the street, that there were things about Robotech too astounding to believe. He saw the distant air engagement too.

Somehow Rick knew, deep down, that life was never going to be the way it had been fifteen minutes ago. Things had changed forever.

# CHAPTER
# EIGHT

*Dear Diary,*
*Launch day's really been fun, even though Jason's making himself a bit of a pest. I met a couple of really dreamy guys, pilots, I guess—a very tall blond one and a cute little dark-haired one.*

*I'm going back out this evening to sing at the municipal center picnic. Maybe they'll be there! I might—hey! I think something's going on outside. More later.*

From the diary of Lynn-Minmei

IN SDF-1'S BRIDGE, VANESSA STUDIED HER SCREENS AND gave Gloval a concise report. "Twenty-four unidentfied objects are descending from space, projected landing point twenty to thirty miles west of Macross Island, sir. They're definitely not ours."

"Why didn't we detect them before?"

Vanessa looked to the captain, adjusting her big aviator-style glasses. "When the main guns fired, they sapped so much power, our radars malfunctioned."

Gloval reflected on that. "That first wave of attack ships —it was just a decoy. Very clever strategy. Lisa! Recall Lieutenant Commander Fokker's team immediately!"

Lisa, studying her data displays, said, "They're still engaged in combat with the first attack wave, sir. I doubt they can break away without suffering heavy losses."

Glovad nodded stiffly. "I understand. Thank you."

Vanessa updated, "The unidentified crafts have landed in the ocean twenty-five miles west of us. They seem to have submerged, sir."

Gloval could no longer put off giving Lisa the unpleasant command. "Call *Prometheus* and order them to send out reconnaissance choppers."

"I already have them awaiting your go-ahead, sir. They'll be on station in five minutes."

"Mind reader," Gloval growled, though there was real fondness in his voice.

"Yes, sir," Lisa said, cheeks coloring a bit.

There was only a moment in which to be relieved that Gloval wasn't rankled at her for anticipating him; those recon helicopters racing to confront the new alien arrivals were quite capable in their own way, but they weren't Robotech ships. And that could be very bad for the helo crews.

People had crept forth, very hesitantly, to gawk up at the towering knightlike figure that had been VT one-two-zero. The Battloid stood straddle-legged in the middle of the street. As pieces of sheetrock fell from its shoulders and bits of rubble rained around it, it appeared as if it were waiting for a trumpet to sound the call to arms. It took a few faltering steps, nearly toppling over.

"What is that?" one man breathed.

"A giant robot!" a second misguessed.

"Could be an alien invader!" a third ventured. There were already a thousand rumors abroad as to exactly what had happened to Macross Island and to the human race in general.

A few yards away, Lynn-Minmei crouched with her uncle and aunt in the doorway of their restaurant, the White Dragon, unsure what to do. Jason had been outside playing somewhere when the chaos began, and there was no sign of him.

"It's stopped moving; it's just standing there now," Minmei said, looking up at it. She got ready to make a dash, to go look for her cousin.

Suddenly a small figure in bib overalls and yellow sweatshirt dashed out from behind a crumpled trailer, passing by the metal fighting machine's feet, close enough to touch them.

"Wow! Hey, Minmei! Come lookit what's out here! An honest-to-goodness giant robot!"

She caught him up in a hug, as relieved as her Uncle Max and Aunt Lena were. "Oh, Jason! What if that thing had stepped on you?"

Jason pushed her away with the unconcern of the very young. "Aw, I can take care of myself." Then he broke loose, heading for the stairs, a compact little whirlwind.

"I want to get a good look at that thing! C'mon; we'll go upstairs and look out the window!"

Minmei hurried after. She yelled, "Jason, wait for me!" as her Aunt Lena called, "Don't let him fall out the window!" then went back to trying to figure out what to do with the shambles that had been a thriving business only minutes before.

The two Barracuda naval attack helicopters from *Prometheus* approached watchfully, encountering only calm sea.

"This is PHP two-zero-two," the flight leader radioed. "We're approaching target area. Negative sightings of alien craft so far."

Lisa's reply came after a burst of static. "Roger that, PHP two-zero-two. Maintain maximum surveillance; bogies are suspected to be submerged. Prepare to deploy sonobuoys."

Her transmission was just ending as the blue water broke for one, then another, then half a dozen rounded shapes. They bobbed up, shedding water, bulbous and gleaming metallically, with odd projections—tubes—suggesting old-fashioned magnetic mines.

The floating objects turned, the tubes aligning and sighting. All at once they spat lines of dazzling brilliance up at the Barracudas. More and more of the rounded shapes bobbed to the surface, joining in the barrage.

The flight leader barely blurted out, "We're being fired upon!" when the crisscrossing beams found the second chopper and blew it to pieces in midair.

"Let's get out of here!" the leader screamed, firing a missile and preparing to run even as the beams converged on his ship. The chopper became a fireball. The pilot's scream was cut off in midtransmission.

Back on the bridge, Lisa reported woodenly, "They're gone, sir."

Gloval glared out the forward viewport. "And here I am with an untested ship, an inexperienced crew—" *And very little time to make my decisions.*

The hatch slid open, and Russo strode onto the bridge, puffing on his cigar and clutching his expensive lapel, seemingly in control. But he was pale and sweating; Lisa could see that and smell it. Under the hail-fellow-well-met exterior, the senator was so frightened that he was in danger of passing out.

"Well, Captain, it's lucky for us we got this ship finished in time to fight off the invaders. When d' you take off?"

The curious timing had occurred to Gloval, too—that the aliens should arrive at this very moment. His own conclusion was that the final activation of the SDF-1's huge, mysterious sealed power plant had somehow drawn the invaders. But he had no time to think about that now.

In answer to Russo's question, he simply *hmphh*ed.

Russo's eyebrows beetled. "You *are* ready, aren't you? Why haven't you taken off? *What are you waiting for?*" He glared up at the captain.

Gloval's upper lip curled. "You must think I'm out of my mind. I can't take this ship into combat with a crew of raw recruits who've never been in space before! What's more, this ship hasn't even been tested yet; we don't even know if it'll fly."

His commitment to his oath of service made him add, "If you order me to take SDF-1 up, I'll obey. But it'll be against my better judgment."

Claudia and Lisa were standing rigidly at their stations, pretending to take no notice. But Sammie turned to Kim and whispered, "D'you think he's serious?"

"I think he means it." Kim nodded after a moment's thought.

Sammie gave a toss of her long mane of wheat-colored hair. "Wow," she whispered with a tremble.

"I *am* ordering you to take off, Captain. Understand?" Russo was saying.

Kim frowned, "What's the matter, Sammie? I thought you *wanted* to go into space."

Sammie's eyes were big, frightened. "I do . . . I think." *But all of a sudden, it's real!*

"Let it be your responsibility, then," Gloval came back to Russo, "because I'm telling you, it could be suicide. We don't understand half of SDF-1's systemry yet!"

Russo's lip was quivering, but he bristled, "It sounds to me like you're saying you've no confidence in your crew. Is that what you're telling me, Gloval?"

Gloval looked quickly to Lisa and Claudia, who turned back to their duties to avoid being caught watching the confrontation. "I didn't say that."

"Then what *are* you saying? Earth has spent untold resources on this Robotech ship, and I don't want to see it destroyed on the ground."

"Senator—"

"No, Captain! No more excuses; take off!"

"Very well. As ranking official, you may take that seat over there. We'll be under way in a few moments."

Russo almost swallowed his cigar. Claudia had to stifle her snigger. "What?!" the senator exploded. "No! That is, I have too many other things to do on the ground. You're *not* to take off until I've left this ship, is that clear?" The terror in his voice was unmistakable.

"Whatever you say, Senator." Gloval showed a thin smile.

Pulling himself together, Russo beat a hasty retreat. To the bridge gang he said, "Well, girls, we're all depending on you. So don't let us down!" The hatch closed behind him.

Gloval stared at the hatch. *We aren't ready for combat. We just aren't ready!*

Minmei joined Jason at the top-story window. They were gazing up at the immobile war machine from about the height of its waist. The titanic chest had been holed by enemy fire.

"Wow, look how big it is!" the boy squealed with delight.

"Be careful, Jason," Minmei scolded, holding him back so he wouldn't climb out onto the ledge.

"I wonder where it came from?" Jason yelled happily.

As they watched, the cyclopean head tilted far forward as heavy servomechanisms hummed, leaving the torso uppermost.

Down in the street, people were exclaiming, "Look! It moved its head!" "It just fell out of the sky and wiped out those buildings!" "It's as big as a building itself!"

"See? Its back opened up!" Jason cried, pointing. Minmei gasped. A co-pilot's seat rose on a support pillar, lifted into sight by some inner mechanism. It was empty.

Jason's brows came together. "There's nobody running it!" Machinery whirred again, and the post moved higher, raising the first seat to reveal a second mounted below it. In that seat was Rick Hunter.

Getting out of his seat, looking down, Rick ignored the furor of the crowd below. "What's going on here? What's happened to me?"

"The pilot looks confused," Jason commented; he'd been hoping for someone a little more impressive.

"Maybe he was injured in the crash," Minmei suggested. But something about the young man was familiar.

"I must be seeing things," Rick muttered. "This *used* to be a fighter plane."

He spotted Minmei and Jason. He recalled the girl from somewhere but couldn't take time to try to place her just now.

"Excuse me, but, uh, what is this?" He indicated the Veritech. "I mean, what does it look like to you?"

Minmei took a moment to absorb the question. "Some kind of robot, I think."

"Oh, great," Rick sighed, relieved. "When I got into this thing, it was an aircraft. I thought I'd gone nuts."

"A convertible airplane?" Minmei and Jason both echoed. "You must be joking," Minmei added. She thought he wasn't bad-looking, however, and wondered how old he was. Not much older than she was, she judged.

"I'm as puzzled as anybody about it."

"You're kidding!" she said. "You're the pilot and you don't even know what it is?"

"No, I'm not a military pilot. I'm just—just an amateur!" *Satisfied, Roy?* "It's all, um, a big mistake. I'm not supposed to have it."

"An enemy spy!" Jason squawked.

Minmei gave him a little shake to quiet him. *"Jason!"*

"Spy?" Rick yelped. "Look, this was the army's idea, not mine!" He shook his head, looking down at the Battloid. "Look at all the damage!"

Helicopters were approaching from the distance, and traffic was venturing forth again. "Will you have to pay for it?" Minmei wondered.

Rick's stomach felt like it was doing somersaults. "Me? I hope not." A truck was insistently blowing its horn down by the Battloid's automobile-size feet. "What?" he yelled angrily.

The driver hollered up, "Get that thing off the road! I have a truckload of military supplies to deliver and I'm in a hurry, Mac! Now, move it!"

Rick stood up, surrendering to the inevitable. "I don't know how it works, but I'll try."

"Good luck!" Minmei called. She'd decided he was kind of cute.

"Thanks." *She has a real nice smile.* He'd have to remember his way back here.

"And please be careful."

He gave her a broad grin and a wave. "Sure. I will." He got back to his seat. As it lowered, he tried to think of something else to say but could only come up with, "So long!"

"I hope I see you again sometime!" Minmei called.

Back in the cockpit, Rick told himself, "Well, all I can do is throw a few switches and hope for the best, I guess." The giant head swung back into place.

Taking the control grips, he panned the screen before him. "At least I can see where I'm going. If I can just figure out how to get there."

But as the Battloid stirred, preparing to walk, he felt a distinct lack of confidence, something he was unused to.

The machine seemed to want more of him than the mere pushing of buttons.

The Battloid lifted its foot to step, lost balance when it brought it too high, and swayed, about to topple over backward. The crowd that had gathered to stare at the Battloid panicked and began to bolt, yelling and milling. Rick howled in dismay.

Just as the war machine was about to crash into the buildings behind it, back thrusters flared for a quick, intense burn. The Battloid was pushed back to a precarious balance. Then it went off kilter in the opposite direction, staggering toward the little balcony over the White Dragon from which Minmei and Jason watched, open-mouthed.

The two saw that it wasn't going to stop; with wails of fright, they turned and fled just as the Battloid crashed through the wall where they'd been standing, collapsing that whole portion of the building. It came to rest like a drunk who'd passed out across a bar.

Minmei coughed and spat out plaster, checking Jason, whom she'd shielded under her as she went down. "Please tell me you're okay!"

"I am!" Jason said brightly.

Rick's voice came over the Battloid's PA system. "Are you two all right in there?"

"Yes!" Minmei yelled.

In the cockpit, Rick tilted his helmet back to wipe his brow. "Thank goodness!" He couldn't bear the thought of hurting an innocent bystander.

Besides, the girl was real cute.

# CHAPTER
# NINE

*Clearly, as Gloval said, SDF-1 was in part a booby trap. He was too busy to think of it, and I wasn't a trained military man, so it didn't occur to us until it was too late that that particular sword might cut both ways.*

Dr. Emil Lang, Notes on Launch Day

**T**HE MOMENT CAME IN A WAY NO ONE HAD FORSEEN even an hour before; SDF-1, all running lights flashing, prepared to launch for the first time.

"Gravity control systems through bulkhead forty-eight are green light," Sammie relayed to engineering. "Please confirm, over."

From all over the ship the reports came in; the messages went to every corner of it. It was no longer a question of waiting for a perfect checklist; the dimensional fortress was going—now.

"Priority one transmission from HQ, Captain Gloval," Vanessa announced. "Armor One has completed recovery procedures and is departing now to join Armor Ten at Rendezvous Point Charlie."

Gloval grunted acknowledgment and added, "Thank you, Vanessa. Claudia, check the reflex furnace and see if we've recovered full power yet."

Claudia studied her equipment, listened to a brief intercom message, and said, "Ready condition on furnace power, sir."

Once more, Gloval wondered about those enormous, enigmatic, and unprecedentedly powerful engines. "Reflex power" was a term Lang used; even his closest assistants scratched their heads when Lang scribbled equations and tried to explain why he called it that and what he *thought* was going on inside the power plant.

Not that it mattered; all Gloval wanted was for his ship to function, to be battleworthy, for however long it took. A few days—perhaps.

*Or a day. Just give me one day!*

"Very good. Antigravity: full thrust."

"Aye aye, sir," Kim sang out. "Full thrust." The mountainous bulk of the SDF-1 trembled and was somehow alive under them. The bridge gang went through individual countdowns and checklists, their voices and those from the intercom overlapping.

Then Claudia's rang out clear as an angel's through the ship, and over Macross Island. "Ten . . . niner . . . eight . . ."

A hundred thousand thoughts and fears and prayers hovered over the island, almost a tangible force in themselves.

". . . two . . . one . . ."

"Full power," Gloval ordered. "Activate the antigravity control system."

The entire city vibrated slightly, as the hundreds of thousands of tons of SDF-1 rose from the ship's Gibraltarlike keel blocks; their unique absorption system adjusted to the sudden unburdening.

The ship rose smoothly, casting its stupendous shadow across the island. "The gyroscope is level, sir," Lisa reported tersely.

Gloval eased back in his chair, hoping it was a good omen. "Well done."

He'd barely said it when a tremor ran through the great ship. Below, he could see the upper-hull/flight deck actually *quake*.

SDF-1 lurched, then listed hard to port, throwing people from their feet. There was a lot of yelling; the intercom was bedlam.

"What in blazes is going on?" Gloval thundered, grasping the arms of his chair to keep from being thrown across the compartment. "Trim the pitch attitude immediately!"

"It must be the gyroscope," Claudia said, struggling to stay at her station.

"No, look!" Lisa was pointing out at the upper-hull/flight deck.

Bulges had appeared, like volcanic domes being thrust up against the hardest armor ever developed; the tearing of metal sounded through the SDF-1 like the death throes of dinosaurs.

The convexities of armor broke open like overripe fruit, yielding complex cylinders of advanced-design systemry. The cylinders, each the size of a railroad tank car, rose majestically into the air, trailing power leads and torn support frameworks.

"The gravity pods are breaking away!"

Gloval rushed up behind Lisa to see for himself. "What is it? Oh, no! They're tearing away from the ship instead of lifting it!"

Everywhere it was the same; the physics of the disaster was inflexible. Dozens of gravity pods tore lose, continuing their ascent as they'd been charged to do, breaking their way through any structure in their path (or, to put it another way, conventional gravity was dragging the SDF-1 down around them).

"This can't be happening!" Gloval breathed, not so much distraught by the probable outcome the disaster would mean for himself and his command as by the utter catastrophe it meant for Earth.

"The ship is losing altitude, Captain!" Lisa cried.

Gloval groaned. *"Please! Tell me I'm dreaming this!"*

"Pardon, sir?" Lisa said.

He hadn't realized he'd spoken aloud. "It's a nightmare."

SDF-1 fell faster, its few operating thrusters unequal to the task of easing it down. All through the ship, people knew that calamity had occurred and waited with varying attitudes to find out what their fate would be.

With alarms hooting and wailing, the ship crashed back onto its keel blocks. Under the velocity of even a cushioned fall, the titanic weight made the monolithic blocks crack, give way, and collapse or drive themselves down into the Earth.

But the impact-absorption systems built into them saved the ship from greater damage and spared lives, before the blocks were overloaded and defeated. SDF-1 settled down with its hull against the rubble and soil and hardtop, but the ship's back hadn't been broken or its hull breached.

The bridge wasn't so different from any other section: outcries and screams and incoherent yelling. In moments, the noise died away and military discipline reasserted itself. SDF-1 rested at a 15-degree list to port.

"Is anyone hurt?" Gloval's voice cut through the confusion. Everyone else chimed in that they were uninjured, then shut up; the captain's voice must be heard, uninterrupted, at a time like this; and though the bridge gang was untried in space, they knew their duty and they knew their orders.

Gloval strode back toward his seat. "I want a full damage report. Give me a computer readout on every system onboard!" The SDF-1 was a fish in a barrel for the time being; he had only minutes in which to act.

"*Yessir!*" the five voices responded as one, giving the words a choral sound.

Gloval looked infinitely tired. "They'll never let me forget this."

"You shouldn't blame yourself for this, sir," Lisa said softly.

Gloval lowered himself into his chair, shaking his head to contradict Lisa.

"I am the captain," he said simply.

In the street outside the White Dragon, a very peculiar salvage operation was in progress.

The Battloid had been rigged with cables attached to two seafood delivery trucks. The civilian populace had always been sympathetic to the military's mission, and by now news broadcasts had made it apparent to most people that a new and awful war had begun and that, like it or not, everyone was a part of that war for the time being. So the truckers and other bystanders were doing their best to get the Battloid righted.

The big box-jobs gunned their engines, tires spinning and squealing, laying down large black patches of rubber and raising reeking clouds of smoke. The trucks backfired, and their engines labored.

Slowly, the armored mechamorph came away from its resting place, toward a vertical position. Rick, sweating over his controls, sat with hands hovering over them, hesitant to court further misfortune by interfering.

The Battloid was standing again—for the moment. It reached the vertical and slowly began to tilt the other way. Volunteer helpers and onlookers let out a wide assortment of exclamations and yowls and scurried for safety; the drivers leapt from the cabs of their trucks and hotfooted it.

Minmei and Jason hugged each other and shouted, "Oh, no!" at the same instant.

Rick grabbed for the controls desperately. At the very least, he had to try to keep this insane metal berserker from doing more damage to the restaurant.

The Battloid lurched, trying to find its balance. Rick tried his best but couldn't seem to do anything right. Again, it was as if the machine was waiting for him to do something more than merely manipulate controls.

The Battloid took a lurching step, and its legs became entangled in the cables; it twirled clumsily and fell backward toward the opposite side of the street, its back crashing against an empty building that had taken heavy damage from the enemy barrage.

It sank down, crunching the building, until it came to rest with its backside halfway to the street, heels dug into the pavement. When Rick was sure the machine was stable for the time being, he wiped his brow again. "Oh, why me? How come these things don't happen to other people?"

The triumphant Veritech squadron flew in tight formation, making its way back to the *Prometheus* and the dimensional fortress.

Roy was in the lead spot, of course. "This is Skull Leader, Veritech squadron, to SDF-1. Am returning to base. We have met the enemy and pretty much cleaned their clocks. They've withdrawn from Earth's atmosphere."

Lisa's face was on the display screen. "Commendable work, Commander Fokker, I'll—"

She was abruptly moved out of the way by Claudia, who said "Let me talk to him! Roy, how many of them did *you* shoot down?"

"Only ten this time," he said nonchalantly. But the dog-fight would be a legend by that night, the hardest rat-racing he'd ever seen. Every millisecond was going to be analyzed and refought a hundred times among the flying officers.

"You're slipping, Roy," Claudia told him, but her tone wasn't critical at all.

"Well, don't worry, Claudia; I'll make it up." *Something tells me I'm going to get plenty of opportunities!* "Do you have any word on the VT one-zero-two?"

Lisa crowded back onto the screen. "That section-eight case! He landed in Macross City in a Battloid, and he's doing more damage than the invaders."

Roy laughed. "Thanks, Lisa."

"Who is he? He's not registered as a fighter pilot."

"Don't worry; I know him."

"Well, he sure needs help." Lisa scowled.

"I'd better go check on him." Roy switched to the tac net. "This is Skull Leader to group. You guys head on back to *Prometheus*. I've got some business to take care of in town. Captain Kramer, you take 'em home."

"Will do, boss."

Roy peeled off from the formation and, increasing his wings' sweep for higher speed, plummeted for Macross City. "I should've known better than to leave him alone," he muttered.

Even in a city that had known a peppering of energy bolts and alien rockets, it wasn't too hard to spot the mess made by an out-of-control Battloid. "Aha! That you, Rick, old son?"

The war machine was resting against a building. "Hi, Roy! It's me!"

"Had a busy day down there, huh?"

Rick sighed. "You might say that, Big Brother."

People in the streets spotted the approaching aircraft. The skull insignia was well known; but things had a way of being unexpectedly dangerous today, and nobody was up for taking any more chances.

Everybody sprinted for cover again. Roy switched his ship to Guardian mode for the descent—the mechanoid/eagle configuration that allowed more control in the tight quarters of a city street. It settled in on the bright blue flare of its foot thrusters, chain-gun cradled in its right arm.

In another moment Roy's ship had mechamorphosed to Battloid. Its shoulder structure gave it a look of immense brute power, like a football player. Rick felt like rubbing his eyes. "I must be dreaming this; I don't believe it!"

Jason, crouched with Minmei behind a fallen cornice, yelped, "That airplane became a robot too!"

"Amazing!" Minmei murmured. It was all so strange and almost magical—it made her wonder what the young pilot's name was.

"A few small repairs and you can take that Battloid back into action," Roy said blithely.

"What're you talking about?" Rick yelled over the net. "I don't even know what this thing is, and if you think I'm qualified to operate it, just take a good look around the neighborhood!"

But he watched his screen in utter fascination as Roy's war machine shifted its weapon from its right arm, drew out a long, thick band as sturdy as a heavy-cargo sling, and settled the weapon over its left shoulder, all as casually as an infantryman going to sling-arms.

Rick gaped. No control system in the world could do that. Maybe a battery of computers, *if* the sequence was worked out precisely in advance. But what Roy had done had more of an on-the-spot look to it.

It brought to mind what Roy had told Rick about the Robotech flight helmet—the thinking cap: "You don't just pilot a Robotech ship; you *live* it."

"If you can fly a jet, you can operate a Battloid," Roy began. "I'll tell you what to do. Gross movements are initiated by manuals—the legs are guided by your foot pedals, for instance."

"*Which* foot pedals, Roy? I've got about fifty controls in here!"

"Fifty-seven, if you want to get technical. But that's not the important part. Just button up and listen; I'll explain while I'm making repairs."

The skull-insignia Battloid extruded metal tentacles, tool-servos, waldos, and a host of other advanced repair apparatus. In moments the one Robotech war machine was repairing the other. Welding sparks jumped, and damaged components were replaced.

"The secret's that helmet," Roy said. "You generate general movements or sequences with your controls, but the Robotechnology takes its real guidance straight from your thoughts. You've got to *think* your ship through the things you want it to do."

Rick couldn't help being skeptical in spite of everything he'd seen. "Now you're gonna tell me these junk heaps are *alive*?"

"Close enough for me," Roy said noncommittally, "although you're going to have to make up your own mind about that. We still don't understand the power source— the same power source that runs SDF-1 but we know that, somehow, it's not just a—a blind physical process. It's involved with life forces somehow; with awareness—with *mind*, if I'm not getting too fancy for you."

"*I* think you're bucking for a medical discharge, mental category."

Roy chuckled. "See for yourself. Just pay attention and I'll tell you how it's done."

# CHAPTER
## TEN

*When it comes to testing new aircraft or determining maximum performance, pilots like to talk about "pushing the envelope."*

*They're talking about a two-dimensional model: the bottom is zero altitude, the ground; the left is zero speed; the top is max altitude; and the right, maximum velocity, of course. So, the pilots are pushing that upper-right-hand corner of the envelope.*

*What everybody tries not to dwell on is that that's where the postage gets canceled, too.*

*The Collected Journals of Admiral Rick Hunter*

FOR THE NEXT FEW MINUTES ROY REPAIRED RICK'S downed machine while he briefed his friend on the secrets of operating Robotechnology.

"These Battloids are classified top secret," he finished, as he made the last reconnection. "And you've gotta trust me on this one: There *is* a reason for it." All the repair tackle had neatly withdrawn itself into the skull Battloid's huge body.

"There, that oughta do it," Roy said. "Now switch on energy and depress those foot pedals slowly, like I told you."

Rick did, and *thought* his way through the maneuver as Roy had instructed. He focused his mind's eye on the act of getting back to his feet; *something* at the other end of the helmet's pickups sensed and understood.

Carefully, Rick Hunter's red-trimmed Battloid levered itself up, gaining its feet to stand shoulder to shoulder with Roy's.

"*That's* it," Roy said. "See how easy it is?"

More than easy; it was exaltation. It felt as if there was a feedback or reciprocation mechanism in the control system; Rick felt as if he *were* the Battloid.

Several stories tall. Indestructible. Armed with the most advanced weapons the human race had developed. With the power of flight in a way that did indeed make the *Mockingbird* seem primitive, and metalshod fists capable of punching their way through a small mountain.

Rick drew a deep breath, dizzy with the feeling.

"That's it!" Roy encouraged. "See how easy it is?"

"Wow, you learn fast, don't you?" said a voice from street level over the battloid's external pickups.

Rick looked down at Minmei and Jason. He automatically guided the Robotech machine so that it leaned down toward the girl. "Thanks."

A voice from the distance—Minmei's Aunt Lena—called, "Minmei! Jason! Come on!"

Minmei waved up at Rick. "See you later! We're being evacuated!" She trotted off with Jason in tow, long, slim legs moving with unconscious grace.

Off the shore of Macross Island the breakers came in, crashed, and sent up high fountains of foam, and the waters pulled back to regroup yet again for their eternal assault on the beach.

But the next breaker brought a different kind of assault.

Zentraedi Battlepods launched straight up out of the water on their thrusters: scout versions, officer versions, and the standard models configured to carry a variety of heavy weapons and equipment.

Their biped design, the legs articulated backward, resembled that of an ostrich. They landed on the shore and began advancing in long leaps like monstrous kangaroos, sensors swinging for information, weapons ready for the kill. They arranged themselves in skirmish formation and covered miles in seconds.

Soon they loomed across a ridgeline, looking down on Macross City.

* * *

At Breetai's command post, the report was patched through. "The recon and Battlepods have landed, Commander. We're ready to attack."

Exedore's protruding, pinpoint-pupiled eyes swung to regard his lord. Breetai leaned to a communications pickup.

"Attention all gunnery crews! Prepare to give covering fire to the recon assault group."

The command "Ready All Guns" and subsidiary orders rang through the armada. The long muzzles were run out and ranged in. In their sights was Macross City.

"We better get moving, Rick," Roy told his friend. "We still have a war to fight."

"I'm still pretty unsure of myself with all these robot controls! I'm not ready for combat."

"Not robot; *Robotech!*" Roy corrected automatically. "Look, pull the control marked G, and we'll switch to Guardian configuration."

Rick complied, muttering, "What the heck is a Guardian? Here goes!"

As the Veritech shifted and mechamorphosed, converting to a bird of prey/war machine, Roy explained. "The Guardian controls operate almost exactly like those of the fighter plane. You can fly it without any problems."

"I've heard that before," Rick reminded him.

On a hill overlooking the city, the crowds waited to be admitted to the underground shelter system. Because of the dangerous nature of research and experimentation going on in the city and the fact that Macross would be a primary military target for any aggressor, the shelters had always had a high priority in the island's construction projects.

Minmei and her relatives were waiting fretfully with the thousands upon thousands of others. The emergency personnel were working as fast as they could, but moving the huge population underground was time-consuming at best.

The job facing the civil defense crews was overwhelming, and to top it off, many people had stopped in the foothills to try to find friends or relatives before moving below.

But that wasn't what made Minmei halt in midstep.

"My diary!" She had been keeping it since she was old enough to hold a pen, xeroreducing her writing so that each page held weeks of entries in a single, thick little volume. In it were all her thoughts, ideas, memories, stories, the lyrics for her songs, her poetry and secret longings, and the most important letter she'd ever received in her life—Minmei's diary *was* her life.

"I have to go back for it!"

"Don't be foolish, child!" Lena cried. "There *is* no going back." Jason watched wide-eyed; he was too young to have known Minmei before she'd come to live on Macross Island, but he already adored her.

Minmei ducked away from her aunt's restraining hands and avoided Uncle Max's effort to stop her. Older people just didn't understand!

"It won't take me a minute to get it, don't worry!" Then Minmei was off, gamine legs flying.

"Come back!" Aunt Lena moved to follow, but two CD workers, too late to restrain Minmei, blocked her way. Uncle Max and Jason and the others stood watching as Minmei's fleet figure disappeared down into the city. Over all loomed the fallen SDF-1, blocking the sun.

Breetai studied the fire-mission computer models. He gave a grudging nod of satisfaction.

"All guns standing by for bombardment, Commander Breetai," a tech reported.

"Good. Level everything in the path of the assault forces but be careful not to damage that battle fortress. I want to take it intact!" Once the Battlepods had established a beachhead, his plan could be implemented, and Zor's masterpiece would belong to the Zentraedi.

*Then let the Robotech Masters beware!* Breetai thought.

Lead elements of the armada opened fire; those farther back in the dense cloud of warships couldn't fire without the risk of hitting another Zentraedi vessel.

A torrent of alien bolts rained down like a hellish spring storm, in a kill-zone that encircled the dimensional fortress. Buildings seemed to melt like candles in a blast furnace, riddled by thousands of narrow, high-intensity beams, collapsing in clouds of plaster and concrete dust.

Death was everywhere among the CD teams, emergency personnel, antilooting squads, and others who'd bravely remained behind. Dying screams and the shrieks of the wounded rose on the bolt-splashed heat waves. Zentraedi Battlepods watched it all impassively from their vantage point: wingless, headless armored ostriches bristling with sensors and heavy weapons. The shelters and the masses waiting to enter them were noted, but those were of no importance; Breetai was only interested in the SDF-1.

"They're invading the city!" Rick yelled from his Guardian's cockpit. It was only by accident, he realized, that he'd crash-landed outside the kill-zone.

"Yeah; it looks like it was evacuated just in time," Roy said, surveying the blasted landscape from his higher vantage point in the Battloid.

He also had updates on the refugee situation and the various assembly points. "If you're worried about your girlfriend, we could go check on her."

Roy shifted to Guardian mode and showed Rick how it was done; the two Guardians skimmed away like jet-powered skaters, foot thrusters riding them on a blasting carpet mere inches off the ground, safe from most of the enemy fire.

"Do we have a fix on where that bombardment is coming from?" Gloval snapped.

"A fleet of spaceships, numbers uncertain but very, very high. In lunar orbit," Vanessa told him promptly.

Gloval rubbed his jaw. "Beyond the range of our missiles."

Lisa looked up from her monitors. "Captain, an alien assault force is approaching from the east, range eight miles."

It was her job and her prerogative, so she added, "We need air support, sir."

Gloval gave a quick nod that shook his cap a little. "Call for it."

*    *    *

The Zentraedi Battlepods leapt from the cliffs around the city and began their fast assault. They moved with the high speed and precision of advanced Robotechnology, hopping nimbly or skating quickly at ground level on their foot thrusters.

At the outskirts of the city they opened weapons ports and missile rack cover plates, then opened fire. Missiles left scorching, corkscrewing trails in the air, converging on SDF-1. Pulsed laser beams strobed and flicked at targets of opportunity.

The initial barrage met with strong defenses. Most of the missiles were jammed by ECM techs or intercepted by countermissiles; the beams were either repulsed by SDF-1's highly reflective surface or failed to do more than warm the great ship's armor at that range and in those atmospheric conditions. Still, the situation was about to get grim if Gloval couldn't change the tactical equations.

"This is SDF-1," Lisa transmitted calmly. "Attention all strike elements: We are under attack and need immediate assistance. Incoming Veritechs, switch to Battloid mode." The tac nets were silent; the situation seemed hopeless. Lisa considered the fact that, in spite of all the beliefs she'd embraced, perhaps humans *weren't* destined to rule Earth. Just then, Gloval played his hole card.

Through a sky crowded with spherical missile explosions, the Veritechs swooped with supreme confidence, dodging the intense ordnance eruptions all around them.

More VTs formed up on the lead formation. In seconds it was a gathering of vengeful eagles. "Roger, SDF-1," Captain Kramer drawled. "We're comin' in. All Veritechs switch to Guardian mode."

Below, the round-bodied, hopping Zentraedi war machines were laying waste Macross City, shooting indiscriminately and ravaging for the love of it. Kramer disliked net discipline as much as Roy did. So he said:

"Skull Team, area four-one. Vermilion Team, area four-four." Kramer gave the other ground-strike assignments, just as Roy would have done. The two had been wingmates long enough for Kramer to know it by heart.

And long enough for Kramer to know how to send the Veritechs on their way: "Awright, boys; let's get on down there an' wrassle 'em around some."

The ships dived in tight formations; the pilots only *talked* imprecisely.

So used to having their own way, the Zentraedi Battlepods, didn't seem to understand that with the arrival of the Veritechs, the odds had changed.

In moments, the Veritechs found, fixed, and fought the enemy, and the aliens began to get an unwelcome message.

Zentraedi Battlepods, headless and ominous, were being blown away right and left by Robotech ships in Battloid mode. The giant mechanical infantrymen had all the skill their human pilots had absorbed; if their close-in weapons were somewhat inferior to the Zentraedi's, it mattered very little in the street-to-street, house-to-house, often eye-to-eye close quarters of urban combat.

Alien Battlepods stalked and stomped through Macross city, cannon muzzles angling and firing at will, rockets twist-trailing everywhere, leaving an inferno behind them.

An elite Zentraedi strike squad had encountered nothing that could impede it. Its members didn't know that a computer-assisted gunsight was zeroing in on the squad leader —until it was too late.

A powered Gatling gun opened up, a thousand times louder than a buzz saw, shell casings flying up in a steady stream. The high-density depleted transuranic slugs used in Terran Robotech bullets were very heavy and delivered devastating amounts of kinetic energy on impact. A generation before, 30-mm autocannon had been capable of blowing tanks apart. A lot of improvements had been made since then.

The Battlepods found that they'd dropped into a very angry wasps' nest and that the stings were deadly. Then the squad leader disappeared in a high-density barrage.

A pod swung its upper and lower plastron cannon muzzles, its operator deciding where to direct his fire next. All at once a Battloid broke through the building next to it, bringing up the muzzle of its Gatling to knock the pod back off balance. The pod was twice the defender's size, three times its mass. But the stroke sent the offworld vehicle reeling back.

The pod staggered, legs flailing, ending up against a metal utility pole, bending it. The Battloid leveled its Gatling and opened fire with a sound like ripping cloth amplified to the point where it was deafening.

The Zentraedi pod abruptly became an expanding sphere of flame, gas, and debris. The Battloid whirled, gun held at high port, looking for more enemies.

All across the city it was the same; as wave after wave of pods descended or leaped ashore, the Battloids engaged and overcame them using tactics distilled from SWAT teams and infantry rifle outfits. The battloids handled themselves like grunt fireteams in fantastic enlargement.

And the Zentraedi learned that the price of Earth, foot for square foot, promised to be very high indeed.

Rick skimmed along behind Roy, twisting and dodging through the war-torn maze that was Macross City. SDF-1's bow was hanging like a threatening hammer above them as tracers drew lines of light through the air, missiles exploded, and alien blasterbolts hyphened all through the combat zone around the dimensional fortress.

The side of an apartment building was blown loose and collapsed in pieces. Rick zigzagged around it, his Veritech still skating along in Guardian mode as he tried to put together in his mind why that girl Minmei was suddenly so important to him that he'd go through *this* for her.

# CHAPTER
# ELEVEN

*In a Veritech y'got every kinda way a pilot can die* and *just about every kinda hurt-alert a leg infantry might run into, see: Exceptin' possibly trench foot, though I wouldn't bet on it.*

Anonymous Wolf Team pilot, quoted by Zachary Foxx, Jr., VT: *The Men and the Mecha*

**M**ORE PODS GRASSHOPPERED INTO MACROSS CITY, all plastron cannon firing.

A damaged pod, hit on descent by SDF-1 missile crews, blazed like a fiery comet, punching through one building and laying a track of devastation across the roofs of three more before colliding with a last in an inferno that sent rubble in thousand-foot arcs.

Nearby, Battloid gunners swung their muzzles from target to target. The pods were falling back on every front. There was word over the net that some guy in Vermilion, out of ammo, had actually downed one with a Battloid roundhouse, and *worked* it good with the Battloid's feet.

Elsewhere, Minmei ran for her life.

It seemed so easy at first: the diary in her hand, the way back to the shelters unobstructed...until the pods had dropped into the neighborhood on every side.

Minmei didn't know where she'd lost the diary; she'd only thought to save her all-important letter. Now she thought only about living. She raced through the streets, the long legs flying, midnight sheets of hair flying, as the pods closed in. Blasts and rockets demolished the buildings around her, and burning wreckage nearly smashed her flat a dozen times.

But bless them, there were also those fantastic robotlike defenders, like the one who'd nearly caved in her aunt's restaurant. They were everywhere, leaping and charging and firing, giving even better than they got. They were like armored giants, but none of them were around now. And now was when Minmei needed one.

A Battlepod stomped after her, hooflike feet sinking deep into the pavement with every step. Minmei understood then that hers was only a little life, of no significance on the grand scale of things. There were so many things she'd never done and so little time to reflect on the things she had—the harshness of it hit her in an instant: the miracle that was life, the irreplaceability of each moment.

The Battlepod was almost upon her, armorshod hooves pounding the street. The very vibrations of it threw Minmei headlong, scraping her elbows and hands and knees, as explosions crashed all around. She was not quite sixteen years old, but she understood in that moment that war had no eligibility requirements.

Gigantic pod feet crashed behind her. Minmei cringed, hands over head, waiting for death to take her. An enormous hoof descended.

Just then an amplified voice said, "Oh, no, you don't!"

She heard an explosion and a tearing of metal and felt waves of heat scorching her back. There was a rending of armor and a ground-shaking crash. Somehow, none of it hurt her.

Minmei gathered her nerve and opened her eyes. The pod had been knocked back through the air, one leg dangling loose, in flames. She'd been protected by great metal wings.

It was another example of those things people were calling Robotech, this time in the metal eagle form they seemed to take on at will. There was something familiar about this one's voice.

"Take it easy, honey; you're okay," Roy said over external speakers. "We'll protect you."

Roy turned to Rick. "Take care of the girl! I'll keep the pods off our backs!"

Minmei struggled to her feet while the skull-and-crossbones machine reared, mechamorphosing and growing taller and manlike in a way that put her in mind of some miraculous origami. The second, the red one she recognized from her aunt's restaurant, stayed in the man-bird mode, objecting, "You can't handle them alone!" in another voice she remembered.

Roy brought his Gatling up, covering the area. "Don't argue with me! I'll draw their fire while you get her out of here."

Rick, using controls and mind-imagery, eased the Guardian over, extending its left hand, until fingers the diameter of telephone poles were ready to grasp her. He raised the cockpit canopy to call down, "Don't move! I'm going to pick you up!"

For a damsel in distress, Minmei showed a certain skepticism. "I thought you were an amateur."

The anthropomorphic hand gently enfolded her; Rick sweated bullets, concentrating, and knew that he would never try anything like this with a mere physical-control system. Only Robotechnology allowed such fine discretion.

Minmei had a fleeting feeling that she ought to be wearing a white gown and wondered if she was to be carried to the top of a skyscraper or dragged into the middle of a fight with dinosaurs.

In a way, of course, that had already happened. "Huh? *Oh, no!*" she cried as the fingers closed around her.

"Trust me; I can do it!" Rick called down to her.

"Do I have to? Ohhhh!"

But the grip, though firm and secure, didn't mangle her or crush her into jelly or even hurt—at least, not much. Which was just as well, since there were alien pods releasing flights of missiles high overhead.

"Get outta here, Rick! Fire your jets!" Roy hollered, bringing up his Gatling and sweeping it back and forth at the incoming missiles, hoping to cut into the odds a little.

The Guardian's foot thrusters blared; Minmei howled, and they were airborne, zooming away from the attack.

Roy got a number of the missiles, detonating them, which in turn knocked out quite a few others—"fratricide," as the ordnance people called it—as they either veered into one another or detonated from the force of the first explosions. But survivors got through, bearing down on Rick, who didn't dare go faster with Minmei in hand for fear that the air blast and maneuver forces would injure or kill her.

He could only duck and dodge, engaging his jamming and countermeasures gear as Roy had taught him, and hope for the best. Missiles sizzled by all around to impact far down the street.

Minmei hid her head in her hands, then looked up to see that Rick was yelling something at her, too distracted to remember the external speakers. "What're you saying? I can't hear you!"

Roy spotted a pod just as his radars and other instruments picked it up; it was making a stand on a ridgeline above the housing project which had been gouged into the side of a hill. The Zentraedi pod launched itself off the ridge at him; Roy brought his muzzle around and trap-shot it in midair. It rained down in fire and broken fragments.

His fields of fire were clear for the moment. He raised Rick on the tac net. "How's it goin'? Everything okay?"

"I'm all right now, Roy—"

"I don't care how *you* are; how's the *girl*?"

"Huh? Um, okay. So far." Rick began a steady, smooth ascent to get above the battle and out of the range of the pods in Macross City.

"She's a taxpayer. If anything happens to her, you answer to me."

Rick grinned at Roy's screen image. "Don't forget, Big Brother: I saw her first."

"That's how it is, huh? We'll discuss this later!"

Roy got back to business at hand, leaving Rick to ponder Minmei, whose hair was being whiplashed in her face by the ship's airspeed. They'd already gained enough altitude for it to be pretty cold out there; she couldn't take much of it, in addition to the strain it would put on her simply to breathe.

"Boy, I've gotta figure a way to get her into the cockpit," he whispered.

It was exactly then that his instruments beeped an urgent warning. "Uh oh . . ."

In Macross City, an alien pod fitted for heavy weapons stood up from its concealment behind a demolished mall. It was mounted with two large racks of rockets, like fire-breathing Siamese twins. Missiles came spiking at him, superheating the air with their trails.

He cut in all countermeasures, going into a booster climb, going ballistic. He rammed the stick up for a push-over, losing a few of the seekers, unable to tell if the maneuver forces had simply knocked Minmei out or killed her.

Wishing he had Roy's skill at this sort of thing, Rick dodged, white-faced with the thought that he would fail, would let Minmei down and lose both their lives.

Miraculously, he avoided them all—almost.

A hit at the elbow joint of the arm holding Minmei blew the joint in half. Minmei fell away, screaming, as if in slow motion. It seemed to Rick that he could hear the scream echoing away.

He banked, diving after her, though all the books and experts would have said that there wasn't a thing in the world he could do to save her. He concentrated on those fingers—thought and thought hard.

The telephone pole fingers of the Robotech hand slowly opened in answer to his thinking-cap command, and Minmei found herself floating in midair. The ground, the sky, the wind—nothing seemed to be moving but she and the giant hand.

She realized she was still screaming, and stopped, pushing herself free for whatever good it would do. Then there was something next to her, matching speeds and distances. She seemed to be floating—swimming outside the canopy, some dream mermaid, kicking and struggling toward him, her eyes so big and terrified and pleading that the sight of them almost paralyzed him.

Earlier that same day, Rick would have said that no aircraft in existence could do what the Veritech was doing now. It drew close to Minmei, canopy easing open (he would have said that an aircraft canopy would be torn away like a piece of tinfoil if subjected to aerodynamic stresses like those), in close obedience to his commands and images.

Her black hair stood back, stark, around her face; the white legs kicked like a swimmer's. She glided toward him, arms outstretched. In that moment he knew that if he didn't save her, life would cease to have any meaning.

Still there was the buffeting of the air and the slipstreams created by the fighter itself; they tore at him as Rick rose up, safety harness released, to draw her into the fighter. No ship, not even a Robotech ship, had ever been subjected to such exacting demands.

Gripping the windshield frame, he grabbed for her hand, missed, grabbed, and missed again, the whole time *imaging* the Veritech's precise positioning at speeds approaching the blackout point. One-armed, its aerodynamics radically changed, the fighter struggled to comply.

They drifted like zero-gravity dancers; it seemed so silent and slow and yet so high-speed, with the air shrieking past them and death only an instant away.

Then, somehow, their fingers were together. Later, Rick never remembered shaping the image, but the Veritech altered its death dive to come around and *catch* them, Minmei drifting into the rear seat, Rick into the front.

A last ripping air current almost carried him away, but the descending canopy pressed him back in to safety, although he didn't recall giving the command for it to close.

*Maybe if the pilot lives the ship, the ship lives the pilot?* he speculated.

He grabbed the manual controls and got the Guardian stabilized again. Behind, there was a last grand explosion of several alien missiles committing fratricide. The Guardian's foot thrusters blowtorched; Rick trimmed his craft. He descended through debris and smoke for a shaky landing, trembling and wiping his brow while Minmei at last gave in to sobs in the rear seat.

"We're safe now. Please don't cry." Rick turned toward her.

The Guardian was in a slow, easing descent, its feet only inches above the streets of Macross City. Minmei wiped her nose on the back of her hand.

"I'm all right now. *Oh, no!*"

Her eyes were wide as saucers—such a strange blue, he thought again—focused over his shoulder.

Even as he whirled, an image of what the Guardian should do sprang to mind; its heels caught the pavement, digging in as the thrusters retrofired.

A Battlepod had backed around the corner of a building at an intersection dead ahead—damaged and covering its own retreat, later reports indicated. The Guardian took it from behind, wings hitting the backs of its knees, neatly upending it.

The Guardian slid for nearly a hundred yards, upside down, Rick and Minmei howling as the pavement tore at the canopy, until it came to a rest.

The Guardian got to its feet; so did the pod, which seemed rather unsteady and showed heavy damage.

"You okay? *Oh, no! Minmei!*" She was pale and unmoving, slumped in the rear seat.

*And why? Because these creatures, or whatever they are, came across a billion light-years to invade us? For more war? FOR MORE WAR?*

"Yahhhhhh!" Furiously Rick gripped the trigger on his control stick, the chain-gun pelting the pod with a hail of high-caliber, high-density slugs.

The invader's armored front disappeared in a welter of explosions, shrapnel, and smoke. There were secondary explosions, and the machine fell to the ground like a dying ostrich, strangely articulated legs rising up behind as the rest of it crashed down.

Rick found that he was still thumbing the trigger on his control stick—to no avail; the Gatling's magazine was empty. He took his hand away, breathing a sigh of relief or despair—he wasn't sure which.

And then he heard a sound of metal creaking and shifting.

In the back of the downed pod, a hatch was thrown open. A hatch three yards across.

A figure emerged, helmeted and armored. It was on the scale of the pods—taller than most of the buildings around it. Its helmet's faceplate was a cold and untelling fish eye of green.

It was human-shaped, and it came Rick's way. And for the first time in his life, he froze. Couldn't leave Minmei, had no ammo left, and besides—the sight of the thing had him completely rattled. It was as big as a Battloid.

The ground reverberated under its feet; just as Rick thought things couldn't get any worse, its arms reached up and wrenched off a helmet the size of the Veritech's cockpit, dropping it tiredly.

The face might have been the face of anybody on the streets of Macross City. The monster made bass-register rumbling noises, unintelligible—not surprising in view of how long and muscled its vocal cords must have been if they followed human form.

It staggered and teetered toward the grounded Veritech. Rick froze in his seat—nothing to fire and unwilling to eject or otherwise abandon Minmei. A terrible basso growling shook the air; one metalshod foot of the giant alien warrior squashed a car.

The titan reached toward the Veritech; he quite clearly knew who his enemy was and what Rick had done to him. Dying, he would still have his revenge. Rick sat frozen.

There was a burst of high-decibel, buzz saw sound from somewhere. The alien, fingers not far from Rick's canopy, suddenly looked blank and vulnerable. He toppled to the ground and didn't move again, his weight bending and collapsing his body armor.

The alien pitched onto his face, his back showing the deep penetrations of Veritech Gatling rounds. He'd nearly made it to his objective; his right hand clutched the Guardian's immobilized left foot. The ground shook at Roy Fokker's approach, his Battloid shouldering its weapon.

Rick couldn't shake off his terror. "What was it? What was that thing, Roy?"

Roy's reply sounded flat, tight. "That's the enemy. Now

you know why we built the Battloids, Rick. To fight these giant aliens." Roy's Battloid toed the corpse with an armored foot.

Rick felt like he was losing his grip. Maybe it was a good time to, but he didn't have much experience in the practice. "But—that guy looks just like a human being!"

Roy snorted, "Yeah. If you ever saw a human fifty feet tall."

# CHAPTER
# TWELVE

> Lisa turned to me and yelled, "I am getting sick of that
> name!"
> And I thought, Mr. Rick Hunter, whoever you are, if you
> know what's good for you, you'll start thinking along the lines
> of an alias.
> She had no idea what you'd brought us, Roy!
> None of us did.

> Lt. Claudia Grant, in a note to Lt. Commdr. Roy Fokker

**R**OY AND RICK LOOKED DOWN AT THE DEAD GOLIATH
who still had one hand clasped around the Guardian's ankle
in final rigor. Rick was just starting to get over the shakes
but was still numb with the idea that beautiful, innocent
Minmei, so full of life, had had that life taken from her in
such a meaningless and appalling way.

His panic reassailed him as he realized that there were
more aliens like this one—that the pods and the ships
beyond the atmosphere were crowded with them—that a
plague of them had come to obliterate the Earth.

"I guess you understand now why we kept this secret,"
Roy said.

"Engineering reports backup rockets are fueled and
ready for firing," Claudia said. "How's the evacuation pro-
gressing, Lisa?"

Lisa was still watching Gloval worriedly. "All civilians
have been safely transported to shelters. Macross City is
deserted except for combat units."

Gloval squared his shoulders. "Very well. Bring up the booster rockets. We'll be blasting off immediately."

Lisa blurted, "I hope the standby boosters *work*," before she could think better of it.

Gloval gripped her shoulder, calm in the eye of the storm, hiding the fact that he harbored the same misgivings. "They'll work, Lisa; *they* were designed and built on *Earth*."

But they'd never been tested under full power.

Gloval glanced around. "All right? Blast off!"

Tight-lipped, Lisa responded by manning her station; the rest of the bridge crew chimed in, "Yes, sir!"

The boosters rained blue-white fire, then flared to full life like chained supernovas, their fury backwashing against the hardtop, raising mist and debris, setting blazes, raising steam clouds from the leaking water that flowed through the streets, melting nearby metal. SDF-1 rose slowly, for the first time in a decade, sustained on fusion-flame.

"Attention Skull Leader." Lisa's voice came over the tac net. "SDF-1 is taking off. Request air cover."

Roy's Veritech mechamorphosed from Battloid to Guardian mode. "We're on our way. Over."

Roy's ship rose on its foot thrusters, hovering when Roy realized that there was no sign of life in Rick's fighter.

"C'mon, Rick; let's go! Get the lead out! What's the matter with you?" He went ballistic, climbing.

Rick reached out and shut off his commo, blanking Roy's image. He hadn't led a sheltered life, but nothing had prepared him for the kind of carnage he'd seen in the last half hour or the fear and hatred he'd known. Or for the dismay and grief he felt over the lifelessness of the beautiful young girl slumped in the seat behind him.

SDF-1 rose on its thrusters. Rick sat, prepared to see it go without him, unable to touch the controls of an aircraft.

He leaned back, lowering his head, catatonic and lost.

Roy, off to rejoin the other Veritechs and provide cover for the dimensional fortress's withdrawal, suddenly realized that Rick hadn't followed along behind.

"Rick! Come in, Rick!" No use; he couldn't raise his young friend.

*Poor kid's had to take on more than he could manage*, Roy decided. *Well, I can't just leave him back there.*

He got back on the radio. "Skull Leader to Control. Lisa, I'm going back to pick up something I left down in Macross City. Captain Kramer can run the fighter group till I get back, over."

Lisa frowned out at him from a display screen. "Why are you turning back? Over."

"Rick Hunter in fighter VT one-zero-two is still back on the ground, and I have to get him out of there."

Lisa's expression showed her sense of outrage. "That pilot's an imposter! I've gone through all the rosters and I find no record of such a person."

Roy was bringing his ship through a wide bank. "Easy enough to explain. He's a civilian, so he isn't listed in the military registries."

Lisa's hand flew to her face. "A civilian? But I thought —ohhh...!" *And I ordered him to get his fighter into the air!* She could hear Sammie and the others whispering among themselves: *"What?" "Did he say civilian?" "Who is he?"*

Back in Macross, the firefights flared with even greater fury as more pods entered the battle in long, two-footed hops.

Two pods and a pair of Battloids were squared off at a range of one hundred yards—practically close quarters— the red tracer streams and the blue energy bolts crisscrossing over the devastated cityscape.

Rubble was tossed into the air and whole walls were blasted to bits as large chunks were gouged or vaporized from the pavement.

It was a nearly even match, but another pod arrived and opened up just as one of the first two went down in a hail of armor-piercing autocannon fire. Still another Zentraedi showed up, to concentrate its chest cannonfire along with the others'. A Battloid, blown in half at the waist and leaking fire and explosions, crumbled and disappeared in a detonation.

The second Battloid shifted to Guardian mode, skimming away at ground altitude, trying to get clear. The pods leapt after, closing in for the kill. All at once the two pods were split open like bursting fruit by direct hits from a pair of Stiletto missiles launched by a diving Veritech.

Roy did a tight bank and came in again. Another Stiletto tore the lead pod's leg in half, toppling it, and the pod blew open like an overtaxed boiler.

Seeing the Guardian was safely on its way home, Roy did a wingover and went down lower, searching through the drifting smoke, steam, and dust.

Rick was brought out of his shock and torpor by a sound. He discovered that he'd been slumped against the instrument panel, head resting on his arms.

He moaned a little, then realized what had snapped him out of it: The girl was coming around, making little groaning noises.

"Thank heaven she's alive," he said aloud to himself. Those endless moments of the midair rescue came back to him again—the look in her eyes and the thought of how important she'd become to him.

He shook off his grogginess and glanced around to take in his situation. The enormous corpse was the first thing he spotted.

"I've gotta get us away from here. She might panic if she sees that."

He reached for the instrument panel, trying to clear his head and recall how things worked. He punched up a take-off sequence, muttering, "I hope this thing'll fly."

But instead of taking to the air, the Guardian lurched and slammed into the pavement, held down by the corpse's death grip, the ship's nose hitting the ground so hard that Rick was nearly jolted into unconsciousness.

He lay, pale and panting, feeling cold even though sweat poured from him. His eyes were glassy; he couldn't take them off the terrible sight of the dead alien.

"What happened?" Minmei asked, just having come to. "What's wrong? Why're you trembling like that?"

When Rick didn't answer, she leaned forward. "What are you looking at out there? What's there—"

The thought of how the sight might subject her to more

pain brought him out of his paralysis. "No! You mustn't look out there!"

She resisted the temptation to do just that; she'd come to trust him. "Why, what's wrong?"

As she was saying it, the ground began to vibrate to colossal footsteps, the approach of another war machine. Rick, remembering his Veritech was immobilized and out of ammunition, gazed up in dread.

But the swirling clouds of the battle parted to reveal Roy's ship in Battloid mode, shouldering its autocannon. "I hate to interrupt you two, but you can't sit around here forever. C'mon; let's go!"

But he could see there was no question of repairing Rick's battered ship this time and saw that the dead alien's grip wouldn't be easy to release, short of blasting the hand off at the wrist. "That big palooka seems to have formed a permanent attachment to you guys."

Fortunately, there was a quicker and less messy way to handle things. Roy's Battloid extruded a long metal tentacle ending in a special waldo. With it, he opened a small access plate in one of the downed Guardian's nacelles, cutting in the rescue overrides manually.

In another moment Rick and Minmei felt themselves jostled around as the cockpit and nose separated entirely from the rest of the machine. Roy caught it up neatly and tucked it into a special fitting on the underside of his Battloid's right forearm.

"Amazing, isn't it?" Rick got out.

"It's—realy incredible" was all Minmei could manage to say.

"How's *that* for convenience?" Roy asked. He never got their answer, because at that moment another alien war machine—a pod armed with heavy missiles—sprang from behind a gutted building and zeroed in on the Battloid.

"Hang on, you two!" Roy leapt his Battloid clear just as the pod fired a volley of energy shots. Bringing up his autocannon, the skull leader peppered the pod and sent it crashing backward, riddled and burning.

But more pods were rising from concealment or springing down from the roofs of adjacent buildings. Roy was already shifting to Guardian configuration and jetting away, the aliens galloping in pursuit, firing and firing.

One pod nearly caught him, the vast torso of it filling the sky to starboard. But Roy completed the mechamorphosis to fighter mode and shot away into the sky while salvos ranged around him, thrusters going full-bore.

Two pods stationed on the cliffs at the edge of town poured intense fire at the Veritech as it climbed directly at them. Rick heard Minmei echo his own moan of fear.

Roy stayed dead on course, releasing more missiles when the time was exactly right. The pods went up like a pair of Roman candles, and Roy zoomed into the clear, headed for SDF-1.


The dimensional fortress, its protecting fighters deployed all around it, had achieved a low orbit.

"Shifting to horizontal propulsion," Lisa's voice rang through the fleet, and the enigmatic main engines sent a river of force through the primary thrusters at the ship's stern. Blue infernos raved, and the SDF-1 gathered speed, moving for a higher orbit.

"Stand by for fighter retrieval," Lisa went on. "All planes return to carrier bays. Over."

"This is Sepia Three. Roger, Control, returning for retrieval."

On the flight decks, the crews prepared for the feverish, dangerous work ahead. The fleet was still on combat alert, subject to attack at any time. Every attempted landing must be a "trap"—successful—because there was no time to waste on "bolters" that would have to be repeated.

The teams swarmed to their mother ship; everyone from Gloval on down sweated each second of the retrieval. "Lisa, please report whether we have all fighters safely aboard," Gloval said after an eternity.

"Yes, sir." The answer came quickly. "Those were the last two, sir. All others are accounted for except for Commander Fokker and VT one-zero-two."

"Good. I don't think we have to worry about Commander Fokker." Gloval rose. "Vanessa, show me the current orbital data for Armor One and Armor Ten."

Vanessa punched up the information. "Yes, sir. They're both approaching Rendezvous Point Charlie right on schedule. We should be making contact with them in about two-niner minutes."

"Very good. Claudia, any sign of enemy craft?"

"No, Captain. It's all clear."

"Excuse me, Captain, but isn't that strange?" Lisa asked. "After launching a massive attack from orbit, why isn't the enemy continuing their attack? It doesn't make sense, does it?"

Gloval usually kept his own counsel but admitted now, "That's bothering me too. There has to be a reason they're just playing with us. They have the advantage, but they don't attack. But why?"

The bridge crew exchanged troubled looks with one another.

Roy's fighter climbed smoothly out of the atmosphere, making for the dimensional fortress. Inside, though, things were a little stormier.

"She doesn't *want* to go to the ship, Roy!" Rick insisted. "She wants to go back to Macross Island!"

Roy, lips pulled back in anger, snarled at Rick's image on his screen. "Are you crazy? Macross is crawling with aliens! It'd be suicide for her to go back there! Did she give you any reason?"

Minmei butted in, "I'm worried about my aunt and uncle back in the shelter, with all those invaders around them!"

"They're perfectly safe there," Roy insisted. "The shelters are impregnable; this is what they were built for."

Minmei looked winsome even when she was being stubborn. "But I still want to go back to Macross. It's my home!"

Roy shook his head slowly. "I promise, as soon as this trouble's over, I'll take you back there personally."

"What d'you mean *you'll* take her?" Rick blurted. "*I* will!" He heard Minmei make a little shocked sound and realized how possessive he'd sounded. "Uh, that is . . ."

"Hold on a second, Rick," Roy said, and switched his

attention to the mammoth ship looming before him. "This is Skull Leader to SDF-1, over."

Lisa's tone was vexed. "Did you find him?"

Roy answered wryly, "He was annoying a young lady. I had to rescue her as well."

"You rat!" Rick snapped.

Lisa had both screens up on her board, looking Rick Hunter over and not missing Minmei, who was leaning in over his shoulder. Hunter was obviously a wet-behind-the-ears kid and a discipline problem to boot, she saw. As for the girl—well, she was pretty in a way, Lisa supposed, if you liked that type.

"So *that's* our civilian pilot," Lisa said. "I wondered why he didn't know how to fly his aircraft."

Rick recognized those as fighting words. "Who's that old sourpuss, Roy?"

Lisa drew back as if he'd thrown ice water in her face. *Old sourpuss?* The rest of the bridge gang was very discreet about swapping startled but amused looks.

Roy couldn't help laughing out loud. "That old sourpuss is our Control and the ship's First Officer, Lisa Hayes. And if she looks *old* to you, you're not as grown up as I thought, kid."

Lisa grimaced and cut in, "Now, listen up, Commander Fokker! You'd *better* have a good explanation for turning a Veritech fighter over to an amateur civilian pilot! You could face a court-martial for this, or hadn't you thought about that?"

Luckily for all concerned, she didn't notice that Gloval was stifling his laughter off to one side. He hastily resumed a straight face.

"Ooo, she's mad," Roy said blithely.

"As for you, Rick Hunter," Lisa bore on, "you're in a lot of trouble, whether you know it or not!"

Somehow, gallantry seemed to melt away now that there was no danger and people were talking about legal proceedings. He gestured to Minmei helplessly. "This whole thing's because of her, you see . . ."

Minmei didn't seem offended, but she confided, "I think

you'd better apologize, Rick. Women her age can get awful mean, you know."

Lisa Hayes silently counted to ten, trying to keep from putting her fist through the screen.

"Bridge Control, this is Skull Leader requesting landing instructions," Roy reminded her. "Give us a bay number— you old sourpuss."

This time there was no controlling it, and the rest of Lisa's bridge gang broke up in giggles. She clenched her fists but somehow kept her rage contained.

"Roger. Bring your plane into bay zero-niner." *And I hope it's the last I see of you, Rick Hunter!*

# CHAPTER
# THIRTEEN

*It is no exaggeration to say that we found the inhabitants of the planet surprising. Quite tenacious and determined in battle, and yet not as suicidal—not as mindlessly ferocious—as, for example, the Invid.*

*But if they surprised me, surely, I thought, we would awe them by an overwhelming application of force. The thing upon which I did not count was how very much like us they were.*

Exedore, from his Military Intelligence Analysis Report

THE BEACHES OF MACROSS ISLAND WERE NOW A STAGING area for the Zentraedi withdrawal. Immense saucer-shaped landing craft pulled themselves along the shoreline, their huge access hatches lowered over the breaking waves.

With the SDF-1 gone, the pods had no further reason to be on the island; the shelters were of no interest to them, and no serious effort had been made to breach the human fortifications. Ironically, the Zentraedi's iron warrior code kept them from realizing the value of hostages; hostages were of no significance at all to them, and it never occurred to them that humans might be different.

Wave after wave of pods bounded into the ships, some trailing damaged parts or showing the effects of Veritech hits. There was plenty of room in the landing ships that would bear them back aloft; the pods' ranks had thinned considerably. The saucers lifted away, shedding seawater.

Breetai received the report in his command post. "Recon force now returning to group orbit."

"It appears only half of them survived," Exedore observed.

"Where is the battle fortress now?" Breetai demanded of his techs. Though the missing pods represented a negligible loss, he seethed over it. That Zentraedi warriors should be thus resisted by mere primitives!

"It has passed through the uppermost atmospheric ranges and achieved orbit," a voice reported. "It is apparently on its way to rendezvous with the other orbital units."

"What is your plan, Breetai?" Exedore asked.

Breetai considered. "It would be a simple matter to shoot them down, but I don't want that ship damaged."

Wisely, Exedore didn't point out that notwithstanding Breetai's preferences, that was the specific order that bound him: To capture the dimensional fortress intact. "Once they're out of Earth's gravitational field, they can execute a hyperspace fold, taking them beyond the range of our weapons—perhaps to escape us completely across spacetime once again."

Breetai nodded. "You have a point there. Perhaps I'd better apply a little restraining force to slow them down a bit."

He turned to give the order in his rumbling basso, his gleaming skullpiece and glittering artificial eye catching the light. "Prepare a laser bombardment!"

The order was repeated all through the fleet, as guns were run out in their turrets and casemates—slender, tapering Zentraedi-style barrels like gargantuan steel icicles.

The order resounded through the fleet, "All gun crews stand by for total bombardment of target area. Stand by for order to fire."

Rick and Minmei were speechless at their first view of the SDF-1's interior.

They raced along in a four-seater troop vehicle driven by Roy, who showed his fondness for high speed and squealing tires. They barreled through holds and compartments so vast that there was no feeling of being inside.

Instead it was like driving through an immense metal metropolis studded with lights of all descriptions, reaching up and up, the levels disappearing into a dim ceiling/sky. Rick couldn't imagine what such stupendous amounts of unoccupied space were for.

"I've got a little surprise for you, Rick." Roy smiled. "Wait'll you see it." He made another turn with two wheels off the deck.

At last he brought the jeep to a virtual panic stop, tires screeching, so that Rick and Minmei were thrown off balance. "Well, here we are." He hopped out jauntily. "Come on!"

Rick glared, helping Minmei up. "Was that really necessary? She could've been hurt!"

Roy ignored the comment because, of course, he was confident that he'd never let that happen. He flicked on a bank of overhead spotlights. Sitting in a small hangar bay was the *Mockingbird*.

"Golly, Rick! Look at that!" Minmei exclaimed.

"Somebody left this thing behind," Roy said casually, "so I had it stashed here and serviced."

The little plane's booster rocket covers had been replaced, and the way the ship sat on its landing gear let Rick know that it had been completely refueled.

"My racer!" He jumped out of the carrier, dashing to his beloved *Mockingbird*, all but dancing around it. "I thought I'd never see it again! You saved it!"

He had Roy's hand in his, pumping it, ready to give his friend an exuberant hug. "Oh, thank you, Roy, thank you—"

Roy disengaged himself. "Hey, cut it out, Rick! Take it easy! I just thought you'd be more comfortable flying in this thing than in one of our Veritechs. *Mockingbird* doesn't turn into a Battloid."

"I don't know what to say, Roy!"

"I've seen that plane before," Minmei said, joining them. "It was in the air show this morning, wasn't it?"

*Yeah, about a million years ago*, Rick thought. But as he was about to explain, Claudia's voice came over the PA. "Attention all hands. We are approaching rendezvous with Armor One and Armor Ten. Report to your docking stations immediately! All hands report to stations!"

Roy was already leaping back behind the wheel of the carrier. "I have to get going now. You two stay here and don't wander around. If you start exploring, you'll get lost."

The tires chirped as he broke traction briefly. "You can't imagine how huge this ship is, so stay put!" Then he was gone.

The Armors and their tenders and destroyer escorts were coming up quickly, strung out in a line so that they could be mated to the SDF-1 in order.

"We have perfect docking alignment," Vanessa announced.

"The enemy ships are preparing to dock, sir," a Zentraedi tech reported.

"All right," Breetai replied. "Tell our gunners to fire their beams *between* the fortress and the other vessels and at the target ships themselves. I don't care how many of the smaller ones are destroyed, but the large one must not be damaged!"

The command was relayed as the long, slender Zentraedi cannon swiveled and came to bear. Then the order was passed: "Gun commanders may fire when ready!"

The Zentraedi beams seemed to light up the universe.

A quick, orderly docking sequence became a bloodbath as alien beams zeroed in from far away, without warning, punching through hulls and turning ships into flowering explosions.

Destroyers, tenders, and escort ships were hit, and Armor Three went up in a ball of fury that lit the SDF-1's bridge in a harsh glare. Wreckage and debris rode the winds of the explosions as though tornado-driven.

Gloval, knocked from his feet, drew himself back up. "Vanessa, what's the enemy's position?"

The bridge crew calmly went back to work. "The current attack is from the exact same location as the first one: They're about ten thousand miles from here in a higher orbit."

Lisa said, "Reporting: *Miranda*, *Circe*, and Armor Three completely destroyed, as well as numerous smaller vessels and heavy damage throughout the Orbital Force."

"They're tearing our fleet to shreds!" Gloval snarled. "And what about *our* damages?"

"We've taken no direct hits, Captain," Sammie declared, and Kim confirmed, "No damage anywhere, sir."

"What's our position?" Gloval snapped, squaring away his cap.

"We're just closing our initial orbit," Vanessa told him. "Approaching our original position over Macross Island, distance approximately one hundred miles."

Gloval made up his mind. "Claudia, take us down over Macross Island. At two thousand feet altitude activate the fold system for a position jump."

Claudia debated whether she should question the order; this was a wartime situation. But at certain critical times allegiance to duty could demand something more than mere obedience. "Are you sure you want to do that, Captain? The fold system hasn't even been tested yet!"

"I am well aware of how risky it is, Claudia, but you can read the situation displays and tactical projections as well as I."

She could, and had, as they all had. The alien fleet had already been deployed in an inescapable net and was drawing the net tighter around SDF-1. "If we stay in this position, we'll be totally defenseless," Gloval added.

"But we're not even sure how the system works!" Lisa reminded him.

"That's why I'm bringing us as close to Macross as I dare," Gloval said calmly. "All Doctor Lang's calculations and preliminary findings are based on experiments conducted at that location."

He looked around at his bridge gang. He wasn't used to explaining orders, but it was important that his reasoning go on the record so that if he didn't survive the engagement, what he'd done might be of use in later decisions.

"We can't just surrender!" he said hotly. "We have to try everything we can first! So ready fold system for a position jump, targeting the area on the far side of the moon, within one lunar diameter of the surface. Get your radar ready for an access check, Lisa."

The bridge gang got to work, speaking into comcircuits, operating their consoles, while Gloval gave orders in a steady voice. "We'll make the jump from precisely two thousand feet above the island."

"Don't we need permission from headquarters?" Claudia asked.

He shook his head. "We don't have time for that."

"But Captain, you know the regulations specifically—" His gaze was white-hot now, making her falter. "Sorry, sir . . ."

Gloval took in a breath. "I know what the regs say, but I appreciate your bringing it to my attention."

"I just wanted to—"

*"Claudia! You've got your orders!"* He turned away, hands clasped behind his back once more.

"Yes sir, Captain," she said through locked teeth, and turned to do as she'd been commanded. "Attention all hands. Priority! Fold system standby! Readying energy at maximum-green at all power sources."

The giant untried fold devices came alight like castles of energy. The crews raced to prepare and make secure for the jump, although there wasn't nearly enough time. The chaos was especially acute in the hangar bays.

Nevertheless, throughout the ship, men and women did their best.

"All hands to emergency stations. All hands, emergency stations. This is *not* a drill, I say again: This is *not* a drill! Prepare for fold operation in T minus five minutes and counting—mark!"

In the labyrinth shelter system under the smoking ruins of Macross Island, Jason shifted uncomfortably. It wasn't that he felt crowded; the shelters had been built with a far larger population and supply requirement in mind—against the day when Macross might be the last human refuge.

But Jason missed his cousin. "I'm getting worried about Minmei, aren't you? I wonder where she went."

"Don't worry about Minmei. She'll be fine," his mother reassured him. "She just went to another shelter, that's all."

His father was quick to add, "Sure! Nothing's going to happen to anyone as smart as Minmei! Isn't that right?"

But among the grown-ups there passed looks hidden from the boy. They'd felt the distant concussions of the terrible battle, and now, for a long time, there had been an ominous silence with no all-clear signal from the military.

"Yeah . . ." Jason conceded, and settled himself down to wait some more, gathering his blanket around him.

"Are you planning on going somewhere?" Minmei asked as Rick ran a final preflight check on *Mockingbird* and made a few last adjustments.

He closed an access panel and turned to her. "I'm gonna take you back to the island like I promised." He knelt to replace his tools in the box and return it to its stowage niche. "You still wanna go back, don't you? Because *I'm* not gonna hang around here one way or the other."

He couldn't bring himself to admit how important it was that she come with him; that wasn't the sort of thing one learned to do working in a flying circus.

The SDF-1 resounded with Sammie's latest announcement: "Attention, all hands. Fold in T minus three minutes and counting."

Minmei offered him part of a chocolate bar that had somehow stayed in her pocket against every conceivable adversity. "Candy?"

"Thanks."

"Rick, what's a fold?"

"Aw, nothing to do with us." He offered her his hand to help her into the cockpit. "Come on; let's go."

She looked into the tiny plane's only passenger space dubiously. "It's so small. Will it hold two people?"

"If they're very friendly, it will." And so, she didn't object when he put his hands on her waist and helped her up into the *Mockingbird*.

Rick handed her his Veritech helmet. "Here; put this on."

She gave the helmet that wide-eyed look he'd come to care so much about. "Ohh!" Then she had it on.

"It's so cute on you, Minmei. You could start a whole new fad."

She snorted in exasperation. "Oh, you!"

He chuckled foolishly and turned to work the bay door. The indicators had already let him know that the SDF-1 was descending, quickly; it was low enough for his plane's turbofan to function.

The first thing he saw as the doors parted was Macross Island, far below. It occurred to him that that was the ship's most likely landing spot, but be that as it might, he had no intention of remaining aboard. These military types had gotten him—and Minmei—into enough trouble.

Minmei saw Macross, too. She was still staring at it longingly as Rick crowded into the single pilot's seat next to her and got her into his lap.

The propfan was turning slowly; he brought it up while he lowered the canopy and began to turn *Mockingbird*'s nose. It would be the trickiest takeoff of his career; the slipstream caused by SDF-1's descent could break the tiny stunt plane in half if Rick didn't do things just right.

"Hang on to me, Minmei."

"It's awful close in here." She squirmed forward, trying to rest against the instrument panel.

"Hey! I can't see to fly if you sit there!"

She leaned back, and he decided that he had to take his shot now, before the SDF-1 got into the heavy air currents lower down. He gunned the turbofan, launched. Counterrotating blades spun.

"I'm sorry, Rick," Minmei was apologizing, "But it's so tiii—yiiite!" as the *Mockingbird* was seized and twirled.

# CHAPTER
# FOURTEEN

> *"Who Dares, Wins."*
> This motto of the Special Air Service commandos of the Royal Air Force of the United Kingdom (latter twentieth century) was known to have been quoted by Gloval, even though his behavior and accomplishments make it clear that he was far from rash.
> Certainly, he proved that he knew what the saying meant that day high above Macross Island.
>
> "Starleap," *History of the First Robotech War*, Vol. VIII

**R**ICK SOMEHOW SUCCEEDED IN KEEPING THEM FROM being smashed into a large gun turret as the *Mockingbird* nosedived, spinning round and round.

"There's nothing to worry about, Minmei; I'm an expert pilot," Rick insisted in what he hoped was a composed voice, fighting his controls and expecting to be slammed back against the SDF-1's superstrong hull. Minmei meanwhile sat with her head buried against his chest, moaning and wishing life would slow down again, even for a moment, so she could catch her breath.

But somewhat to his own surprise, Rick did manage to pull the ship out of its spin, level off, and gain proper flight altitude. "There, okay?"

She got up the nerve to look, saw that things were under control, and couldn't help laughing for joy, hugging him.

Rick Hunter felt very, very pleased with himself and began to wish that the flight could go on forever

Macross Island was clearly defined beneath the dimensional fortress, seeming to draw nearer as SDF-1 descended. "We will enter fold in ten seconds," Claudia intoned over the PA. "Nine . . ."

Gloval watched the dozens of displays and screens with no outward show of the misgivings he felt. The enigmatic sealed engines made the huge vessel tremble, and the high vibrations of the fold generators seemed to cut through everyone aboard.

The seconds seemed to stretch on endlessly, then he became aware of Claudia saying, ". . . two . . . one . . . zero!"

"Execute hyperspace fold-jump!" Gloval ordered. The bridge gang bent to their duty stations to carry out the command.

It seemed to Gloval that he was seeing the view from the bridge in an altered way, that he was perhaps seeing higher into the ultraviolet or lower into infrared. In any case, the superstructure was outlined with strange hot reds, yellows, and oranges that hadn't been there moments before.

*Am I seeing into the thermal part of the spectrum, perhaps?*

But even that didn't explain the strange, almost ghostly images, not quite indentifiable, that suddenly loomed in the air or the way in which vision suddenly altered so that the world looked like a shifting double exposure.

The SDF-1 appeared to be in the center of a hot gas cloud. From it expanded a white-hot globe of light, the same sort that the Zentraedi armada had produced earlier that day. Sounds like nothing humans had ever heard before toned and swirled in the crew's ears, with no apparent source.

The fold-jump globe expanded, defying Lang's theories and calculations, enveloping Macross and its harbor, making even the supercarriers *Daedalus* and *Prometheus* shift in focus and seem to blur into double exposure as the waters crashed as if storm-tossed.

A vibration like an earthquake, far greater than any the Zentraedi attack had produced, shook the shelters, and the refugees thought the worst had come—the worst as they could conceive of it: the end of their world.

In Macross City sudden eddy currents from the fold

swept through the streets, destroying buildings and the remains of downed war machines of both armies. The violent side effects of the space jump maneuver caught the tiny *Mockingbird* too, whirling it like a leaf.

Incandescent motes appeared, growing brighter and brighter, circling like lazy insects or sentient miniature stars. On the bridge, it was impossible to focus on instruments or screens. Lisa sobbed, feeling sick and wrenched from herself, as if she were being torn from life itself.

A globe with the SDF-1 at its center now encompassed the island, the waters around it, and a considerable bubble of sky. The ocean crashed against the force field, without effect.

SDF-1 shifted through the double-exposure changes again, stabilizing at last, then began to fade. In one moment, the spherical force field was immovable in the midst of the furious sea—and in the next, it was gone.

Billions of gallons of water poured in to fill the gap, colliding to send up tidal waves that would race around the planet for days. Air rushed in to take the place of the sudden vacuum, creating a thunderclap like the detonation of a nuclear weapon, only sharper.

Over the rim of the world, where the main Zentraedi elements were forming up for a final attack, the event registered only picoseconds before the glow erupted. It lit the horizon like a "diamond necklace" eclipse. Breetai needed no instruments or tech reports to know what had happened.

"A fold! I don't believe it!"

"Impossible that close to planetary gravity!" Exedore burst out in a rare display of emotion. *These primitives somehow rebuilt the SDF-1 and, with whatever modifications or improvising they did, somehow came up with a superior spacefold process! Or perhaps it's something of Zor's; it doesn't matter. If it still exists, we must have that ship!*

Breetai was uttering his terrible animal growl, fists clenched so tightly that Exedore could hear the squeaking of bones and cartilage under the exertion of those corded muscles.

"I want to know their exact position immediately!"

*   *   *

Out in the farthest reaches of the solar domain it had been cold and dark since the birth pains of the solar system, almost twenty million years before. Here the great furnace of the sun was only a tiny, cold droplet in the night, and Pluto, the only planetary body, nearly forty times as far from the life-giving primary as Earth, maintained a temperature near absolute zero.

But in an incomparable moment, Pluto and its single loyal satellite, Charon, were joined in their lonely, eccentric orbit.

The fold force field appeared, a stupendous orb in space, holding the SDF-1 suspended over an island with a fish-bowl-bottom of ocean underneath it, the smoke of battle still rising from Macross City.

The sphere winked out of existence. By all rights, the waters should have boiled away in the vacuum, all atmosphere not pent up in the battle fortress or the shelters dissipated; and the fragment of Earth that was Macross Island itself should have begun coming apart.

That none of these things happened was proof—reinforcing later evidence—that certain other forces were still at work. The Protoculture-powered globe couldn't be maintained for very long, not even by the dimensional fortress's mighty engines, but secondary effects could; Protoculture-powered phenomena were very different from the raw-power manipulations of the universe that humans had been used to until now.

The ocean waters froze, still adhering to the island fragment, expanding and cracking. Most of the atmosphere began to fall toward the island, frozen air snowing down on it, coating it in seconds with a thickening glacial coat—*despite the fact that instruments indicated no gravity whatsoever beyond the negligible amount such a mass would generate*. Be that as it might, the harbor became a solid mass and the aircraft carriers were rimed with permafrost in moments.

These anomalies have always constituted one of the great mysteries of the Robotech Wars, though subsequent events and discoveries gave the human race some tantaliz-

ing hints as to what may have happened that chilly afternoon some three and a half billion miles and more beyond
Terra's orbit.

Already disoriented and dismayed, with Minmei clinging
to him, and concealing the terror he *wanted* to show, Rick
realized two new and frightening things: His propfan engine
was no longer having any effect, and the entire canopy was
frosting over—fast.

It wasn't as if he needed that; he'd already watched with
horror as Macross turned to a polarscape. It was clear that
there wasn't much gravity in the dark, empty neighborhood, whatever it was. He'd heard *Mockingbird*'s seals
close against low pressure—*no* pressure, he was certain—
and that spelled very bad luck.

Rick watched the blanket of white cover the canopy and
wondered what he could possibly do next, aside from
dying.

"Let's have some light in here!" Gloval ordered; the
fold-jump had drained all systems. The emergencies cast a
weird red glow over everything. Heating units shouldn't
have been needed in the vacuum of space; Gloval wondered
what was wrong.

"Switching to backups, Captain," Claudia said crisply,
and brought lighting back to normal. The bridge gang
blinked a bit but kept to their jobs. Powerful running lights
showed a dust storm of wreckage blowing past the ship,
pieces impacting constantly.

"Radar shows an extremely large object just—beneath
us, sir," Vanessa said. At least, it was "beneath" *relative* to
the battle fortress; but the readings looked very peculiar,
even though the ship's artificial gravity had cut in automatically during the jump.

"Our jump target was the moon; that's what your large
object is," Gloval said.

"No; it's too small to be the moon, sir," she countered.
"I'll put it on one of the main screens for you."

Everybody there looked, and everybody drew breath in
brief astonishment and fright.

"It's coming straight at us, sir!" Vanessa said.

Gloval took a quick look at the readouts and contradicted, "No! *We're* moving toward *it*!"

"It's Macross Island, Captain Gloval!" Vanessa yelled, but Gloval had already seen that and reached his own conclusions as to the magnitude of the disaster. But there were other things that had to be dealt with instantly; reflection must wait for a later time.

"Retro rockets, Claudia! Maximum thrust!"

Claudia worked, tight-lipped, at her station and spared only a moment to say, "It's no-go; I'm getting no response whatsoever from the computer!"

*Damn energy drain!* Lisa thought, even as she sounded "collision" over the PA. "Emergency! Emergency! Prepare for impact! Prepare for impact!"

Helpless, the SDF-1 floated kneel-on toward Macross Island. "It's covered with ice," Sammie reported, looking into her scope while everyone else could see that on the screen. Claudia yanked her away from the scope so she wouldn't get her nose broken.

SDF-1 hit the tilted surface and crunched through the buildings as if they were a bunch of potato chips dipped in liquid nitrogen, sliding side-on across the surface of the worldlet that had been a thriving, jubilant city only hours ago.

Down in the shelters, people already dealing with the difficulties of mass null-g sickness and panic had their problems complicated by an impact that sent many of them flying once again across the shelters—toward walls and ceilings and floors that weren't padded and wouldn't make kind landing places.

Jason wailed and grabbed for his mother's hand; Lena pulled him back from an impact with the wall, and together they spun helplessly in midair, wondering if this was the end.

The rime frost on the outside of *Mockingbird*'s canopy was gone in that uncanny pulling-together force exerted in the wake of the fold—a force that wasn't gravity but had many of its attributes. A force that seemed to make *conscious* distinctions.

But the cold of the outer rime had transferred through the canopy to the atmosphere in the cockpit, forming a thick glaze. Now Rick wiped away a large patch to get a look at what was going on.

"Ooo! Look how beautiful it is!" Minmei gasped, her long dark hair floating weightless. Rick was struck again by her innocence, the purity of spirit that saw beauty everywhere and gave so little attention to danger and evil.

A starfield shone against the blackness of space. Chunks of rock and debris floated by. Rick tried his controls, without effect.

*I'm getting no response at all from the propfan. As crazy as it seems, there's no other answer: We're out in deep space. And that means we're in deep trouble!*

"Oh, my, isn't it romantic?" Minmei sighed.

Rick forced himself to smile. "Yes, it is."

There was an abrupt metal-to-metal collision that jarred the little plane brutally, sending it spinning away. Rick had a split-second glimpse of some kind of large machine casing veering off from its impact with *Mockingbird*.

The two cried out in shock as the plane was spun through the vacuum, to collide with another piece of flotsam. The second hit jolted Rick's nose into the back of Minmei's head, but it also absorbed much of the spinning and brought the ship virtually to rest relative to the junk floating around it.

Rick sneezed mightily from the bump on the nose. Minmei looked startled, then laughed, and Rick joined her.

But she stopped in alarm a moment later. "What's that hissing sound?"

Rick was quick to cover his panic. "Oh, it's perfectly all right. Don't get upset about it."

But the hissing was coming from a hairline crack just under the windshield frame. "You hear all kinds of weird noises in these things." He forced himself to laugh lightly.

*I don't dare tell her our air's leaking out into space!* The flow wafted the ends of stray strands of Minmei's hair toward the crack.

Rick wadded a handkerchief and tried to push it into the crack. *Maybe this'll hold it temporarily.* It didn't seem to do much good.

Minmei's eyes were enormous with fright. "Let's get out of here, okay?"

"Hey, relax; what's your hurry?" Rick could think of only one slim hope of survival. He put the helmet back on her head, and she snuggled into his lap again as he thought, *If the boosters don't work, we're sunk!* "Comfy?"

"Uh huh," Minmei answered. Rick hit his boosters very gently, bringing them up.

He had a certain amount of independent control over each, but that still made steering a very ticklish problem. Attitude thrusters would have been a tremendous help, but there just hadn't been much need for deep-space maneuvering capability in the air circus.

A tiny burn—a mere cough—got the *Mockingbird* under way, infinitesimal spurts from selected boosters were the only way he had to steer. And there wasn't very much fuel in the little rockets.

He was beginning to see where there were some advantages to those nutty Veritechs after all.

"I guess we'll go find the SDF-1," he said. "Something funny's been goin' on around here." The air leak hissed on. At least the frost was melting off the canopy; he gave up wondering how much time they had and concentrated on piloting and spotting the battle fortress.

"There it is!" Minmei said very shortly. SDF-1 was hard to miss: still lodged in the remains of Macross Island, with explosions, tracers, and energy blasts flashing all around it.

The war had resumed.

*Well, you're never gonna believe* this!

From the diary of Lynn-Minmei

**"I**T LOOKS LIKE THEY'RE FIGHTING DOWN THERE!"
Minmei said.

*It doesn't matter; we've got nowhere else to go.* "Don't
worry." He cut in the boosters, nursing them along exact-
ingly to line up his vector, praying no debris got in his way
because there was no hope of dodging anything.

In the fury of the battle back on Earth, human defenders
had overlooked the fact that one of the first Zentraedi landing ships, loaded with Battlepods, had been heavily damaged and forced to set down on Macross once again, unable
to fly. And so it, too, had been transported into deep space
by the fold maneuver.

While the landing ship was no longer operable, the pods
were. They'd immediately resumed their attack on the ship,
no doubt in response to their assigned mission but moved,
too, by the awareness that they were somewhere far from
their fleet and that if they couldn't take the fortress, they
wouldn't survive for long out by Pluto's orbit.

The island in space was now complete bedlam, with alien

mecha massed in suicidal assault waves, while the ship's guns blazed away. Rick Hunter rocketed into the midst of this with a ship he could barely control.

Still, he did the best he could, gradually bringing the little racer in end for end through judicious use of the boosters, his only method of halting being a retrofire. He made microburns, slowing, trying to line up his approach. It seemed hopeless.

Then a bad situation became even worse. All the landing bays were closed, sealed tight. "I forgot, they shut them during combat," Rick said, tight-lipped. Minmei blinked, looking at him as if he'd said it in another language.

A mortally damaged pod went tumbling past them, trailing fire like an erratic meteor, victim of an armor-piercing, discarding-sabot round from SDF-1—so close that it all but singed *Mockingbird*'s wingtip. Rick and Minmei shrank from it in reflex, but it was already impacting the SDF-1.

Rick had to crane around, glancing over the back of the plane, to see what happened. The pod gave up all its destructive power in one great explosion, hitting at the confined area of a recessed maintenance causeway.

It was a million-to-one shot, but the explosion acted as a shaped charge, blowing a gaping hole in the dimensional fortress's armored hide. And it was toward that hole that the plane was going.

Until the explosion's shock wave hit it.

*Mockingbird* was jarred, stopped in midflight, spun. It ended up with its nose more or less pointed at the SDF-1 but moving away from it.

Rick was already feeling a little light-headed, and breathing was an effort. Moreover, the boosters didn't have very much left to give. "Maybe we can get through the hole the invader made!"

Minmei nodded, too short-winded to answer. Rick cut in the boosters, steering as best he could.

Another pilot would have died then. But Rick knew *Mockingbird* well, even under circumstances as bizarre as these. He nursed the racer along with minute bursts of thrust, knowing there'd be no time to flip and retro, hoping he and Minmei could survive a crash.

But they would have to endure one more bad break to even the balance of the sudden luck that had come their way: A thick curtain of armor was descending over the hole, the reaction of an automatic damage-control system.

Rick cut in all boosters full throttle, seeing his only chance of survival disappearing. He cranked up the propfan in full reverse, hoping that it might stop the ship once it hit atmosphere.

He'd calculated that most of the outsurge of air from the breached compartment would have spent itself by the time he got there. There was no point in thinking otherwise; neither boosters nor propfan could take *Mockingbird* "upstream" against the terrific pressure of such a monster air leak.

He wasn't too far off. In fact, he did a piloting job worthy of a place in the record books until the descending armor curtain sheared the racer's uppermost wing off.

Still, the little plane shot into the vast compartment, more or less intact, aimed at a far area of the ceiling. The propfan howled as the blades got some bite in a very thin atmosphere. The armor patch clanged into place.

And there was gravity. *Mockingbird*'s upward climb topped out and became a crash dive. *We almost made it*, Rick realized. The deck whirled at the canopy.

But they'd happened into an area still strung with hoisting cables, rigging slings, and tackle—a jungle of them. *Mockingbird* was successively snagged, whirled, flipped, and caught in a matter of seconds, with more pieces broken from it.

Rick and Minmei felt themselves blacking out but shook it off a few seconds later to discover themselves hanging upside down, the deck only a yard or two below the cockpit dome. The rumble of life-support equipment pumping air back into the chamber was already loud.

*Mockingbird* hung ensnared in the lines and cables, upside down but stable for the time being. A last piece of good fortune: None of the lines had caught across the canopy to hold the cockpit shut and imprison them.

Rick had no reserves left to think of elegant solutions. He hit the release, and the canopy swung down. He lowered Minmei with the last of his strength and, resigning himself to a fall, released his safety harness. He landed on the deck at her feet, saying only, "Oof!"

She knelt next to him. They looked themselves over with wonder, having resigned themselves to being dead. Then they looked at each other and burst out laughing at the same moment.

It was the best, loudest laugh either of them had ever had. Somehow, it was immeasurably important to Rick that he share it with Minmei.

"We just shot down the last enemy Battlepod, sir," Sammie relayed the information.

"Very good." Gloval nodded. "Any contact with headquarters yet?"

That was Claudia's hot potato. "No, Captain. I've tried, sir, but nothing works. We can't raise them."

Sammie broke in, "Are you sure there's no system malfunction?"

"Negative," Claudia shot back tersely.

"None at all," Vanessa said, backing her. "It's operating perfectly."

Gloval didn't want to indulge his fears; he had a pretty good idea what had happened, but if it were to prove true, the consequences would be dire indeed. Still, there was no avoiding the inevitable. "Give me the reading on our position."

Vanessa was prompt and precise in answering. "The planet Pluto's orbit, according to the computer plot."

*"The planet Pluto?"* So much worse than even he had suspected. Gloval dipped deep into the fortitude that develops when death has been cheated a hundred times and comes back for a rematch. Relentlessly.

The bridge gang was gathering around Vanessa, even rocklike Lisa. "Pluto?" "Impossible!"

"It can't be!" Claudia was proclaiming, knowing very well that it was. "I was against this fold-jump business all along!"

More than just about anyone else alive, Gloval knew when it was time to play martinet (rarely) and when it was time to play patriarch (the manner in which he had won every important citation there was, some several times over).

"Now, now, now. Settle down; don't panic." His voice

was calm and sure. It brought order and discipline back to the bridge by its very measured resonance. "All we have to do is refold to get back to where we started."

That made them all exchange looks and get a grip on themselves. Gloval was four steps ahead of everyone, as usual; everything was all right.

Far aft, in the engineering section, Lang stared up and laughed, then doubled over, slapping his knees—a laugh that seesawed between the hysterical and the Olympian. The techs and scientists and crewpeople around him looked at him dubiously.

It had been going on for a half minute or so, and each time he took a fresh look, Lang laughed again. Tears had begun squeezing out of the corners of his strange eyes for what he perceived as a monumental joke.

Before anybody around him could act, Lang forced himself to stop. Cosmic jokes weren't something you could share with everybody; the gift of humor didn't run that deep in some people.

Lang straightened and caught his breath, gathering himself, shaking his head.

"Somebody get me Gloval."

"There's absolutely nothing to worry about," Gloval was saying.

"I hope not, Captain," Lisa muttered, back at her duty station. And that was when the hot line rang.

"*Now* what?" Gloval got it, growling like a bear. "Yes? What? Are you absolutely sure? Stand fast; I'll be right there."

Gloval slammed the handset down. He ignored the questioning faces around him and headed for the hatch. Lisa stood rooted, stunned by the idea that the captain would even *think* about leaving the bridge at a time like this. "Captain? What happened?"

Gloval paused at the hatch. "Doctor Lang informs me that the fold system has vanished into thin air."

The bridge gang let out stifled cries and moans; Sammie

and Kim hugged each other, fighting back tears. Everyone there knew just as well as Gloval what that meant.

"We'll never get back," Claudia whispered.

Outside the hatch, Gloval stopped to fire up his evil-smelling old briar. There was no point in doubting Lang's news; the man was obsessed with Robotechnology but otherwise quite rational. That left Henry Gloval to calculate matters of current orbital positions, distance, life support, and engine performance profiles.

He blew out a cloud of smoke, considering the tobacco in the pipe's bowl. *I'd better cut down; what I have is going to have to last me quite a while.*

"Hmm. Well now," he said aloud. "Gonna be a long trip."

Fantastic as it seemed, Lang was right: The fold engines were gone.

Gloval returned to the bridge to try to salvage this seemingly hopeless situation as best he could.

"I don't know what happened exactly," Gloval shouted into a handset. "But our first priority is to get the civilians onboard this ship as soon as we can!"

He slammed down the handset and turned to his bridge gang. "Well?"

"Captain, we can't raise the *Daedalus* or *Prometheus*," Lisa told him.

His gaze went to the forward viewport. At a distance of a few hundred yards, the titanic shapes of the two super-carriers could be seen clearly amid the cloud of debris and wreckage, the drifting automobiles and furniture, and the more ghastly remains of human victims of the tragedy.

"They're aircraft carriers; all atmosphere would have bled away at once, as soon as the fold force field disappeared." No one needed to be told what that meant; all hands lost in the wake of the jump, like every other unprotected human being. "What a catastrophe!"

But other matters were too urgent for him to dwell on the horror of what those last few seconds must have been like in the supercarriers. Chances of survival and a safe return to Earth were slim, but it was up to him to make the most of them.

Like a handful of others throughout history, Henry Gloval was uniquely suited for this particular moment and situation. History was to record it as a singular stroke of good fortune for the human race.

"Commander Hayes, order a squadron of rescue vehicles to maneuver the carriers alongside the SDF-1. We will make fast to them and get crews working round the clock to make them airtight and operational once again." He shunted aside the thought of what a grisly job the clean-up would be.

Lisa looked surprised. "Captain, is it more important that we link up with them than with Armor One or Ten?"

"Yes. I believe their onboard weapons will still be functioning, and there are Veritechs onboard both of them."

"I hope it works, Captain," Lisa said.

"It must be done quickly," Gloval added.

Claudia muttered, "That's for sure."

Gloval went to stand by the viewport. *All those lives lost! How could I have been so stupid?* But he knew, deep down, that he was being unfair to himself. He'd taken the only option open to him. If he'd chosen another course of action, the SDF-1 would now be in the hands of the alien invaders, and all would have been lost.

"We will also deploy boarding tubes to the shelters and begin transferring all occupants to the SDF-1," he gave the order over his shoulder. "Instruct Colonel Fielding and his staff to drop everything else and begin making temporary living arrangements for them at once. Detail EVE groups five and six to start salvage operations; tell them to bring in all usable materials, with special emphasis on foodstuffs and any water ice they may be able to find."

The bridge gang hopped to it, taking notes, as the orders went on. Inventories of all resources; requirement and capability projections from all division chiefs; long-range scans for any signs of enemy presence or activity.

There was particular attention to that last item. *They found us once*, Gloval thought. *Heaven help us if they do again.*

# CHAPTER
# SIXTEEN

"SOS" signal attempted by
various means by Rick Hunter

**F**AR BELOW THE BRIDGE AND SLIGHTLY AFT, RICK
Hunter strained against a hoisting line. Grease-stained and
exhausted, he persisted, even though it seemed hopeless.
Getting the wing patched back onto *Mockingbird* hadn't
proved impossible—though he wasn't sure how long the
patch would hold—but straightening the frame and repairing the fuselage had him near the limits of his endurance.

The racer still hung upside down, cables and lines looped
under its wings, nose canards, and tail. He loved the ship,
had built it by hand virtually from scratch; the idea of not
saving it was hard to accept, and more important, he had
reached the conclusion that it was the key to his and Minmei's survival.

They'd ended up in a portion of the ship that was completely deserted, unequipped with intercom or other communications gear or any indication as to how to get out.
Rick had quickly decided that if he could just get his plane
working, he could somehow get the armor patch to move,
get back out into space, and reach a landing bay.

Minmei had less faith in the plan, but she'd been silent.

Up to now. But she touched his shoulder as he strained against the line.

"Rick, you'll never get it to fly. Why don't we see if we can get some help by using the radio in your plane? It seems like it would be the easiest thing."

He let go of the line tiredly. "The radio got busted up when we landed. There are pieces of it all over the compartment: it'll never work."

"Oh," Minmei said in a small voice.

Rick reconsidered something that had been in the back of his mind. He held up his Heiko aviator's-model watch, switching modes. "But maybe this'll help us get out of here."

She came closer, watching. "What've you got there?"

"An inertial tracker—a kind of a compass."

Minmei looked puzzled. "But I thought a compass had two arms that go back and forth?" She held her forefingers together to show what she meant.

"Huh? *Oh!*" Rick laughed.

Minmei looked hurt. "Well, the only compass I ever saw was for drawing circles."

They set out at once, Rick showing the way with a flashlight from his emergency equipment. "With *this* kind of compass we'll be able to make our way back to *Mockingbird* if we get lost inside this big old tub and can't find a way out."

They quickly found out that they were in a maze, a limitless world of conduits, cables, hull, passageways, ducts, and bulkheads. Their footsteps echoed eerily.

"I wonder what all these pipes are for?" Minmei said, reaching out to touch one.

"Maybe to cool some kind of energy unit." Rick shrugged.

"Oh." Then, "Yow!" yelped Minmei, snatching her hand back, fingertips scalded.

"You okay?"

"Oh, I'm all right. It was just a little hot."

Rick's eyebrows went up. "Well, now, that was pretty dumb."

"Sorry." But as he started off again, Rick put his foot

right in a puddle of oil and nearly landed flat on his face, flailing and slipping.

"Um, what was that again?" Minmei asked sweetly. Rick grunted and strode off again.

But they came at last to a big compartment filled with scrap, discarded machine parts. "I think it's a dead end," Rick judged.

"You mean,," Minmei said with a tremor in her voice, "we can't get back?"

"You can't go searching for your friend *now*, Roy!" Claudia shouted at the screen.

"But I know Rick's out there somewhere," the Skull Leader insisted. "I can't just abandon him."

As much as Roy meant to her, Claudia couldn't help wishing she could reach through the screen into his cockpit and throttle him. "Listen, you can't just leave your post any time you feel like it! What if—"

Gloval was clearing his throat meaningfully. "Lieutenant Grant, let me talk to him."

She bit her lower lip but answered, "I'll patch you through on channel eight, sir."

Gloval took up his handset. "Commander Fokker, your request is denied. I'm sorry to hear about your friend, but we have over seventy thousand civilian survivors aboard this ship, and we'll need every hand working full-time to ensure their safety."

Roy's eyes narrowed. "Aye-aye, *Captain*. I guess friendship's a little more important to some of us than it is to others. Sorry to bother you, *sir*."

Roy signed off, and Gloval slammed down the handset. "Insolent pup!"

"Hothead," Claudia said under her breath, while Lisa tried to get her mind back on what she was doing, bleary-eyed from lack of sleep. She hoped she never heard Rick Hunter's name again in her life.

"Where are we? What is this place?" Minmei wanted to know.

"I dunno; it's huge," Rick exclaimed. Not that she

couldn't see that for herself; the compartment was the size of a hangar, with piles of crates and equipment. But the astonishing thing about it was the cyclopean hatch at the far end.

"Why don't we climb up and get a closer look at it?" Minmei proposed, heading for a nearby hill of boxes. As he helped her make the ascent, she bubbled, "Maybe there's a doorway at the top that's open and leads to a hallway that leads to the outside! Why, I could be home in time for dinner!"

But while she rushed off in one direction, he spotted markings in another. "Hey, that thing is a giant air lock! Built to scale for those giant aliens!" He suddenly felt mouse-size and very vulnerable out there in the open. "I hope they don't come back... Minmei? Minmei! Where are you?"

He dashed off to find her at a viewport, staring out as if hypnotized, into space. The debris and wreckage were much thicker, drifting past the ship.

"Look at that," she said sadly. "What do you think happened?"

"I don't know where all that stuff came from. It looks like a whole city blew up."

Minmei seemed about to burst into tears. "Could... could all that be from home? From Macross?"

The bridge crew was taking its first break in what seemed like years, sipping coffee, while Gloval was off on a personal inspection of the ship's situation.

Lisa was shaking her head. "If the aliens attack us again, we won't have a chance."

Vanessa said, "We should have standard communications working very shortly! Maybe Earth can tell us what's going on."

Lisa was skeptical. "If we use conventional transmissions, we'll be taking a big chance. The aliens might get a fix on us; we could give away our location."

"Commander Hayes," Sammie piped up from her duty station, "resettlement team five leader wishes to speak to you. He says it's urgent."

Lisa put aside the coffee, knowing she wouldn't be finishing it any time soon.

"Well, this one doesn't go anywhere either." Rick frowned, shining his light on the blank bulkhead before him. "How does your leg feel? Any better?"

Minmei rubbed her ankle. "My leg's a lot better; I just twisted it, I guess. But I'm getting kind of thirsty."

Rick considered that. "I've got some emergency rations in my plane, but I haven't got any water."

But suddenly inspiration struck. "There's water all around us! Just wait right here!"

He sprinted away while Minmei murmured. "I wonder what in the world he's talking about?"

He was back in moments with a length of steel bar he'd spotted. "Ta-dum! I believe madam requested some water? Refreshments coming right up!"

He wedged it into the junction of two pipes and began pulling at it to break them apart. "Careful! Don't hurt yourself!" Minmei warned.

"Harder . . . than I thought," he said through gritted teeth.

Minmei kicked off her shoes. "Let me help you!" Together they threw all their strength into the effort, the pipes creaking. It took everything they had, but at length there was a snapping of metal and the gushing of water.

Luckily, it was tepid rather than superheated. Rick and Minmei fell backward to the deck as it fountained high to fall back on them like a downpour. "We got it! It's a geyser!" Rick shouted jubilantly. Minmei laughed, and he joined in.

After a few moments of it she got up, sopping wet, and went to catch the streaming water in her hands. "Wow, this is wonderful! Well, I think I'll take a shower."

"Huh?" was all Rick could think of to say.

"Well, I might as well take advantage of this while it lasts." She began unfastening the back of her dress, then stopped to glance at Rick, whose mouth was a big O. "Ahh, Rick . . ."

"Oh! Um. I, uh, guess I better go scout around a little, hmm?"

She grinned, nodding. "And don't peek. Would you push that over here so I can use it as a shower curtain?" He lugged a big hunk of sheet metal into place across the open passageway hatch as he retreated.

"Thank you!" she called over the splashing water. He noticed a small hole in the sheet metal and bent to inspect it, just checking of course, putting his eye to it.

Minmei shrieked. Rick was back on the other side of the partition in a split second, visions of menacing alien giants daunting him. "Minmei, what's wrong? I'm coming—"

He slid to a halt. She was gazing at him with a mischievous glint in her eyes, long dark hair plastered flat against her by the falling water, arms folded, still wearing her dress. "I *thought* I saw something, there by the shower curtain."

"Your imagination, maybe?" he said weakly.

"Su-uure." She nodded sarcastically.

"Yeah." He coughed. "Well. Excuse me, I—" He turned and hurried off.

Minmei lost track of time, singing and humming, luxuriating in the feel and taste of the water. Then she heard a sound, too faint to identify.

She, too, thought of alien giants. "Rick? If that's you, stop playing tricks!" She felt a wave of panic. "Rick, you answer me right now."

A small roll of cloth was tossed through the gap in the makeshift partition. "Brought you some fresh clothes," he called. "It's an extra work shirt I had in the *Mockingbird*."

After Rick grabbed a quick shower, they started back for the plane, guided by his inertial tracker and the markings he'd made at various passageway junctions in the course of their explorations.

Rick tried not to be too obvious about ogling Minmei. The shirt was baggy on her but barely covered the tops of her thighs. Her lovely, coltish legs seemed to go on forever.

She was in high spirits—it seemed to be her natural state. "That was just what I needed! I feel a whole lot better now. And thanks for the shirt, Rick."

"You're welcome—"

"Even if it *is* a bit big." She flopped the empty cuffs around to demonstrate, giggling.

Minmei capered over to a highly polished metal panel, which reflected her image like a dark mirror. She made a comical face, sticking her tongue out and crossing her eyes, waggling the overlong sleeves. "'The Creature with No Hands!' *Nyyah!*" She laughed.

They'd come back to the compartment where the *Mockingbird* hung suspended. Rick went over and sat beneath it, on a pallet improvised from shipping crate padding he'd scavenged. He picked up a couple of flat cans.

"I dug out my emergency rations. Here: This one's for you." He tossed it to her.

"Oh! Thank you!" She looked delighted, as she so often did. Minmei found more delight in life than anyone Rick had ever met.

She watched him detach the fork that came with the can, trigger the lid release, and peel it back. "Let's see if this stuff's any good." He dug into the brownish concentrate paste, making approving sounds.

Minmei didn't follow suit, suddenly looking troubled. "Shouldn't we be conserving these in case we have to make it last?"

"I'm not worried." He shoveled in some more. "We'll be out of here soon."

"Yeah, but what if we're not?"

He tried to sound confident. "I used to be a Junior Nature Scout; I'll get us out of here."

She looked at him archly. "Well, I'll bet you didn't get any merit badges for pathfinding, did you?"

"Now, stop worrying," he told her, around a mouthful of food. He swallowed. "I promise you I'll find a way out of here." He suddenly lowered his fork, looking down despondently at the deck. "But that *was* one badge I didn't get," he confessed.

She made him jump by giggling into his ear. "I *knew* it!"

"Hey, what's so funny?"

She was laughing into her hands, unconcerned with their plight for the moment, making him smile involuntarily.

"I was sick the day they gave the test! At least *I* know what a compass looks like!"

Minmei laughed harder and harder. Rick couldn't resist and joined in.

Later they sat on the padding, backs resting against a crate, under *Mockingbird*. "I'm real worried about my family," she confessed.

"Don't be. I'm sure they're safe in the shelters," he insisted, making it sound as positive as he could.

She was blinking sleepily. "Oh, I hope so. Y'know, there was a shelter right next door to our house."

"Well, there you go; they're all fine."

She yawned against the sleeve-covered back of her hand. "I suppose." Her head settled against his shoulder.

Rick was so surprised that he didn't move or speak for some time. "Um. Are you going to sleep?" She was breathing evenly, eyes closed. She looked more enchanting than ever.

"Wake up. You can't go to sleep like this; you'll get a stiff neck."

He reached around her shoulders from either side, about to ease her down into a more comfortable position. His elbow brushed against something alive that was poised behind him on the crate.

With a shrill chitter, a fat gray mouse bounded across Minmei's shoulder, scampered along her arm, and ran down the length of her bare leg, springing away into the dimness. Minmei awoke with a scream, to find Rick's hands on her shoulders.

"Ah. Um."

She gave him an appraising look. "Hmm. Maybe I'd better move. *You* stay here, and *I'll* sleep over there." She rose lithley and went to another pile of padding a few yards away.

"Hey, it was a mouse," Rick protested.

"Mm-hmm." Minmei ignored him. She was young and very, very attractive; she'd learned that she had to be careful. She kneeled to pull aside a fold of the padding and rearrange it more to her liking. As she did, a fat, furry gray form bounded out of hiding and went racing off into the darkness.

*"There's a mouse!"* Minmei covered the distance back to Rick in a single hysterical leap.

He sniffed. "You don't say. I seem to recall mentioning something about that, but you didn't believe me."

She hung her head, then looked at him again. "I'm really sorry, Rick. From now on, I promise I'll believe you."

He struck a noble pose. "In that case, fair lady, I shall defend you from these fearsome creatures!"

"Oh, thank you." Minmei stifled another yawn.

"I think we'll be all right for tonight," he added, looking around the compartment as she rested her head on his shoulder once more. Her eyelids were fluttering tiredly. "They're more scared of us than we are of them."

*What's more important*, he didn't say out loud, so as not to discourage her hopes of escape or rescue, *if they can survive here, we can.* He tried to fight down the feeling that their situation wasn't very promising.

"So if you want to sleep—" he started to say, then realized she was dozing, snuggled against him.

"I'll be darned. Wish *I* could fall asleep like that." He made himself comfortable as best he could, leaning back against the crate, concentrating. He considered every option and plan he could think of, certain of only one thing.

He wouldn't let Minmei down.

# CHAPTER
# SEVENTEEN

> *If Breetai and company were confused by human behavior
> as applied to war, one cannot help but wonder, in light of sub-
> sequent events and Zentraedi responses, what they would have
> thought if they could have looked into the remotest corner of
> SDF-1 and observed the behavior of two castaways.*
>
> Zeitgeist, *Alien Psychology*

R ICK WAS BROUGHT OUT OF HIS MUSINGS BY A SCRAPE
of metal—a screech, really—that set his teeth on edge and
had him alert for danger.

He'd grown used to the endless dripping of water con-
densed on or leaking from pipes, not even registering it anymore, and could identify most of the ship's sounds—giant
circulation systems and the vibrations of far-off machinery.
But this one was something new.

It was Minmei. "Let's see: Yesterday was Thursday.
Now Friday..." She held a triangular piece of scrap metal
in her hand, one edge sharpened against the deck, finishing
the line she was gouging in *Mockingbird*'s upside-down fuselage, under the starboard nose canard.

There were two of them, irregular verticals cut deep into
the racer's vulnerable skin. She'd picked a spot where there
was room for quite a few marks, he saw.

"Hey! What're you doing?"

She turned to him with a smile, happy to be doing something that yielded tangible results, however slight. "I'm
keeping a record of how many days we've been stranded

here." She offered him the improvised cutter. "Would you like to help?"

It had obviously never occurred to her that his Heiko had a day/date function. Rick kept the fact to himself; her personal calendar seemed to lift her morale. "No thanks. You're doing fine. I'm gonna get back to work."

"See ya." Minmei grinned and watched him walk off, slinging his clipboard around his neck for another exploration-survey mission.

*That was a brand-new paint job!* He blew his breath out. It didn't matter anyway; *Mockingbird* would never fly again. *Some help* she *is! Well, I don't suppose too much else can go wrong today.*

Which was just when he clunked his forehead against a low-hanging pipe. Recoiling back in pain, he hit another with the back of his skull. Hissing in anger and pent-up frustration, he berated himself for not wearing the Veritech helmet as a hardhat.

But he refused to turn back. Marking off the different routes and possible escape paths available to them had seemed easy at first, until he'd come to realize what a tremendously complicated and far-reaching maze they were trapped in. He'd come to so many dead ends that he constantly saw them in his dreams.

Banging on pipes and bulkheads with the metal bar had produced no results, and even sending shorts and longs over a severed power cable was a failure. Depression was hard to fight off, and he couldn't bear the thought of what would happen if he didn't come up with a solution soon.

There was one long shot he hadn't mentioned to Minmei yet, not so much because it was a life-or-death risk for him but rather because, if he tried it and failed, she would be alone. Still, his alternatives were fewer and fewer with every passing hour.

When he finally dragged himself back to the plane after more fruitless searching, he was pleasantly surprised to see that he hadn't been the only one hard at work.

"Well, Rick, how do you like our new home?" Minmei asked him, eyes shining.

Rick broke into a smile for the first time he could recall. "It's great!" was all he could say.

Minmei had somehow figured out how to get the parachute out of the back of the pilot's seat—maybe after reading the ejection instruction plate, it occurred to him. It couldn't have been easy with *Mockingbird* hung upside down eight or nine feet off the deck.

More than that, she'd draped it over the ship to make a roomy red and white striped tent. And best of all, she'd located the survival gear, set up the tiny camp stove, and put together a meal whose smell had his mouth watering until his jaws hurt.

The compartment lights were going dim according to SDF-1's twenty-four-hour day/night schedule. The two moved in under the tent, Rick sitting tailor-fashion while Minmei knelt by the stove, stirring with a plastic spoon.

"By making stew we can make our supplies last longer," she explained. Rick repented of his earlier thought—that she couldn't pull her own weight.

"That's right; I forgot," he said, determined to make it up to her. "You're in the restaurant business."

She was sprinkling bits of what seemed to be seasoning into the stew, only he couldn't remember spices being listed on the rations contents listings. Whatever she'd done, she'd come up with something that smelled heavenly.

"No, the White Dragon was my Aunt Lena's restaurant," Minmei responded, shrugging. She thought a moment, then added, "Actually, I want to be an entertainer."

Rick cocked his head in surprise. "You're planning on being an actress?"

"Well, I studied acting, singing, and dancing." She'd been dishing up his portion. "Here."

"Thanks." He was silent for a while, taken by the image of Minmei dancing. Then, "That doesn't exactly prepare you for something like this, huh." Ruefully, he looked down at his clipboard and the growing map of dead ends.

Five days went by.

\* \* \*

"Can you believe they're rebuilding the city *inside* the ship?" someone was saying as Lisa Hayes entered the officers' wardroom. "It's amazing."

She saw by his insignia that he was a Veritech pilot off the *Daedalus*, one of the few who'd been in the air during the spacefold jump and had thus been spared. He and his kind were like specters these days, watching whole new groups of pilots being crash-trained to fly the fighters that the carriers' dead could no longer man.

His comment about the refugees and their rebuilding was grudging. Open area of any kind in a naval or space vessel was always held dear, and now—

"You can leave the trays, steward," Claudia was saying at the table where she waited for Lisa. "Thank you very much. It smells wonderful."

"Yes, ma'am." The steward served awkwardly, a new recruit; everybody with military training had been tapped for higher-priority work these days, and it was most often serve yourself. But things were tough all over, and complaints were very few. This particular steward, Claudia had found out, was to be posted to a gunnery class next shift.

"So he expects me to volunteer and go out and get this castaway shelter module all alone, and I sez, 'Sir, I'm brave but I ain't crazy!'" the VT pilot continued.

"So you didn't volunteer," his tablemate said. "But did you go?"

The first pilot shrugged unhappily and made a zipping motion with his hand, thumb and pinkie spread to indicate a Veritech's wings. They both laughed tiredly.

*Some things never change*, Lisa thought. Contrary to what most civilians thought, real combat veterans seldom bragged among themselves of their heroism; it was a mark of high prestige to go on about how scared you were, how fouled up things were, how hairy the situation had gotten, how dumb the brass were. Because among them, everyone *knew*; boasts were for outsiders.

"Oh, *there* you are," Lisa said, collapsing into a chair across from Claudia.

Claudia lowered her coffee cup. "What's the latest on the refugees?"

Lisa pursed her lips, weighing the answer. "We finally have them divided by city blocks and the construction's going on twenty-four hours a day."

Claudia's dark eyes were unfocused with fatigue and with the strangeness of what had happened and what was going on.

She could only manage an understatement. "Really? That's incredible."

Gloval had known at once what must be done. His relentless effort to get the Macross survivors and as much salvageable and recyclable material aboard as was possible had yielded amazing results. It was the only way the humans could make the long voyage home.

Miles-square purse-seine nets had been devised overnight by the engineers to collect what could be collected of the wreckage. There'd been too many acts of individual valor to count or keep track of. Not the least of them was the work of the disposal teams, whose grim job was to remove the dead from the supercarriers and other areas where they were encountered.

Hold after hold in SDF-1 that had been reserved for future missions and future purposes that would never come to be were now filled with wreckage, and there were material stores that could be used as well. Robotech fabrication machines aboard the SDF-1 were the most advanced devices of their kind ever developed—the equivalent of an industrial city packed into a few compartments, minifactories that could replicate a staggering assortment of manufactured goods and materials.

As for blueprints and plans, they would be child's play for the SDF-1's computers, since all records of the city's construction, from the first permanent building constructed ten years earlier to the last, were in the ship's data banks.

More importantly, Gloval understood before anyone else aboard just what the long trip to Earth would entail. The civilians couldn't be expected to simply sit in packed emergency billets and twiddle their thumbs; that invited complete social breakdown, and disaster for the SDF-1.

The secret was well kept in subsequent mission reports and in announcements to the refugees, but it was Gloval's liaison officers who planted the seed of the idea: *Why not rebuild Macross City?*

The gouges of Minmei's calendar had multiplied: four verticals with a crosshatch now, and two more besides.

Now Rick dreaded returning to the small light cast by the miniature camp stove, dreaded having Minmei pretend she wasn't disappointed by another day of bad news.

She'd begun explorations too, to double their chances, over his strenuous objection at first—but with his unspoken acceptance as things became more and more desperate.

Now he sank wearily onto his pallet, while she stirred the thin soup that was the very last stretching of their rations. He hadn't been able to find out how the mice were subsisting, but it wouldn't be very long before he and Minmei would be forced to start trying to catch them. He doubted that even she could make mouse stew taste very good.

He sat, trying to figure out how to phase his difficult decision.

"No luck, huh?" Minmei said. "Why don't you rest?"

"Minmei," he began, head lowered on his knees, "I don't know what else to do. This ship is like a big prison maze."

"Yeah," she said without looking up, "a big prison floating somewhere in space."

It was an opening he hadn't expected, a chance to make his plan look hopeful, to make her optimistic. "That's it, of course! We're in space!" He tried to sound as though he'd just realized the implications of that.

She looked startled. "What about it?"

"That's our way out of here! Out that air lock we found and into another, somewhere farther above!"

She didn't understand. "We can't do that; we don't have any spacesuits."

He was already on his feet, the Veritech helmet taken down from its resting place. "My flight helmet will protect me. I'll float out, get help, and come back down here for you. It's simple! It'll work!"

He flipped up his flightsuit collar and ran his fingers along the automatic closure to show her how it formed a pressure seal and a collar ring that could be fitted to the helmet's.

She looked terribly confused. "Yes, but—"

"Now, I'm going to need your help," Rick said as he led the way with the flashlight. "So I'll show you how to use the air lock controls, okay?"

She trailed behind unwillingly, hands clasped behind her, silently accepting his help as they began ascending the mountain of packing crates and boxes again.

They reached the Zentraedi-scaled utility shelf near the power panel; it was the width of a country lane. The control dials were the size of wagon wheels, the buttons as big as her bedroom window. "You sure you understand everything?" he checked again.

"Mm-hmm." Then she said in a rush, "Without oxygen tanks, though, Rick? *How're you going to breathe?*"

"There's air in the helmet and some in the suit. I won't need much time." But he hurried along before she could pinpoint the problem that he'd already spotted: They'd explored the ship in every direction and found no nearby air locks. From this one, it would strain his scant supply of air to the very limits to reach another, even if one lay just beyond their prison.

He turned and started off before she could say anything more. "Wait!" cried Minmei, running after him. "I'm having second thoughts about all this! Rick?"

She ran after him, back around the turn in the shelf. "Where're we going?"

"I want to show you: You can stand by this big viewport here so we can communicate if we have to." The viewport was bigger than a movie screen.

She gasped and threw both hands up to her mouth, feet going pigeon-toed, eyes enormous.

He prepared his most matter-of-fact voice. "Minmei, what is it *now*? You've gotta stop this constant worrying—huh?"

She wasn't looking at him. She was gaping over his shoulder at the viewport. He whirled. "Look . . . at . . . that!"

"I've never seen anything like it!" Minmei breathed. "What kind is it?"

At first he thought it was some kind of new prototype spacecraft, silvery and sleek, and he was already trying to figure a way to signal it. Then he was afraid it might be an alien ship, although it didn't look anything like a pod. But a second later he calmed down and saw what it really was, which was only slightly more fantastic than possibilities one and two.

"Offhand, I'd say it's a tuna," Rick ventured. "I didn't know they grew that big."

This one was as long as *Mockingbird* and appeared to be intact and whole. Why the forces of explosive decompression and vacuum hadn't turned it into something more like a radar-waved football, he couldn't imagine; he was unacquainted as yet with the very singular peculiarities of a Protoculture-generated force field.

It floated along like a schooner, as if it was keeping pace with them. "That sure is a big tuna fish," Minmei observed, licking her lips.

"*Real* big," Rick conceded. He turned to her, and they both yelled "*Yay-yyy!*" at the same instant, pressing their noses and palms up against the viewport. "I wonder if there's a way I could snag it out there," he said longingly.

They turned to each other, chorusing, "Tuna fish!"

Rick made sure the ring seal was as tight as he could make it. Seals at his wrists and ankles were reinforced with all the tape he'd been able to find and some turns of twine. The collar closure was wound tight with layer upon layer of cloth strips.

He realized he couldn't hear anything and opened the faceplate again. Minmei was yelling down to him, "Be careful out there! Wave when you're ready!"

He gave her the wave and closed the faceplate again, carrying his looped line back into the oversize air lock. Minmei said, "Here we go!" to herself and strained against a wagon wheel dial.

Rick did his best to keep calm as the inner hatch came down with a finality that made the deck jump and the air bled away. Next to him were a pair of heavy tanks of some kind; he clutched them close. He felt the ship's artificial gravity easing off him.

When the air was gone and the outer hatch was open, he took careful bearing and pushed himself off, trailing the long rope behind. His suit was already becoming a steam-bath.

The tuna was obliging in that it didn't move much, but his aim was off. He threw one of the tanks from him in one direction, Newton's third law driving him off in the other.

There'd be no time for fumbling; if he missed, he'd have to go back in and refill his suit with air, get more ballast, and try again. Exhausted and depleted, he didn't know if he had the strength for that and didn't want to find out. He tucked the second tank into the looser cloth windings.

He pinwheeled, unused to zero gravity, forcing down the appalling thought of how he'd die if he lost control of his stomach now and gave in to zero-g nausea.

Then he was drifting toward a lifeless eye the diameter of a dinner platter. He spread his arms and bulldogged the tuna. The big fish spun slowly as Rick clung to the left side of its head. He belayed a loop around a pectoral fin as insurance.

He tried heaving the second tank to get the tuna moving toward the lock, but without much luck; the thing was weightless, but its *mass* hadn't changed, and its mass seemed immovable.

The line he'd played out behind him reached its end, stretching just a bit, an expensive composite made for deep-space work, stronger than steel. Rick was jolted, realizing that if he hadn't looped the fin, he'd have been snapped loose from the fish like a paddleball.

The line's elasticity absorbed the fish's movement and contracted, starting the tuna moving back for the lock. Rick felt his air getting short and fought the urge to use the fish as a launching platform—to kick off for the air lock and hope he could recover it later. He and Minmei could survive for a while longer without food, but not forever, and the fish would probably be the difference between life and death for them both.

He held on, straining at the line to speed things up. The air lock seemed a long way away, and his air very, very thin, making him groggy, while the fish moved as slowly as a glacier.

He shook his head to clear it, concentrating. Everything was blurry. Wasn't there some book about an old fisherman who hung on somehow? Rick was pretty sure his father had made him read it, but he couldn't recall it.

The hatch was before him. Had he been napping? He didn't have time to get out of the way, and the tuna trapped him against the deck, plowing him along. He felt some tiny seam give, and the air pressure in his suit began dropping.

He shoved hysterically, fighting his way out against the impossible mass, kicking off and fetching up against the miles-high inner hatch. He slammed it with his fists, breath and consciousness slipping away—forever, he knew, if he didn't get air soon.

The hiss got louder, and he located the stressed spot just as it began to go, holding it together with his hand, hooking one foot on some kind of cross member, hammering and hammering with his free fist. He didn't notice the jarring of the outer hatch.

Nor did he notice the return of gravity until it flipped him off the inner hatch. He sagged against the armored door, now only able to thump it feebly, the world going red in his vision, then increasingly dark.

# CHAPTER
# EIGHTEEN

*That suppressed longing of the Flower of Life, which desire generates the incalculable power of Protoculture, has its human equivalent. The interlude of the castaways is rich in insights as to those Greater Forces, so much more powerful than mere guns or missiles, that manifested themselves in the Robotech War.*

Jan Morris, *Solar Seeds, Galactic Guardians*

RICK ALMOST FELL TO THE DECK ON HIS FACE. THE inner hatch had risen without his noticing it, and there was air all around him. Unfortunately, his helmet was still sealed.

Minmei raced for him, screaming something he couldn't hear. He reeled and staggered. At last, between them, they got the helmet off; he devoured air, his chest straining against the flight suit, sobbing on the exhale, but alive.

Minmei got a shoulder under his arm, steadying him as he sank to all fours. "I was so worried! I thought—" She didn't finish it.

"At least . . . I got the tuna back in," he labored. Catching his breath a bit, he straightened up and looked back over his shoulder into the lock, at his catch.

The fish had been thrust back when he kicked off from it and had been completely severed by the outer hatch; only the glassy-eyed head remained in the lock, and everything behind the gills was out drifting once more on some new vector

"Or some of it, anyway," he amended. He wondered

whether Minmei's aunt had taught her any recipes appropriate to the occasion.

"Hu-uuuh!" Rick observed, and sank to the cold deck.

*Ushio jiru*, a great delicacy, was more suited to the preparation of the porgy, exploiting the flavor and use of piscine parts Westerners usually discarded. The version Aunt Lena had taught Minmei, however, did *not* start "Take one fish head one and one-half yards long."

That didn't make Rick's mouth water any less as the hapless fish sat staring at them out of a big vat; *Mockingbird*'s jet fuel flamed through jury-rigged burners, and a delicious smell wafted out through the compartment.

"Why are you sitting there with such a sad look on your face?" Minmei prodded Rick. "You caught a fish in outer space! You were wonderful out there!"

Glumly, he sat with face cupped in hands. He'd underestimated her and had made a pact with himself to be honest with her from now on. "Thanks, but that little fishing trip ruined our chances of going out along the ship's hull." He showed her the rent that had appeared in his suit in the last instants before she had opened the inner hatch and saved him.

"We have no way to fix it. I don't know *what* we're gonna do." He hugged his knees, forehead sinking down against them.

"Maybe we could cut a hole in the roof and then climb right up," she proposed—anything to keep him from losing hope.

His head came up again. "I've already thought about that. I took some tools and climbed up to the ceiling yesterday. But it's like armor; I couldn't even make a dent in it."

Minmei gave the mountainous fish head a poke with her long sheet-metal fork. "What about an explosion?"

"What would we explode? The last of our fuel will run the camp stove a while longer, but it wouldn't even warm up this armor all around us."

Minmei prodded the fish head a little, trying to set it so it wouldn't topple. They'd lashed together some pitchforklike cooking tools, but those were pretty clumsy. They couldn't afford to spill the *ushio jiru* or waste any of the fish head; they might not have any other source of food for a long time.

She looked at the flame beneath the vat and wondered what would happen to them when the food, the fuel—perhaps even the air and water—finally gave out.

Minmei's tally of the days had grown: four verticals crosshatched with a fifth, and another group of five, and two more besides, for a total of twelve. Neither of them mentioned the count anymore.

They would leave the stove on, a tiny orange-yellow flame, for just a little while after the compartment lights went out each night. It was unwise from the standpoint of conservation, of course, but it helped their morale a lot, talking for a while in the peaceful quiet of their tent before going to sleep. Rick found himself looking forward to those moments all day as he dragged himself around the maze, his hopes dashed over and over by dead ends.

But he was already thinking about the moment when the stove would flicker out for the last time. There was always the wood from the many packing crates, of course, but Rick wasn't sure what danger an open fire might constitute to the air supply. He was already mapping steam and hot water lines, looking for the best and nearest place to do their cooking, and trying to interpret the utility markings in order to improvise a little light during the night cycles and recharge his flashlight once *Mockingbird*'s batteries were completely dead.

"And so I practiced as hard as I could—I didn't do much of anything else, I guess," he told Minmei. He was lying with his head pillowed on his arms, staring up at *Mockingbird*. Minmei lay across from him on her pallet, resting on one elbow. The soft light made her skin glow and her eyes liquid and deep.

"My dad grumbled a bit," he went on, "but he taught me everything he knew, and I came back to win that competition the next year. And I won it eight times in a row, even though I was only flying an old junker plane."

He stopped, wondering if it sounded like he was bragging. Then he dismissed the thought; Minmei knew him better than that. And he felt like he'd known her all his life—no, like he'd known her *always*.

She sighed, laying her head on her hands, watching him. "Rick?" she said softly. "Do you think I'll ever get to fly with you again?"

He put all the conviction he could into his answer, trying to sound matter-of-fact. "Why, sure! Once we get rescued, I'll take you up whenever you want. That is, if you'll sing for me now and then."

She lay back, gazing up at the play of firelight on the inverted cockpit canopy. Their isolation had become their world, filling dreams as well as days.

*Sometimes I dream of falling in love.* She'd never dared mention it to him.

Minmei began singing, a song she'd written and never shared with anybody before. It took him a second to realize that he didn't recognize it.

"To be in love
  My hero he must take me where no other can
  Where silver suns have golden moons,
  Each year has thirteen Junes,
  That's what must be for me
  To be
  In love."

"You've got a beautiful voice." He'd said it before; though he tried to think of some flowery new way to tell her, it always came out the same way.

She looked over at him again; he couldn't tell if she was blushing or not. "Thank you, Rick." She averted her eyes for a second, then looked to him again. "If I could do one thing with my life, it would be to sing. I couldn't live without singing."

"It's always been planes for me," he answered, even though she already knew that. "All I ever wanted to do was fly." Then he felt awkward for repeating what he must have told her a hundred times already.

But Minmei sat up, embracing her knees, nodding

gravely. "I know how you feel, Rick. Sometimes you can't be happy unless you do what you dream about."

"So you're sure that being an entertainer is what you want from life?"

"Yes, I guess." She added in a rush, "But what I really want is to be a bride."

He was suddenly alert and wary. "Ah. You mean, married?"

She nodded, the long hair shimmering in the stove's light. "In my family, there's so much love—well, I've told you that already, haven't I? You'll simply have to meet them! They're wonderful and—that's the kind of joy I want in my life."

"I guess you'll probably make somebody a terrific wife," he said noncommittally.

She was suddenly sad again. "Thanks, but now I'll never have the chance."

"Don't you even *think* that, Minmei! I *know* we're gonna get out of here somehow!"

"It's been twelve days. And I'm sure they must have given up searching for us by now." Her voice had shrunk to a whisper. "We'll never get out of here."

He didn't know what to say. Before he could decide, there were squeaks and chitters and a faint rattling.

"It's those mice again! I'll get them this time!" Relieved at a chance to work off his frustration, he grabbed an empty can and sprang to the opening of the tent.

He hurled the can, and it clunked and bounced in the darkness, scattering the mice.

She was standing next to him. "We're never going to make it out of here alive. We're going to be here forever."

Her hands were clasped, and she was gazing sadly into the darkness. She suddenly sounded bitter. "We've been here too long. They've all forgotten about us by now."

"Minmei, I don't want to hear that kind of talk!"

"It's true! We've just got to face it." She stood with her back to him, looking out into a void darker than deep space. "We'll live our entire lives right here in this ship. I'll never know what it's like to be a bride and start a whole new life."

She was weeping, unable to go on, her shoulders shaking.

"Minmei," he said gently, "you will. I'll show you."

She sniffed. "How can you do that?"

"Um, we can have a ceremony right here. We can pretend."

She turned and came back to him, cheeks wet. "Oh, Rick, do you mean it?" He nodded slowly; Minmei wiped away her tears. "Then let me borrow your scarf?"

She unknotted it and drew it from around his neck, a long, white flier's scarf of fine silk, spreading it and carefully arranging it as a bridal veil.

"Minmei, you look beautiful. I—I guess I should be the groom, huh?" he said haltingly, then rolled his eyes at his own stupidity.

Minmei said nothing, holding her hand out. He took it. "Is this what we do next?"

She started to nod, then broke from her role, close to tears again. "Oh, Rick, why doesn't someone come and *find* us? *I want to go home!*"

"But you will, I promise you."

She squeezed his hand hard. "I'm just so scared." It sounded so small and forlorn in the huge, empty compartment.

"I know; so am I." He took her shoulders in his hands. "Come on, I'm telling you: We're gonna get out of here! There's got to be a way! We can't give up! I've never been a quitter, and you shouldn't be either!"

She pulled back out of his reach. "Stop it. That's all just silly talk! You know what's going to happen! We're going to die here!" She turned away, sobbing.

Rick stared at her, not knowing what to say. She was not quite sixteen, very much in love with life. "Minmei, it's not silly talk. I really believe it. You mustn't give up. I'm doing my best." He gestured vaguely. "I'm sorry."

She turned back to him. "No, Rick; I'm the one who should apologize. It's just that—" She threw herself into his arms. "I'm being so stupid—"

He held her close. "That's not true."

She turned her face up to his. "Kiss me, Rick."

"If you're sure . . ."

She closed her eyes, and they kissed.

It seemed to them that their lips had barely touched when there was a concussion that shook the deck, shook that whole part of the ship, like the crack of doomsday, nearly sending them sprawling. The *Mockingbird* and their camp disappeared under tons of metal alloy. They barely kept their feet, holding each other in their arms.

Suddenly there was something—*the Leaning Tower of Robotech!* Rick thought wildly—canted to one side in its lodging place, having penetrated the deck above, the one totally immune to Rick's tools. Light shone down into the compartment.

*Not just light; it looks like SUNLIGHT!* Minmei thought, though she didn't understand how that could possibly be. Wasn't it night all over the ship?

Long shafts of artificial light—flashlights—probed down into the dust and smoke of the sealed-off compartment. There were voices.

"What was that? An enemy missile?"

"Looked to me like a bomb!" Human figures were gathering around the jagged entrance hole of the metal juggernaut that had struck daylight into Rick and Minmei's prison.

"Naw," somebody drawled. "New converter subunit from the ceiling level, according to Control. Mounting gave way."

The beams played this way and that while the castaways watched, too astounded to speak. Then one light found them, and another, and in a second four or five converged on them.

"Hey! There's somebody down there!"

"It looks like a coupla kids!"

They held each other close, not sure what might have happened to the rest of the universe in twelve long days and nights. The harsh flashlight beams sent shadows away from them in different directions.

Then a familiar voice said, "Why, that looks like Minmei down there!" It came from a squat, broad figure gazing down at the very edge of the abyss.

Minmei's grip on Rick tightened. "It's the mayor! Rick, Rick, we're saved!" She hugged him but then let go, moving into the center spotlight to wave.

Rick dropped his arms to his side and wondered why he wasn't as ecstatic as he thought he'd be.

It took only a few minutes to get a crane rigged with a bucket to lift them out; there was construction equipment all over that part of SDF-1. They were lifted up into more intense light than they'd seen in nearly two weeks. But that was hardly noticeable, insignificant against the shock of the new world in which they found themselves.

"Are we dreaming or something?" Minmei clung to the bucket's rail. "What in the world is going on here?"

They were looking around them at broad streets and tall buildings, signs, lamp posts, marquees, and throngs of people. They were looking at Macross City, except that far overhead was the expanse of a spacecraft's metal "ceiling." A far-reaching lighting system had already been set up to give Earth-normal illumination. The crowds were pointing at them and gabbling and yelling.

"I can't believe it," he muttered. "The whole city's here."

The bucket set them down to one side of the hole in the deck. Minmei was about to climb out when she gasped and pointed. "Oh, Rick, *look!*"

He remembered the corner well; he'd done enough crashing around on it in a Battloid he couldn't steer. Except these buildings all looked new, bright with fresh paint.

"The White Dragon and Aunt Lena's house are right here!" She was already clambering out of the bucket.

*There's no place like home*, Rick thought sourly, not remembering whether or not he'd clicked the heels of his ruby slippers.

He felt a little woozy, and there were a lot of confusing images, one on top of another, after that. A tiny dynamo came dodging out of the crowd. Jason threw himself into Minmei's arms, and the cousins hugged each other and cried.

Mayor Tommy Luan was slapping Rick on the back and

saying things like "As you can see, m'boy, the entire city's been rebuilt! Now, we've got to get you rested up and hear what happened to you; you've been gone for almost two weeks!"

Minmei's Uncle Max had more to add, pumping Rick's hand with the powerful grip of a lifelong worker. "I appreciate the protection you provided our baby girl!"

"Uh, don't mention it," Rick said vaguely. He suddenly wanted very much to sit down. Then he caught other nearby voices.

People were gathered around Minmei, Macross City people who knew her and regarded her as part of their extended family, not a castaway and a stranger—not as they would regard Rick.

"Oh, it was so frightening down there," she was telling her audience, wide-eyed. "You have no idea!"

"Oh, I can imagine," a woman said, while people nodded and murmured in agreement.

A godlike voice echoed through the strange, metal-boundaried world of the new Macross City, startling Rick. "Attention! Message from the bridge!"

He thought it was a voice he'd heard before somewhere, but he was too disoriented to place it. "The disturbance in Sector Seven-X was caused by a construction accident. There were no injuries. The damage will be cleared up very shortly. All divisions revert to normal status."

*Where'd I hear that voice before?* he wondered.

Minmei was regaling people now; she had the crowd in the palm of her hand. "Oh! And the *mice*!"

The onlookers laughed in anticipation, though they had no idea what the mice story was all about. Rick waited for her to catch his eye and draw him into the center of attention, but she was focused on her performance now.

*A bad dream*, he told himself, not sure if he meant the long wait below or coming back to a too-bright, too-loud, too-strange world.

"Well, m'boy, you must be one happy fella right now, by golly, huh?" Tommy Luan said, and slapped him on the back again in a man-to-man fashion. The mayor was built like a barrel weighted with cannonballs; the slap sent Rick teetering over to the deck.

It felt nice and comfortable there. He didn't have the strength to get up anyway and didn't think anybody would miss him if he just napped for a little while.

# CHAPTER
# NINETEEN

*Heroism? Perseverance? When it comes to the story of Macross City and its citizens, we're talking about a whole lot of new superlatives for those concepts.*

Mayor Tommy Luan, *The High Office*

*IT FEELS SO MUCH LIKE HOME,* MINMEI THOUGHT, WIPING down the table, *even though it's not.*

There were little differences that let her know she wasn't really in the original White Dragon, but she could ignore them—ignore them happily—after her imprisonment in the deserted portion of SDF-1.

So, waiting for her uncle and aunt to return, she cleaned the place up the way she'd done back in Macross City. The furniture felt a little strange, lighter and far stronger than the wooden stuff she was used to, fabricated by Robotech equipment out of reprocessed wreckage; but it looked close enough to the original tables and chairs to make her feel like she was home again. She worked happily, humming, not realizing that the tune was the "Wedding March."

The front doors swept apart, just like the ones back on Macross Island, and her uncle and aunt came in. "We wasted half the day standing on line for this," Uncle Max was grousing, shaking a food ration package no bigger than a good-size book.

She thought again what a strange pair they made, her

uncle broad and substantial as a boulder, barely coming shoulder-high to his willowy, serene wife. And yet when Minmei thought about what it meant to be completely in love, she often thought about these two.

"We're lucky to have anything," Lena reminded him gently.

The SDF-1 had been equipped and supplied for a variety of missions, but not for feeding tens of thousands of refugees. Aeroponic and hydroponic farms and protein-growth vats were already in operation, but for the time being the dimensional fortress's stores, and the supplies salvaged from the shelters, were the extent of the food supply. Those were quite considerable, rumor had it, but rumor also had it that SDF-1 faced a very long trip back to Earth, and Captain Gloval was being careful.

"Hi, you two!" Minmei said brightly. "Welcome home! How'd it go?"

Aunt Lena tried to put on a cheerful expression. "About as well as could be expected, I guess."

"I'm feeling much better now," Minmei said, gesturing around to show them the progress she'd made toward putting the place in order. Uncle Max looked around despondently; it was so much like the White Dragon that was gone forever.

"I'm glad to hear that," Aunt Lena said. "And how's Rick? Is he up yet?"

When the medics released him, Aunt Lena and Uncle Max had insisted that Rick stay in a spare bedroom in the rebuilt restaurant until he was fully recovered. "I suppose he's still in bed," Minmei said. "I haven't heard him moving around up there."

"I'm not surprised." Lena smiled. "After watching over you for two weeks, he probably deserves a rest."

Minmei grinned. "I guess you're right about that. Oh, by the way, are you going to leave everything like this or will you reopen the restaurant?"

"What d'you mean reopen the restaurant?" Uncle Max exploded, though she could hear the sudden hope in his voice.

Minmei gestured around at the stacked chairs and boxed

flatware and bundles of table linen. The White Dragon, which originally stood at the virtual center of Macross City, had served as a kind of field test for the engineers seeking to help the Macross City survivors rebuild their lives, an experiment to see if a piece of the city could be reproduced down to the last detail. There were working dishwashers and ovens and sinks and rest rooms, freezers and refrigerators, lighting and a sound system.

The only thing that was different was that there were no garbage pails or dumpsters. A system of oubliettes was being built into the new Macross City because everything —*everything*—would have to be recycled and reused. It made perfect sense to Minmei, who'd known thirst and hunger and other privations well in the past two weeks; anyone who couldn't see that was just being stupid.

"We have everything we need," she pointed out. "It'll be fun!"

She saw a rekindling in Uncle Max's eyes, but he said slowly, "Maybe so, but it'd be awfully difficult to run a restaurant when these are all the rations they give at one time." He shook the book-size box. "For four of us, for today."

"But you kept your place open all through the war!" Minmei cried.

Uncle Max ran his hand through the tight black curls on his head. Aunt Lena looked shocked, but happy. "*Whff!* That was much different," Max said. Then he reconsidered. "Well, the army *had* imposed rationing then too . . ."

"But—we're living inside a spaceship, Minmei," Lena said.

"But the main problem right now isn't shortages, right?" Minmei reminded her. "It's distribution and control. We've got thousands of people spending half the day on line! How's anybody gonna get anything *done*? That's the ultimate in stupidity!"

She saw that they were getting the point. "Aunt Lena, once the authorities know you're reopening the White Dragon, they'll give you all the supplies you want! And it wouldn't surprise me if they put us all on salary as food distribution specialists!

"And people can pay us with their ration cards; the army pays at least part of the overhead; there's room for a little markup, I would think; the tips are pure profit, whether they're in military script or in goods or service IOUs; and we'll get that new bookkeeping computer they're setting up to keep track of cost/profit margin!"

She was out of breath but triumphant. And she could see from their faces that she'd sold her aunt and uncle. "What d'you think?"

Uncle Max rubbed the back of his neck, wanting very badly to believe it. "I suppose it doesn't sound like a bad idea, after all."

"I guess so," Aunt Lena allowed. She drew in a great breath, looking at Minmei. "Doing business as usual is the answer to a lot of problems, right?"

Minmei nodded until her hair was rippling around her.

*"Right!"* barked Uncle Max. "Let's get cracking! Full steam ahead!" He laughed, full-throated, at the dark starburst of happiness in his wife's eyes and at Minmei's gasp.

"Wait just a second!" Minmei dashed off, hair whipping behind her. "I'll be right back! I'm just gonna change my clothes!" Mandarin dresses were no problem at all for computer-directed fabrication units that had reproduced alien technologies.

Uncle Max expanded his chest in pride. Aunt Lena put her arm around his broad shoulders and said, "I'm glad she's excited."

He nodded. "I only hope we're not making a mistake about this."

Lena kissed him tenderly. "We're not."

"Careful, that's it," Uncle Max instructed anxiously as he and Minmei carried the little stand out onto the sidewalk in front of the restaurant. "Now turn it around. Good!"

*"Everybody'll* see this!" Minmei said excitedly. The stand was covered with a bright red and yellow silk cloth announcing the restaurant's name in Chinese characters. Minmei's elegant mandarin dress was made of the same stuff. She'd arranged her hair in large buns with a braid to one side, weaving a rope of pearls into the coiffure.

She was so intent on her work that she almost collided with the mayor and his wife, who stared in surprise. "Well, well, what's all this about?"

Minmei replied, "A little surprise, Mr. Mayor. We're reopening our restaurant!"

Tommy Luan's eyebrows shot up. "Have you all gone completely crazy? Has it ever occurred to you that we're at the edge of the universe in the belly of a spaceship?"

"Why, no, we never thought of that," she said tartly. But then she gave him her sunniest smile. "But honestly, that doesn't mean we shouldn't make the best of things, does it? I think we can still have normal lives. After all, this is still our good old hometown, isn't it?"

She indicated the town. It was already an everyday thing for traffic to be moving around the streets—not just military vehicles but cars and trucks that had been salvaged after the spacefold jump as well.

One thing was for sure, the mayor knew: When the diversion of rebuilding the city was over, and that would be soon, the refugees would need something else to occupy them. And as she so often did, Minmei had seen to the heart of things.

"By gosh, you're right!" the mayor said excitedly. To get back to life as usual—how grand that would be! His head was suddenly swimming with ideas for restoring normality to refugee life, but he was distracted as a four-seater troop carrier pulled to the curb with a squeal of tires and a beep of its horn.

Three Veritech pilots sat there, gazing at the restaurant as if it were a three-headed dinosaur. "We saw it but we couldn't believe it!" the jeep's driver said. "Are you really open?"

"We certainly are!" Minmei said proudly.

They looked a little dazed as she led them inside, seated them, and brought glasses of ice water. "Welcome to the first Chinese restaurant in outer space," she beamed, distributing menus.

"Thanks; it's an honor to be here," the driver said. "Hey, you're that girl Minmei everybody's been talking about, huh? I'll bet you had some incredible adventures."

"Sometimes it was pretty scary," she admitted.

The biggest of the three, the one who'd been sitting in the back of the carrier, said in a sly tone, "I heard it was just you and whatshisname, that kid, alone for two weeks. What'd you do all that time?"

She blinked. "What do you mean?"

"Oh, I think you know," the big guy said.

"C'mon, it's obvious," the third one said.

"You make me sick!" she fumed, turning her back on them.

"You mean nothing happened?" the big one persisted. "Nothing at all?"

She whirled. "Yes, that's exactly right!"

"Speaking of whatshisname," the driver said, "is he still around? I mean, I heard he was living here or something."

Minmei answered carefully. "Yes, he's renting a room upstairs from my aunt and uncle. Why?"

The driver shrugged. "You're saying that with all you two went through together, nothing happened? You didn't fall in love or anything?"

"Don't be ridiculous! Rick is just a friend! Now, are you three gonna order or are you gonna leave?"

Rick, poised on the stairs, had heard enough. As the pilots hastened to order chow mein, he turned and went back up to his room.

He sat on his bed and stared glumly at the wall. *So, we're just friends, huh?* He remembered the feel of her in his arms, the electric thrill as they kissed.

*After everything that happened, the next day we're just friends.* He knew Minmei could be stubborn, but on this subject she was just going to have to change her mind.

The engineering section was a hive of activity where every tech, scientist, and specialist available was working twelve-, eighteen-, sometimes twenty-hour days.

Gloval, by his own order, was ignored as he entered, not wishing to break anyone's concentration even for a moment. "Doctor Lang, what do you think? Is the main gun usable or not?"

Lang gave Gloval a brisk salute from habit. The strange whiteless eyes were still mystical, dark. "Look at this schematic, sir."

Lang projected a diagram of SDF-1 on a big wall screen. "This is a first-level depiction of the primary reflex furnace, our power plant. And there you see the energy conversion unit for the main gun. Between the two is the energy conduit for the fold system."

He gave a bitter smile. "*Was*, I should say."

"Which means that after the fold system disappeared, the gun's power source was separated from it, correct?" Gloval asked. "What are you planning to do, since we haven't much spare conduit left?"

And, ironically, conduit was one of the very few things the fabricators couldn't reproduce with materials at hand. But the main gun was SDF-1's hope of survival; Gloval studied Lang, hoping the man had an answer.

Lang assumed the tone he'd used in his lectures back on Earth. "The SDF-1's construction is Robotech construction, sir. That is, the ship is modular, as our Veritech fighters are modular. Variable geometry, you see."

Lang ran a series of illustrations to show what he meant. "So, simplistically speaking, we should by all rights be able to reconfigure the ship, altering its structure in such a way as to bridge the gap that now exists between the main gun and its power source."

It was all a little breathtaking and bold; the proposed reconfiguration, with modules realigned in new shapes, was radically different from the SDF-1 as she now existed.

Gloval felt very uneasy. Lang went on, "The problem, very simply, is that until this modular transformation is completed, the main gun *cannot* be fired."

Lang gestured to the diagrams. "There are going to be major changes, both internally and externally. Of course, the rebuilding of the city and the other modifications made by and for the refugees were never planned for in the ship's construction. I anticipate considerable damage. It's going to be quite a mess for a while."

Gloval was staring at the diagrams, haunted by the awful scenes he'd been forced to witness out the SDF-1 bridge viewport after the spacefold. Mention of structural conversions and damage automatically made alarm bells go off in any seasoned spacer's head; despite Lang's cool calculations, the risk wasn't just of damage—it was of utter disaster.

"Don't we have any other way to fire the main gun, Doctor?"

"You mean besides a modular transformation, sir? No other way that I know of."

Gloval turned away from the screen angrily. "We just can't! The people are only now getting used to being here, trying to patch their lives back together. To subject them to such chaos and perhaps lose more lives—no, it would be just too much."

But a small part of him feared that the decision wasn't that simple; events could force his hand.

# CHAPTER
# TWENTY

*The Rick Hunter who crashed in that hold would never have listened to Roy Fokker. The one who came out—
Well, it's just funny how things happen sometimes, isn't it?*

*The Collected Journals of Admiral Rick Hunter*

"**C**AN I HAVE TWO MORE ORDERS OF EGG FOO YONG and a milk shake, please?" the air crewman yelled over the din in the White Dragon.

"*Milk* shake?" Minmei shivered at the thought, but she put the order in anyway. Uncle Max didn't seem to mind in the least; he was happier than she'd ever seen him, doing the work of three men back in the kitchen, performing miracles with stove and wok.

And the place was packed; word had gotten around even faster than Minmei had hoped. The SDF-1 liaison officers were overjoyed at this solution to their food distribution headaches and provided incentive packages to get the whole population to resume as normal a life as was possible under the circumstances.

Minmei turned, then burst into a smile. "Oh, hi, Rick!"

But he gave no sign of having heard her, slouching toward the door with hands in pockets. Minmei watched him go, her brows knit, suddenly worried and confused.

*  *  *

The hangar bay was dark, quiet as a tomb. *Very appropriate*, Rick thought.

He pulled the bright red-and-white striped chute off the dashed remains of *Mockingbird* just enough to be able to gaze down at a flattened section of engine. The racer was wreckage and would never be anything else again. He still couldn't bring himself to accept that, and so he forced himself to stare, to acknowledge.

He shook his head. "Boy, what a mess."

"Hey, Rick!" It was Roy, stepping into the little circle of light. "Now, show me this junk pile."

Rick came to his feet, fists balled. "Listen, buddy, this is the racer I won eight international championships in. You call it junk? I oughta knock your block off, Roy!"

Roy kneeled to take a better look at *Mockingbird*'s remains. "Actually, it's very *nice* junk. But—them's the breaks, kiddo."

Rick seemed about to explode.

"Hey, I've got an idea." Roy grinned. "Let's take a walk, okay?"

Rick looked startled. "I've never seen you so depressed in my life," Roy went on. "What you need is exercise!" He came over to put an arm around his friend's shoulders. "Try it! You'll like it!"

Roy's walk took them to the uppermost part of SDF-1 for an astonishing view.

From the lounge of the officers' club, Rick found himself looking down on the *Daedalus*. "Wow! An aircraft carrier connected to the Robotech ship?"

There was a long elbowlike housing holding the carrier fast. Rick could see that the ship had been patched and made airtight and was in service. All six bow and waist cats appeared to be in operation. As he watched, an elevator brought up two Veritechs for launch.

The Thor-class supercarrier, almost fifteen hundred feet long, had undergone a lot of other modifications. Most conspicuously, its "island"—the towerlike superstructure that had once dominated the flight deck and been the *Dae-*

*dalus*'s bridge—had been removed to leave the deck perfectly flat. All flight operations had been combined in the SDF-1's command center, and the salvaged materials and equipment had been used in the design changes.

The Veritechs spread their wings, not for the sake of aerodynamics but rather because the wider placement of thrusters gave them better control. The hookup men and cat crews, now spacesuited and still color-coded according to their jobs, went through the time-honored routine.

As Rick watched, a bow cat officer pointed to his "shooter," the man who actually gave the order to launch. The cat officer signalled the Veritech pilot with a wave of a flashlight, pointing toward the bow, dropping to one knee to avoid being accidentally hit by a wing.

The fighter was accelerated off the flatdeck's hurricane bow at almost 200 knots—not because airspeed was necessary in the airlessness of space but to get the Veritech launched and clear of the ship in a hurry, as it would have to be in combat, so as not to be a sitting duck for alien pilots.

The Veritech banked and soared away. Rick had to remind himself that it was flying in total vacuum; Robotech control systems made the operation of a fighter very much a matter of thought, and the Veritech pilots were used to thinking in terms of atmospheric flying. And so the Veritechs flew that way; it was wasteful of power, but power was something Robotech ships, with their reactor drives, had in great supply.

Rick watched longingly. "Terrific."

"How'd you like to fly one again?" Roy clapped Rick on the shoulder.

Rick spun on him. "What are you saying?"

"Join us, Rick. Become a Veritech pilot and stop all this moping around."

Rick's expression hardened. "I don't want to be a fighter pilot."

"Oh? You'd rather drag yourself around the SDF-1 like a lovesick idiot? Well?"

Rick broke loose of Roy's hand, turning away. "Roy?" he said over his shoulder.

"Yeah?"

"Roy, I think I'm—I mean, do you think it's possible for girls to change overnight? Completely?"

"How's that again?"

"Can a girl simply change from what she was the day before?"

"I don't think you have to worry about that. Minmei thought you were depressed, and it was *her* idea for me to bring you up here and have a little chat."

Roy slapped him on the back, knocking a little of the breath from him. "So just cheer up and go back to Minmei, kid; she's waiting for you."

He walked off, chuckling to himself, but paused to call back, "Oh, one more thing: Girls like her can be sort of flighty sometimes, know what I mean? You better be careful some guy in uniform doesn't catch her eye. See ya."

Across the solar system, maintaining position relative to Earth's nearby moon, the Zentraedi armada hung like a seaful of bloodthirsty fish.

Breetai returned to his command post in response to Exedore's request. "Trans-vid records of the aliens, you say?"

Exedore kowtowed to his lord. "Yes, they were just recovered from a disabled scout pod. And they confirm absolutely the eyewitness accounts of our warriors. If you would care to study them, Commander..."

A projecbeam drew an image in midair. The recorder's point of view was a fast-moving, almost bewildering sweep through the carnage and fury of the battle in the streets of Macross City. Explosions and fire were everywhere, but now and again there were split-second glimpses of the aliens, mostly fleeing or falling.

"I believe you'll find this intriguing," Exedore said. Then suddenly a pod loomed close by one of the inhabitants of the planet, and for the first time Breetai got a feeling of scale.

His voice reverberated in shock and anger, a guttural to shake the bulkheads. "*So!* It's true! *Micronians!*"

The trans-vid record cut to another shot that left no doubt: a human figure falling to its death from a high building, knocked off along with debris by the enormous foot of a pod.

"Precisely," Exedore said delicately.

"So the inhabitants here *are* Micronians, eh?" Breetai scowled. The conflicting emotions held by the Zentraedi toward normal-size humanoids—"Micronians," as the giant warriors contemptuously referred to them—welled up in him. There was disdain and hatred but also something strangely close to fear.

"I brought the trans-vids to you as soon as I saw them," Exedore said. "They present us with a very unpleasant new situation. During my researches into the origins of the Micronians in our most ancient records, I encountered a decree from our dimmest histories.

"It directs us to shun contact with any unknown Micronian planet—and threatens disaster if we do not heed it."

Breetai's face looked like a graven image. "So I'm to keep my hands off this Earth, eh? *Bah!*"

"It is my considered opinion, m'lord," Exedore insisted, "that we must cease hostilities with this planet immediately. We now have a fix on the battle fortress; I consider it prudent counsel that we make its capture our priority." The pinpoint pupils bored into Breetai, unblinking.

Breetai knew that Exedore would drop his usual deference only for a matter of vital importance. Breetai, like all Zentraedi, had absorbed his race's legends and superstitions along with its lore and warrior code. Like them all, he felt a twinge of apprehension at the thought of defying his heritage.

It was in his mind to object—to say that Exedore's stricture came from the days when the Zentraedi's numbers were fewer, their ships less mighty, their weapons not as powerful. But he considered Exedore: the repository of most of the lore and learning of the Zentraedi race. In a way, the diminutive, physically weak Exedore *embodied* his people. And Exedore seemed to have no doubts about the correct course in this instance.

"Very well, then. We will execute a spacefold, immediately and pursue the dimensional fortress."

Exedore bowed. "It shall be done."

"And see to it that an appropriate reconnaissance vessel is sent out at once upon completion of the fold maneuver."

Exedore knew what "appropriate" meant; they had discussed Breetai's strategy for dealing with the SDF-1. Exedore bowed again. "Yes, m'lord."

"Oh, you're back, Rick! Anything special on your mind?"

Rick paused with his knuckles poised to rap on Minmei's door. It was a red door she'd chosen to decorate with a whimsical pink rabbit's head bearing her name. He'd wavered quite a bit before finally drawing a deep breath and preparing to knock on it.

Only to find her standing in the hall behind him. "Uh, nothing, Minmei—really . . ."

She burst into one of those captivating laughs, eyes crinkling. "I'm sure! C'mon in, Rick." She opened the door and led the way. "Make yourself at home."

It was a bright little room, painted in shades of blue and yellow, easy on the eyes and not overfurnished. Bed, lamps, bookshelf, and a handmade throw rug; a few flowers very beautifully arranged—*thoughtfully* arranged—in a small antique vase. There were stuffed toys, too, and a favorite purse. It was a room of seeming clashes that somehow gave the impression of oneness—like its occupant.

Minmei sat on the bed. "Oh, could you open the window?"

"Right; glad to."

He slid the window aside, not that the air in the rest of the ship was very much different from that in Minmei's room. But here over the restaurant it was a little warmer than outside, and with the window opened more of the slight, never-ending breeze from the SDF-1's circulation system could be felt. It was as much like getting "fresh air" as people in the dimensional fortress could expect.

Minmei folded one leg under her. "So, what happened?"

"Not much. But it's nice to be back here." He looked around her place to avoid meeting her gaze and to give himself time to build up courage to say what he had to say.

His eyes lit on an envelope lying on her dresser. "Hey,

don't tell me you got mail!" He picked it up and looked it over.

"That's what I went back for," she said, watching him. "That and my diary—when you rescued me." She shivered, remembering the concussions of the pod's titanic feet crashing down, nearer and nearer, behind her.

It had plainly been reread over and over. "A love letter, hmm?" The thought made him so depressed that he ignored the warmth in what she'd just said.

"Don't be silly! You can take a look at it if you like."

He did. It took him a minute to figure out what he was looking at. "What's this all ab— A *singing audition*? It says you, um, got to the preliminaries."

Her eyes were dancing. "That's right! I can hardly believe it!"

He read on. "This says you were accepted for the Miss Macross competition. *Miss Macross?*"

He wondered for a moment why she'd never told him about that in the long imprisonment they'd shared down in SDF-1's sealed nether regions. But then, he realized there were things he'd never shared with her, either.

"Uh huh!" Minmei was giggling.

Rick put the letter down slowly. "Well, I guess it's no surprise. Minmei, you really sing well."

"Thank you, Rick." But the joy abruptly changed to a faraway look, a sadness. She rose from the bed and went to the window to look out on Macross and the bulkheads and overheads that hung in the distance like the end of the world.

"But this isn't the Earth, and people there have forgotten about this contest, so it's all kind of pointless, isn't it? Who cares if I'm a star *here*?"

It was the first time he'd seen her great thirst to be famous and successful; in their imprisonment it had seemed such a distant, implausible thing. But now it was clear that it was what she lived for.

He looked at the letter again. "Minmei, don't be sad. You can always audition again when we get back to Earth."

"*If* we get back to Earth."

He had no ready comeback for that. They both knew

how desperate the situation was, how terrible the enemy. As they gazed at each other a skycrane went by the window, floating a prefab condo module toward its destination. The illusion of home all around them only made them that much more homesick.

"Rick? Do you ever dream?"

He was surprised, answering hesitantly. "I used to have a dream. Now it's a pile of junk in a hangar bay up on the flight deck levels."

*"Mockingbird."*

"Yeah." *And I won't let my father down! I'm not going to be part of this war or* any *war! So—I guess I might as well get used to being a passenger.*

"I'm never gonna have another dream again, Minmei. They hurt too much when they die."

She hung her head. "Oh, Rick."

He wondered if it had occurred to her that he wasn't just talking about *Mockingbird*, wondered if she ever remembered that one kiss . . .

# CHAPTER
# TWENTY-ONE

*They still thought of mechamorphosis, of transformation and in fact transfiguration, as an unlooked-for last resort and a sort of desperate aberration. There was no point in my telling them that it was all in the nature of Robotechnology; they would come to understand that for themselves.*

Dr. Emil Lang, *Technical Recordings and Notes*

**"W**E REGISTER A DEFOLD REACTION," REPORTED a voice from the monitor-lit cavern of the sensor operations center, "at the following coordinates."

Up on the bridge, Vanessa forced down her dismay as she relayed the information to Captain Gloval. "Radar reports unidentified object, bearing six-two-seven-seven, possibly of alien origin."

The information was pouring in quickly; Lisa correlated it at her duty station. "Enemy starships," she confirmed.

Gloval rose slowly and crossed to peer over her shoulder. "So, they've come at last." He stood looking down at the huge "paint," the wide splotch on the radar screen that indicated the enemy.

Claudia and the rest of the bridge gang took a moment to gaze too.

"All right, then," Gloval said. "Prepare to repel attack and launch an immediate counterattack."

"Aye-aye, Captain." Lisa moved with precision, sounding the alarms that were her province, speaking into a handset.

"Enemy attack. I say again, enemy attack. This is not a drill. Scramble all Veritechs. Scramble all Veritechs."

As general quarters sounded, the SDF-1 and its attached supercarriers became scenes of frantic activity. Men charged to their planes, some of them to fly combat for the first time, as plane crews and launch crews, flight controllers and cat crews, all braced for the manic haste.

The hangar decks and flight decks were in a well-ordered turmoil. Elevators raised flight after flight of fighters to the flatdecks' waist and bow cats, and even more Veritechs blazed angrily from SDF-1's bays.

Roy Fokker pulled on his helmet, checking out his own ship's status and the rest of Skull Team's as well. It so happened that they were taking off from *Daedalus* after a familiarization mission; Skull's usual berth was in a bay on the dimensional fortress.

But they were all experienced naval aviators. The hookup man had made the connections to the bow cat, and the blast deflector had been raised from the deck behind Roy's Veritech. The cat officer had her right hand up high, two fingers extended, waving it with a rapid motion.

This particular catapult officer, Roy knew, was a good one: Moira Flynn, who'd been reassigned to SDF-1 from the *Daedalus* and had thus been spared the horrible fate so many of her shipmates had suffered in the wake of the miscalculated spacefold. Moira and the other old hands had worked like coolies in the reorganization, training new crews for the fearsomely dangerous job of working a flight deck.

Troubleshooters made a last quick eyeball inspection of the fighter in a fast walkdown along either side and found no reason to abort launch. The cat officer registered their thumbs-up reports; some things hadn't changed much since the early days of carrier flying and visual signals were the communication of choice, even though the suit helmets had radios. Verbal communication among so many people would have made any communications net chaos.

The hookup man was clear, and Moira Flynn pointed to Roy. Fokker replied with a sharp salute to signal his readiness, cutting his hand away from the brow of his helmet smartly.

The cat officer turned to point at her shooter to alert the

man for a launch, then turned as in some punctilious dance to make a last check that the deck was clear for launch. Roy felt his stomach get tight, as it always did.

The cat officer turned back to the fighter, kneeling in what looked like a genuflection so as to be clear of the launch in case of catapult or Veritech malfunction. Lieutenant Flynn gave final, ritual clearance, pointing along the track of the cat, with her flashlight, into the void, in a pose like a javelin thrower who'd just released.

Her shooter hit the button, brought both hands together in signal, and ducked, as per procedure.

Roy felt himself shoved at 200 knots along *Daedalus*'s deck. All the catapults had had to be recalibrated because, while there was gravity on the flight decks now thanks to equipment from SDF-1, there was no air resistance.

Skull Leader's fighter shot forth over the ship's hurricane bow, going out straight as an arrow to avoid a collision with ships being launched from the waist cats. Another Veritech was about to be launched from the center bow cat, and it would bank starboard. A third was about to be guided into the slot of the third bow cat; a fourth was about to be guided into the slot Roy had just abandoned.

The Veritechs launched, one after another, all over the reconfigured SDF-1. The blue novas of their drives lit the darkness of the solar system's edge as they formed up and went to meet their enemies once again.

It promised to be a proper park someday, but now it wasn't much more than a patch of unproductive soil atop a castlelike upthrust of interior equipment overlooking Macross City. But somebody had planted trees and shrubbery, and somehow they were being kept alive. Rick suspected that it was the work of homesick Macross refugees rather than any official project. Up here, the gigantic citycompartment's overhead lights were close.

Minmei led the way to the low railing. "What a view!"

Rick grunted, shuffling along behind her with his hands in his pockets. He supposed that she was right; the city lay at their feet, and there probably wasn't a better vista of human-type scenery within a billion miles. He sank down on the wide railing, looking at the ground rather than at the city.

Minmei didn't notice his depression, too taken with the scene. "It's so—" she started to say, just as the general quarters alarms cut loose and Lisa Hayes started making her announcements. Rick recognized the voice and decided he disliked it more than he'd thought possible.

"Will we be all right?" Minmei asked him as another voice started to yammer about air raid warnings.

He kicked a bit of dirt. "Don't worry. Roy'll take care of it. As usual."

She put her hands on hips. "How come you're always talking about Roy's flying? You're just as good a pilot as he is, any day!"

He looked away at that, up to the ceiling lights. Alarms wailed, and he wondered what Big Brother was doing.

Just then, Roy was leading Skull Team in the most furious dogfight he'd ever seen, as wave after wave of pods came in at the SDF-1. Zentraedi energy blasts and missiles flashed in all directions as the dimensional fortress's defensive batteries blazed away. The special Veritech autocannon ammo, designed to fire in airless space, was even more powerful and accurate there than in atmosphere.

There were explosions and more explosions, all in the eerie quiet of vacuum. Except the tac nets weren't quiet; if the explosions emitted no sound, the screams of dying men made up for that.

Every Veritech squadron rehearsal and drill went out the window; in the utter madness that swirled around the SDF-1, the pilots found that they could keep tight with their wingmen and engage the enemy only as the opportunity arose. It was a cloud of dogfighting like nothing that had ever gone before it in human history—fireballs created by exploding spacecraft, perhaps a half dozen of them at a time, and the relentless lancing of beam weapons and autocannon tracers.

"These aliens are a lot better up here than they were back on Earth," Roy told Skull Team, although they were all painfully aware of that already. "Looks like a real rat race this time."

He led his wingman onto a new vector and headed for a cluster of pods that threatened to break through SDF-1's defenses at a spot where two gun turrets had been knocked out.

Pods began erupting in flames as the VTs' shots rained on them; the sally was turned back, but in the meantime three more cries for help came in. Roy told himself to ignore the big picture and just tend to his flying.

"Our special decoy vessel is now within their firing range," the report came to Breetai.

Exedore stood next to him, watching the same tactical display monitors. "I find it strange they haven't fired their main gun yet."

Breetai, arms folded across his immense chest, contemplated the screens. After a lifetime of soldiering, after uncountable contests in battle, he'd come to appreciate a shrewd enemy, and he'd begun to conclude that this enemy commander was either quite shrewd—or insane.

Still, a warrior fought to win. To meet a foe worthy of respect was a thing to be wished for but also a thing to ignite caution in any wise commander.

The metal and crystal of his headpiece caught the light. "What are you planning, my dear Micronian friend?" Breetai murmured.

"Perhaps we should offer them another enticement and see what they do," Exedore suggested.

"Mmmm." Breetai's metal-sheathed head inclined. "Very good idea. Tell the recon ship to open fire, but it is *not* to do serious damage to the battle fortress. Is that clear?"

Exedore bowed and hastened to obey.

Out in the lead of the armada's main body, the recon ship opened up with all batteries. At that distance, it was impossible to be sure an energy bolt wouldn't hit a dogfighting pod; the battling Robotech machines were in constant motion.

But the Zentraedi overlords cared little about that; their warrior code held that lives were expendable. Without warning, a terrible volley hit friend and foe alike and holed the battle fortress.

A pod was blown apart just before two converging VTs could make the kill themselves; another Veritech was singed along a wing surface by the barrage. Attempting to switch to Guardian mode so it could cope better with damage to itself, it was hit by another blast, flying to pieces in a bright globe. Secondary explosions blistered from the SDF-1's hull. Wreckage flew, and precious atmosphere puffed into space.

Lisa was thrown against her console by a direct hit to a reactor subcontrol unit several decks below the bridge. Gloval rose halfway from his chair. "Are you all right?"

She righted herself, nodding. "I'm okay, but what about the hull?"

He came to his feet, studying the damage reports pouring in all around him, gazing out the forward viewport at the eruptions of destroyed pods and VTs, and the blue hail of incoming cannon bolts.

"Just pray," Gloval said tightly.

A call came in from the engineering officer, the shouts of his men and the crackle of fire mixed with the hiss of firefighting foam in the background. "There's been some damage to the reactor subcontrol, Captain, but we'll manage."

"I'm counting on you," Gloval told him, wondering how long the ship could withstand the barrage.

Out in the savage killing ground of the dogfight, pod preyed on Veritech and Veritech upon pod. All was swirling combat, blazing weaponry, max thrust, and desperate maneuvers. The pods, like the VTs, often moved in a way that suggested atmospheric constraints, despite the fact that they were in deep space.

The Zentraedi recon ship continued to pour heavy fire into the SDF-1's general vicinity, though the dimensional fortress sustained less damage than it might have. The alien gunners weren't making it obvious, but Breetai's orders regarding the battle fortress's survival were being followed to the letter.

Still, carefully placed rounds seared through the ship's shields and armor, blowing apart a turret here, a radome there. A nearby hit shook the bridge gang around like dice in a cup and threw Gloval headlong out of his chair, his hat skittering across the deck.

"Thundering asteroids!"

Vanessa was back to her station before he got to his feet. "Captain, damage control reports that the second and fifth laser turrets have sustained heavy damage. They'll be out of action for seven hours minimum."

"Number four thruster is almost completely destroyed," Claudia declared grimly.

"Subcontrol systems report heavy damage and heavy casualties," Lisa added.

Another close hit jarred the ship, lifting a missile-launching tube away from it and scattering wreckage and pieces of human bodies.

Gloval reared up angrily. "That's the last straw! *We're firing the main gun!*"

Lisa heard herself gasp along with the rest of the bridge gang.

Gloval was stone-faced. "Stand by; upon my command, we will execute Dr. Lang's designated modular transformation!"

Kim couldn't keep herself from protesting. "But if we do that, it means the whole town might—"

"Yes, that's right, the damage—" Sammie agreed, breathless.

Gloval glared at them. "I either take this risk or see the SDF-1 completely destroyed. I have no choice! I have to do it."

Outside, the sinister festival of lights grew more intense. Another nearby hit shook the bridge again. Lisa whirled back to her duty station. "All systems attention, all systems attention! Begin preparations for firing the main gun!"

Her voice rang through the rest of the ship, through engineering compartments and fire control centers and living quarters alike. "Modular transformation will be initiated in three minutes, *mark*!"

An engine room tech looked to his squadmate. "They can't be doing that crazy transformation now."

"They're outta their minds," the other agreed.

"Two minutes, fifty seconds and counting," Lisa's steady voice echoed.

The two looked at each other for a moment, then dove for their emergency suits.

The traffic had halted in the city streets below, but otherwise Macross looked the same. Rick and Minmei glanced up at the nearest PA speakers as the voice he'd come to so dislike said, "Attention, all citizens! This ship will be undergoing modular transformation in two minutes. This operation is dangerous; please take all safety precautions.

"Move outdoors at once. Beware of possible quake damage. If possible, evacuate to a designated safety area." There was a slight pause before the echoing voice added, in a softer tone, "And—good luck."

"Transformation? What's that?" Minmei wondered. She and Rick had stayed where they were once the fighting started because it seemed as safe a place as any.

"I dunno; maybe something they came up with while we were—while we were stranded."

"I guess that Roy must be out there in the middle of the fighting," she said sadly, looking out at the city.

"You mean—you think *I* should join the defense force?"

"No, I didn't mean that at all. It's just that airplanes are your dream, aren't they?"

He could see that the war didn't matter very much to her; that wasn't the way her mind worked. But she'd seen that he was sad and saw what she thought to be a remedy to that sadness.

"I guess so. But if I go and join the defense forces, Minmei, I won't be able to see very much of your anymore." Painful as seeing her under present circumstances was, he wasn't willing to give it up.

She was suddenly smiling. "Rick, we're on the same

ship! On your days off or furlough or whatever it is, we can see each other whenever we want to."

"If I survive."

"Oh, how can you talk that way? All the soldiers who come to the restaurant are in exactly the same position!"

"The same position?" He smiled bitterly. "You'd be the one to know, now, wouldn't you?"

She started as if she'd been slapped. "What?"

Up on the bridge, Claudia watched her monitors. "Ten seconds to transformation."

# CHAPTER
# TWENTY-TWO

*And so, my preliminary conclusions lead me to believe these creatures harbor certain unpredictable impulses of a nature as yet unknown to us. It seems obvious that this irrational side to their nature will impede their warmaking ability and work in our favor, assuring us the ultimate victory.*

Preliminary findings summary
transmitted by Breetai to Dolza

**"A**LL SECTIONS ON EXECUTION STANDBY?" GLO-val demanded.

"D and G blocks are running a bit late but they'll manage," Kim sang out.

"Good; continue," the captain said.

"Counting four seconds," Claudia resumed. "Three ... two ..."

"Commence full-ship transformation," Gloval ordered.

The bridge crew took up the quiet, critical exchanges of the transformation, listening to their headset earphones and speaking into their mikes. What would have been soft-spoken bedlam to an outsider was instantly intelligible to Gloval.

Sammie: "Commence full-ship tranformation. J, K, and L blocks, stand to."

Kim: "Number seven reflex furnace, power up. Seven-eight section start engines. Not enough power, J block!"

Vanessa: "Activate main torque-sender units."

And the ghostly voices came back, complaining of trouble with substrata plasma warps, of injuries in a hundred different locations, of machinery that was being asked to do too much, of overtaxed components that simply could not do their jobs, and of civilians who, confused and disoriented, were not prepared for the upheaval that was about to take place. Through it all, the bridge gang worked selflessly, concentrating on their jobs and their responsibilities.

Gloval knew that no matter what was about to happen, he was proud of them, proud to serve with them.

"Full-ship transformation under way, sir," Claudia relayed.

With the ship trembling and vibrating all around him, Gloval drew on his reserves of inner calm, clasping his hands behind his back. Now, what would happen would happen; he'd done all he could, and the odds of numbers or the vagaries of engineering or happenstance or some higher power—or all of the above—would make the final judgment.

"Very good," he told Claudia.

Rick looked down at the city. People had streamed from the buildings, racing this way and that, with no clear destination or purpose. Some seemed to be headed for designated shelter areas, but others darted aimlessly, unable to bear another catastrophe so soon after the last.

Rick didn't particularly care, didn't feel any urge to find refuge. "Y'know, Minmei, sometimes I wish they'd never found us."

"I can't believe I'm hearing that from you! How can you be so spiteful? Oh, *I hate you!*"

He looked back at her. "The same goes for me. If it doesn't mean anything to you that you and I were—"

The vibration had reached a level that nearly knocked him off his feet as enormous pylons, each as wide as a city block, began descending from the gigantic compartment's ceiling. The grinding of the monster servomotors that moved them became deafening.

Rick and Minmei barely had time to get an inkling of what was going on, barely had time to begin to cry out, when the ground at their feet split apart, he on one side and she on the other.

The tower on which humans had so tentatively begun a garden had functions none of them had foreseen. In answer to the reconfiguration order, the tower halves swung away from each other.

Minmei lost her balance and fell, barely catching the brink of a metal ledge that jutted out a few inches below the soil level. The tower part to which she clung pivoted on its supports out over the roofs of the city; screaming, she kicked and scrabbled for purchase against a sheer cliff face of technical components, systemry, and equipment modules.

*"Minmei!"* Rick fought for balance as the tower segment on which he was standing shook, moving into place with a grinding of massive gears. The gap between the halves was growing wider. He took a running start and hurtled out over empty air, barely making the other side.

Rick knelt to where Minmei hung, legs kicking, hundreds of feet above the roofs of Macross. She'd lost one hand grip, and her fingers were slipping form the other.

He threw himself prone at the brink of the abyss and grabbed her wrist with both hands just as she let go. He gritted his teeth and pulled, but the leverage was difficult, and he hadn't had time to get a firm hold.

Minmei's wrist slipped through his grasp a fraction of an inch. She stared up into his eyes, terror consuming her. "Rick, help me!"

Again the monster cam devices rotated SDF-1's forward booms apart in preparation for the firing of the main gun. But other alterations were taking place, too; and the ship, particularly the stupendous hold where the refugees had rebuilt their city, was filled with devastation, injury, and death.

A hull structure the size of a billboard moved to one side like a sliding door to reinforce the new configuration; out through the gap in the ship's side poured a tidal wave of air, ripping up everything in its way, hurling cars and people and trees into space. An inner curtain of armor dropped to close the gap in moments, but not before part of the city had been sucked away to utter destruction.

Elsewhere, more pylons were in motion, this time rising from the floor, climbing up and up, crushing the buildings atop them flat against the hold's ceiling. Debris rained everywhere; the thousands who hadn't sought shelter or hadn't been able to find it were crushed or injured. Falling signs, toppling light poles, vehicles careening out of control, ruptured power lines, and tons of plummeting concrete and steel claimed as many lives as the Zentraedi had.

Roy bagged another kill, a pod that had very nearly bagged *him*, and brought his fighter around to locate Captain Kramer, his wingman, and get his bearings. Then he saw the SDF-1. *"What in the . . ."*

The *Daedalus* and the *Prometheus* were in motion, swinging on the giant elbow moorings that joined them to the dimensional fortress. In the blizzard of explosions and ordnance and fighter drives, the supercarriers swung from positions more or less alongside the SDF-1's stern, port and starboard, to a deployment that left them angled out from the hull.

Roy got a confused impression of movement along the hull, of realignment, of major structural features disengaging and then reshaping themselves. The entire midships area was turning. The great forward booms that constituted the main gun were on the move, and the bridge itself was shifting position. And the overall effect was—Roy stared, trying to believe it—the overall effect was of a *human figure*, a giant armored warrior something like a stylized Battloid.

The flattops resembled pincer-equipped arms, the tremendous aft thrusters were like legs and feet, and the bridge and the structures around it were a blank-visored helmet. And standing high above either shoulder, like uplifted wings, were the booms; with the shifting of the entire midships section, they were now in position to receive energy.

Somehow, Roy found himself accepting the strange apparition as a logical thing; Robotechnology seemed to have, as a primal component, a quality involving shape shifting, and anthropomorphic structures.

"So, that's the transformation," he breathed. *Now, if it only works!*

"Right wing section, modification percentage seventy-five," Kim relayed to Gloval.

"Left wing section, modification percentage at eighty-three. Main gun up," Sammie added. There was more booming and reverberating as the last components were mated and the final connections made.

"Modular transformation completed, sir," Lisa announced. "SDF-1 is now in Attack mode."

"Captain, another enemy assault wave is approaching from one-zero-niner-three."

"Disregard," Gloval ordered. "Fire main gun at designated targets."

"Yes, sir." Claudia thumbed the safety cover off a red trigger button and pressed it with her forefinger. There was a fateful little acknowledging click.

Out between and around the forward booms, the red flash flood of energy began building again, just as it had that day on Macross Island. A wash of energy a quarter mile in diameter sprang across space, instantly destroying all the alien pods in its path as well as pods on the periphery of the beam, out to a radius of a mile and more. They lit up, superheated by the eddy currents, their shields overpowered in seconds, armor heated to cherry-red and then white-hot before the occupants could take any evasive action or retreat.

They simply blazed in the stream of the main gun's volley for an instant, giving off trails like meteors, then disappeared.

The beam hit the decoy reconnaissance vessel and its escort ships, making them pop open like chestnuts in an arc furnace, then run like quicksilver and vaporize.

The glare of it lit Breetai's command post. "What's happening?"

Exedore looked out on the carnage, thinking of the strictures from the Zentraedi ancients. Try as he might, he couldn't fathom the workings or the strategies of these Micronians. He was intrigued, as he always was when he found something new to study, but he was also beset by doubts and misgivings.

Somewhere, somehow, Micronians had evidently given the Zentraedi good reason to shun them. But why?

"I wonder..." he said aloud, only partly in reply to Breetai's question.

"Enemy ships disintegrated!" Vanessa cried. The bridge was in a joyous uproar.

*What those people at NASA used to call a "whoopee,"* Gloval reflected, recovering his hat from where it lay on the deck.

He cleared his throat, and the "whoopee" was over. "Get me a full damage report on all sections immediately," he said. As after-action reports started coming in, the thought of the losses the people in the Macross hold had suffered seriously dampened the festive mood.

In the shattered ruins of Macross, people were moving around again. Ambulances and stretchers and rescue teams swarmed through the aftermath of the latest disaster.

A voice on the PA was saying, "We have suffered grave losses both in the military combat squadrons and within SDF-1. However, we fired our main gun and completely destroyed the enemy attack force that was attempting to obliterate us. We thank and salute the residents of Macross City for their gallantry and courage."

There was more, about where to bring casualties and how the clean-up would proceed. And the rebuilding, of course. Rick Hunter, looking down from the tower, knew that rebuilding had become a part of the people of Macross. Whatever didn't kill them made them stronger and more determined to overcome any adversity.

Minmei stood beside him. Her brush with death had left her in a strange state—flushed with life and yet remote somehow. Rick knew the feeling, knew that all he could do was wait for her to come out of it before they started the long descent to Macross.

"Well, Rick," she said softly. "You said once that you wouldn't mind if the whole town were wiped out of existence, remember? How d'you like it?"

He stared down at the ocean of human suffering before him. "I didn't actually want anything to happen! I never wanted this."

She tried to identify city blocks from the fallen remains of buildings. "I wonder if the White Dragon is still there."

He turned to her. "Minmei, I'm gonna do it." He drew a deep breath. "I'm gonna join the defense forces."

"What?"

"You're right. It's no good, my moping around, especially when we're in the middle of a thing like this. I don't know if my father would understand; I think he would, though. I'm gonna enlist."

They turned to take a last look at the shattered city before going down to be of what help they could. Minmei took Rick's hand.

Roy had Skull Team back in some order, and the other surviving VT teams were forming up too. Instruments indicated that the aliens were withdrawing. Roy didn't blame them a bit, after that shot from the main gun.

Human losses had been considerable, though, and that was from an attack that could have involved no more than a tiny fraction of a percentage of the enemy forces. It was a sobering thought, and he tried not to think too hard about what the next set-to would be like.

No time to sound doubtful now, though. "Awright, boys," he drawled over the tac net, "let's head for home."

Yessir, mosey along. But as the other Veritechs formed up on his ship and their drives lit the eternal night on the solar system's edge—as they returned triumphantly to a ship that was now an armored techno-knight dominating its part of space—Roy couldn't help wondering how many more miracles were left in the magic hat.

*Luck doesn't hold out forever; it never does.* There were too many gaps now in the elite ranks of the Veritechs. Too many; filling them must be top priority, starting today. The very best of the best *had* to be in those seats.

Roy knew who it was that must be persuaded to join the Robotech warriors. *Even if I have to ram his head against a wall!*

The surviving VTs sped home; the Zentraedi paused for cold calculation. Decisions were made, and all eyes looked to the overwhelming distance SDF-1 would have to cross in its journey back to Earth.

Unknowns... the situation was filled with unknowns. And the only good thing about unknowns was that they allowed marginal room for hope.

**The following chapter is a sneak preview of *Battle Cry*— Book II in the continuing saga of ROBOTECH!!**

# CHAPTER
# ONE

*If there was any one thing that typified the initial stages of
the First Robotech War, it was the unspoken interplay that developed between Captain Henry Gloval and the Zentraedi commander, Breetai. In effect, both men had been created for
warfare—Gloval by the Soviet GRU, and Breetai, of course, by
the Robotech Masters. When one examines the early ship's log
entries of the two commanders, it is evident that each man
spent a good deal of time trying to analyze the personality of his
opponent by way of the strategies each employed. Breetai was
perhaps at an advantage here, having at his disposal volumes of
Zentraedi documents devoted to legends regarding the origin of
Micronian societies. But it must be pointed out that Breetai was
severely limited by his prior conditioning in his attempts to interpret these; even Exedore, who had been bred to serve as
transcultural adviser, would fail him on this front. Gloval, on
the other hand, with little knowledge of his ship and even less of
his opponent, had the combined strengths of a loyal and intelli-
gent crew to draw upon and the instincts of one who had
learned to function best in situations where disinformation and
speculation were the norm. One could point to many examples
of this, but perhaps none is so representative of the group mind
at work onboard the SDF-1 than the Battle at Saturn's Rings.*

"Genesis," *History of the First Robotech War,* Vol. XVII

**Z**OR'S SHIP, THE SDF-1, MOVED THROUGH DEEP SPACE
like some creature loosed from an ancient sea fable. The
structural transformation the fortress had undergone at the
hands of its new commanders had rendered it monsterlike
—an appearance reinforced by those oceangoing vessels
grafted on to it like arms and the main gun towers which
rose now from the body like twin heads, horned and threatening.

What would the Robotech Masters make of this new design? Breetai asked himself. Even prior to the transformation, Zor's ship was vastly different from his own—indeed, different from any vessel of the Zentraedi fleet. Protoculture factory that it was, it had always lacked the amorphous *organic* feel Breetai preferred. But then, it had not been designed as a warship. Until now.

The Zentraedi commander was on the bridge of his vessel, where an image of the SDF-1 played across the silent field of a projecbeam. Breetai's massive arms were folded across the brown tunic of his uniform, and the monocular enhancer set in the plate that covered half his face was trained on the free-floating screen.

Long-range scopes had captured this image of the ship for his inspection and analysis. But what those same scopes and scanners failed to reveal was the makeup of the creatures who possessed it.

The bridge was an observation bubble overlooking the astrogational center of the flagship, a vast gallery of screens, projecbeam fields, and holo-schematics which gave Breetai access to information gathered by any cruiser or destroyer in his command. He could communicate with any of his many officers or any of the numerous Cyclops recon ships. But none of these could furnish him with the data he now desired—some explanation of Micronian behavior. For that Breetai counted on Exedore, his dwarfish adviser, who at the moment seemed equally at a loss.

"Commander," the misshapen man was saying, "I have analyzed this most recent strategy from every possible angle, and I *still* cannot understand why they found it necessary to change to this format. A structural modification of this nature will most assuredly diminish, possibly even negate, the effectiveness of the ship's gravity control centers."

"And their weapons?"

"Fully operational. Unless they are diverting energy to one of the shield systems."

Breetai wondered whether he was being overly cautious. It was true that he had been caught off guard by the Micronians' unpredictable tactics but unlikely that he had underestimated their capabilities. That they had chosen to execute an intra-atmospheric spacefold, heedless of the effects on their island population center was somewhat disturbing, as was their most recent use of the powerful main guns of the SDF. But these were surely acts of desperation, those of an enemy running scared, not one in full possession of the situation.

In any straightforward military exercise, this unpredictability would have posed no threat. It had been Breetai's experience that superior firpower invariably won out over desperate acts or clever tactics. And their were few in the known universe who could rival the Zentraedi in firepower. But this operation called for a certain finesse. The Micronians would ultimately be defeated; of this he was certain. Defeat, however, was of secondary importance. His prime directive was to recapture Zor's ship undamaged, and given the Micronian penchant for self-destruction, a successful outcome could not be guaranteed.

With this in mind Breetai had adopted a policy of watchful waiting. For more than two months by Micronian reckoning, the Zentraedi fleet had followed the SDF-1 without launching an attack. During that time, he and Exedore had monitored the ship's movements and audiovisual transmissions; they had analyzed the changes and modifications Zor's ship had undergone; they had screened the trans-vids of their initial confrontations with the enemy. And most important, they had studied the Zentraedi legends regarding Micronian societies. There were warnings in those legends —warnings Breetai had chosen to ignore.

The SDF-1 was approaching an outer planet of this yellow-star system, a ringed world, large and gaseous, with numerous small moons. A secondary screen on the flagship bridge showed it to be the system's sixth planet. Exedore, who had already made great progress in deciphering the Micronian language, had its name: "Saturn."

"My lord, I suspect that the spacefold generators aboard Zor's ship may have been damaged during the hyperspace jump from Earth to the outer planets. My belief is that the Micronians will attempt to use the gravity of this planet to sling themselves toward their homeworld."

"Interesting," Breetai replied.

"Furthermore, they will probably activate ECM as they near the planetary rings. It may become difficult for us to lock in on their course."

"It is certainly the logical choice, Exedore. And that is precisely what concerns me. They have yet to demonstrate any knowledge of logic."

"Your decision, my lord?"

"They have more than an escape plan in mind. The fire-power of the main guns has given them confidence in their ability to engage us." Breetai stroked his chin as he watched the screen. "I'll let them attempt their clever little plan, if only to gain a clearer understanding of their tactics. I'm curious to see if they are in full possession of the power that ship holds."

Henry Gloval, formerly of the supercarriers *Kenosha* and *Prometheus* and now captain of the super dimensional fortress, the SDF-1, was a practical man of few words and even fewer expectations. When it came to asking himself how he had ended up in command of an alien space ship, 1,500,000,000 kilometers from home base and carrying almost 60,000 civilians in its belly, he refused to let the question surface more than twice a day.

And yet here was the planet Saturn filling the forward bays of the SDF bridge, and here was Henry Gloval in the command chair treating it like just one more Pacific current he'd have to navigate. Well, not quite: No one he'd encountered during his long career as a naval officer had ever used an ocean current the way he planned to use Saturn's gravitational fields.

The SDF spacefold generators, which two months ago had allowed the ship to travel through hyperspace from Earth to Pluto in a matter of minutes, had vanished. Perhaps "allowed" was the wrong word, since Gloval had had his sights on the moon at the time. But no matter—the disappearance of the generators remained a mystery for Dr. Lang and his Robotechs to unravel; it had fallen on Gloval's shoulders to figure a way back home without them.

Even by the year 2010 the book on interplanetary travel

was far from complete; in fact, Lang, Gloval, and a few others were still writing it. Each situation faced was a new one, each new maneuver potentially the last. There had been any number of unmanned outer-planet probes, and of course the Armor Series orbital stations and the lunar and Martian bases, but travel beyond the asteroid belt had never been undertaken by a human crew. Who was to say how it might have been if the Global Civil War hadn't put an end to the human experiment in space? But that was the way the cards had been dealt, and in truth, humankind had the SDF-1 to thank for getting things started again, even if the ship was now more weapon than spacecraft. All this, however, would be for the historians to figure out. Gloval had more pressing concerns.

Relatively speaking, the Earth was on the far side of the sun. The fortress's reflex engines would get them home, but not quickly, and even then they were going to need a healthy send-off from Saturn. Engineering's plan was for the ship to orbit the planet and make use of centrifugal force to sling her on her way. It was not an entirely untested plan but a dangerous one nonetheless. And there was one more factor Gloval had to figure into the calculations: the enemy.

Unseen in full force, unnamed, unknown. Save that they were thought to be sixty-foot-tall humanoids of seemingly limitless supply. They had appeared in Earth space a little more than two months ago and declared war on the planet. There was no way of knowing what fate befell Earth after the SDF's hyperspace jump, but some of the enemy fleet—or, for all Gloval knew, a splinter group—had pursued the ship clear across the solar system to press the attack. The SDF's main gun had saved them once, but firing it had required a modular transformation which had not only wreaked havoc with many of the ship's secondary systems but had nearly destroyed the city that had grown up within it.

For two months now the enemy had left the ship alone. They allowed themselves to be picked up by radar and scanners but were careful not to reveal the size of their fleet. Sometimes it appeared that Battlepods made up the bulk of their offensive strength—those oddly shaped, one-pilot mecha the VT teams called "headless ostriches." At other times there was evidence of scout ships and recon vessels, cruisers and destroyers. But if the enemy's numbers were a source for speculation, their motives seemed to be clear: They had come for their ship, the SDF-1.

Gloval was not about to let them have it without a fight. Perhaps if they had come calling and *asked* for the ship, something could have been arranged. But that too was history.

There was only one way to guarantee a safe return to Earth: They had to either shake the enemy from their tail or destroy them. Gloval had been leaning toward the former approach until Dr. Lang had surprised him with the latest of his daily discoveries.

Lang was Gloval's interface with the SDF-1; more than anyone else onboard, the German scientist had returned his thinking to that of the technicians who had originally built the ship. He had accomplished on a grand scale what the Veritech fighter pilots were expected to do on each mission: meld their minds to the mecha controls. There was suspicion among the crew that Lang had plugged himself into one of the SDF's stock computers and taken some sort of mind boost which had put him in touch with the ship's builders, leaving him a stranger to those who hadn't. Gloval often felt like he was dealing with an alien entity when speaking to Lang—he couldn't bring himself to make contact with those marblelike eyes. It was as if the passionate side of the man's nature had been drained away and replaced with some of the strange fluids that coursed through many of the ship's living systems. You didn't exchange pleasantries with a man like Lang; you went directly to the point and linked memory banks with him. So when Lang told him that it might be possible to create a protective envelope for the SDF, Gloval merely asked how long it would take to develop.

The two men met in the chamber which until recently had housed the spacefold generators. Lang wanted Gloval to see for himself the free-floating mesmerizing energy which had spontaneously appeared there with the disappearance of the generators. Later they moved to Lang's quarters, the only section of the unreconstructed fortress sized to human proportions. There the scientist explained that the energy had something to do with a local distortion in the spacetime continuum. Gloval couldn't follow all the details of the theories involved, but he stayed with it long enough to understand that this same energy could be utilized in the fabrication of a shield system for the SDF-1.

Since his conversation with Dr. Lang, Gloval had become preoccupied with the idea of taking the enemy by surprise with an offensive maneuver. With the main gun now operational and the potential of a protective barrier, Gloval and the SDF-1 would be able to secure an unobstructed route back to Earth. And Saturn, with its many moons and rings, was ideally suited to such a purpose.

Rick Hunter, Veritech cadet, admired his reflection in the shop windows along Macross City's main street. He stopped once or twice to straighten the pleats in his trousers, adjust the belt that cinched his colorful jacket or give his long black hair just the right look of stylish disarray. It was his first day of leave after eight weeks of rigorous training, and he had never felt better. Or looked better, to judge from the attention he was getting from passersby, especially the young women of the transplanted city.

Rick was always reasonably fit—years of stunt flying had necessitated that—but the drill sergeants had turned his thin frame wiry and tough. *Nothing extraneous, in mind or body.* Rick had adopted their motto as his own. He had even learned a few new flying tricks (and taught the instructors a few himself). Planes had been his life for nineteen years, and even the weightlessness of deep space felt like his element. He wasn't as comfortable with weapons, though, and the idea of killing a living creature was still as alien to him now as it had been two months ago. But Roy Fokker, Rick's "older brother," was helping him through this rough period. Roy had talked about his own early misgivings, about how you had to think of the Battlepods as mecha, about how *real* the enemy threat was to all of them aboard the SDF-1." "The price of liberty is eternal vigilence'," Roy said, quoting an American President. "There's no more flying for fun. This time you'll be flying for your home and the safety of your loved ones." Of course, Roy had been through the Global Civil War; he had experience in death and destruction. He'd even come through it as a decorated soldier. Although why anyone would have sought that out remained a mystery to Rick. Roy had left Pop Hunter's flying circus for that circus of global madness, and it wasn't something Rick liked to think about. Besides, as true as it might be that the war was right outside any hatch of the ship, it was surely a long way off for a cadet whose battle experience thus far had been purely accidental.

Rick was strolling down Macross Boulevard at a leisurely pace; he still had a few minutes to kill before meeting Minmei at the market. The city had managed to completely rebuild what the modular transformation had left in ruins. Taking into account the SDF's ability to mechamorphose, the revised city plan relied on a vertical axis of orientation. The attempt to recreate the horizontal openness of Macross Island was abandoned. The new city rose in three tiers toward the ceiling of the massive hold. Ornate bridges spanned structural troughs; environmental control units and the vast recycling system had been integrated into the high-tech design of the buildings; EVE engineers— specialists in enhanced video emulation—were experimenting with sky and horizon effects; hydroponics had supplied trees and shrubs; and a monorail was under construction. The city planners had also worked out many of the problems that had plagued the city early on. Shelters and yellow and black safety areas were well marked in the event of modular transformation. Each resident now had a bed to sleep in, a job to perform. Food and water rationing was accepted as part of the routine. The system of waivers, ration coupons, and military script had proved manageable. Most people had navigated the psychological crossings successfully. There would soon be a television station, and a lottery was in the works. In general the city was not unlike a turn-of-the-century shopping mall, except in size and population. Remarkably, the residents of Macross had made the adjustment—they were a special lot from the start—and the general feeling there was a cross between that found in an experimental prototype community and that of any of the wartime cities of the last era.

Nearing the market now, Rick began to focus his thoughts on Minmei and how the day as he imagined it would unfold. She would be knocked out by the sight of him in uniform; she wouldn't be able to keep her hands off him; he would suggest the park, and she would eagerly agree—

"Rick!"

Minmei was running toward him, a full shopping bag cradled in one arm, her free hand waving like mad. She was wearing a tight sleeveless sweater over a white blouse, and a skirt that revealed too much. Her hair was down, lustrous even in the city's artificial light; blue eyes bright, fixed on his as she kissed him once and stepped back to give him the once-over.

Inside the cool and crisp cadet Rick was projecting, his heart was running wild. She was already talking a blue streak, filling him in on her eight weeks, asking questions about "spacic training," complimenting him, the uniform, the Defense Forces, the mayor, and everyone else connected with the war effort. However, Rick was so drawn to her beauty that he scarcely heard the news or compliments; he was suddenly quiet and worried. Minmei drew stares from everyone they passed, and she appeared to know half of Macross personally. What had she been doing these past eight weeks—introducing herself on street corners? And what was all this about singing lessons, dance lessons, and an upcoming beauty pageant? Rick wanted to tell her about the hardships of training, the new friends he'd made, his unvoiced fears; he wanted to hold her and tell her how much he had missed her, tell her how their two-week ordeal together had been one of the most precious times in his life. But she wasn't letting him get a word in.

A short distance down the block, Minmei stopped midsentence and dragged Rick over to one of the storefronts. In the window was a salmon-colored, belted dress which had suddenly become the most important thing in the world to her.

"Come on, Rick, just for a minute, okay?"

"Minmei." He resisted her tugs. "I'm not going to spend my leave shopping."

"I promise I'll only be a second."

"It always starts out that way and, and . . ."

Minmei already had her hand on the doorknob. "Just what else did you have in mind for today, Rick?"

She disappeared into the women's shop, leaving him standing on the sidewalk feeling somehow guilty for even *thinking* about going to the park.

By the time he entered, Minmei had the dress draped over one arm and was going through the racks pulling out belts, blouses, patterned stockings, skirts, sweaters, and lingerie. Rick checked his watch and calculated that he'd be AWOL long before she finished trying everything on. She had entered the dressing room and was throwing the curtain closed.

"And no peeking, Rick," she called out.

Fortunately there were no other customers in the store at the time, but the saleswoman standing silently behind Rick had found Minmei's warning just about the funniest thing she had heard all week. Her squeal of delight took Rick completely by surprise. He thought an early-warning signal had just gone off—and in the middle of squatting down for cover managed to lose some of the items from the top of the shopping bag. In stooping over to recover these, he tipped the bag, spilling half the contents across the floor.

The woman was laughing like a maniac now, the door buzzer was signaling the entry of three additional shoppers, and Minmei was peeking over the top of the dressing room curtain asking what had happened. Rick, meanwhile, was down on his hands and knees crawling under tables in search of the goods—bottles of shampoo, creme rinse, body lotion, baby oil, lipsticks, and sundry makeup containers—all of which had become covered in some sort of slippery wash from a container of liquid face soap that had partially opened. Each time Rick grabbed hold of one of the items, it would jump from his hand like a wet fish. But he soon got the hang of it and had almost everything rebagged in a short time. Only one thing left to retrieve: a tube of tricolored toothpaste just out of reach, bathing in a puddle of the face soap. Rick gave it a shot, stretching out and making a grab for it. Sure enough, the tube propelled itself and ended up under another table.

It was time to get serious. Rick set the bag aside and crawled off stealthily after his prey, as though the tube had taken on a will of its own and was on the verge of scurrying off, like some of Macross City's robo-dispenser units. He squinted, held the tube in his gaze, and, when he was near enough, pounced.

The tube seemed to scream in his hands and immediately worked itself into a vertical launch. But Rick had prepared himself for this; he lifted his head, eyes fixed on the tube's ascent.

The one thing he hadn't taken into account was the height of the table. His head connected hard with the underside, the tube made its escape, and Rick collapsed back to the floor, rolling over onto his back and holding his head.

When he opened his eyes, he was staring up at a rain of brassieres and three pairs of silken female legs. The women owners of these were backing away from the table, high heels clicking against the floor, hands tugging at the hems of their skirts as though they'd just seen a rodent on the loose.

Rick pushed himself out and got to his feet, facing the three women from across the table. They were still backing away from the tabletop lingerie display with looks of indignation on their faces. Rick was stammering apologies to them as they exited the shop, the saleswoman was once again laughing hysterically, and Minmei was suddenly behind him, tapping him on the shoulder, soliciting his opinion of the dress she was trying on. He stood shell-shocked for a minute, laughter in one ear, Minmei's questions in the other, and left the store without a word.

Minmei remained inside for well over an hour. She had two additional shopping bags with her when she came out. Undaunted, Rick once again tried to suggest a walk in the park, but she had already made other plans for the two of them. Her surrogate family, who ran Macross City's most popular Chinese restaurant, the White Dragon, had been asking for Rick, and this would be a perfect time to visit— he looked so "gallant and dashing" in his uniform.

Rick could hardly refuse. Minmei's aunt and uncle were almost like family to him; in fact, he had lived with them above the restaurant before joining the Defense Forces.

They were an odd couple—Max, short and portly, and Lena, Minmei's tall and gracious inspiration. They had a son back on Earth, Lynn-Kyle whom Lena missed and Max preferred not to think about, for reasons Rick hadn't learned, although there was little else that either kept from him. As Rick entered the restaurant they pretended surprise, but within minutes they had his favorite meal spread out before him. While wolfing down the stir-fried shrimp, he regaled them with the barracks stories he had been saving for Minmei. They wanted to know all about the Veritech fighters—how they handled in deep space, how they were able to switch from Fighter to Guardian or Battloid mode. And they asked about the war: Had Gloval managed to contact Earth headquarters? Did his commanders believe that the enemy would continue their attacks? Was Rick worried about his first mission? How long it would be before the SDF-1 returned to Earth?

Rick did his best to answer them, sidestepping issues he was not permitted to discuss and at other times exaggerating his importance to the Defense Forces. It concerned him that the residents of Macross City were not being given the same reports issued to the Veritech squadrons. After all, Macross was as much a part of the ship and the war as the rest of those onboard.

He was about to allay their fears for his safety by telling them that a combat assignment was far off, when he saw Roy Fokker enter the restaurant. The lieutenant's six-four frame looked gargantuan in the low-ceilinged room, but there was something about Roy's unruly blond hair and innocent grin that put people at ease immediately. He greeted everyone individually, made a show of kissing Minmei's hand, and took a seat next to Rick, snatching up the last of the shrimp as he did so.

"Figured I'd find you here," Roy said with his mouth

full. "Gotta get you back to the base on the double, Little Brother."

"Why, what's up?" Rick asked.

"We're on alert."

Rick was suddenly concerned. "Yeah, but what's that have to do with me?"

Roy licked his fingers. "Guess who's been assigned to my squadron."

Rick was speechless.

Aunt Lena and Uncle Max stood together, worried looks behind the faint smiles. Minmei, however, was ecstatic.

"Oh, Rick, that's wonderful!"

Like he'd just been awarded a prize.

Roy stood up and smiled. "Up and at 'em, partner."

Rick tried valiantly to return a smile that wasn't there.

The war had caught up with him again.